PENGUIN CRIME FICTION

LOVE LIES BLEEDING

Edmund Crispin was born in 1921 and educated at Merchant Taylors' School and St. John's College, Oxford, where he read Modern Languages and where for two years he was organist and choirmaster. After a brief spell of teaching (a fact to which he attributed, tongue-in-cheek, his knowledge of the criminal in human nature) he became a full-time writer and composer (especially of film music). Among other variegated activities in the same departments, he produced concert music, edited many science-fiction anthologies, and wrote for many periodicals and newspapers. For a number of years he was the regular crime-fiction reviewer for the London *Sunday Times*. Edmund Crispin (whose real name was Bruce Montgomery) once wrote of himself: "He is of sedentary habit —his chief recreations being music, reading, church-going, and bridge. Like Rex Stout's Nero Wolfe he leaves his house as seldom as possible, in particular minimizing his visits to London, a rapidly decaying metropolis which since the war he has come to detest." Until his death in 1978 Mr. Crispin lived in Devon, in a quiet corner whose exploitation and development he did his utmost to oppose. Penguin Books also publishes Edmund Crispin's *Beware of the Trains, Fen Country, The Long Divorce,* and *The Moving Toyshop.*

LOVE LIES BLEEDING

EDMUND CRISPIN

PENGUIN BOOKS

Penguin Books Ltd, Harmondsworth,
Middlesex, England
Penguin Books, 40 West 23rd Street,
New York, New York 10010, U.S.A.
Penguin Books Australia Ltd, Ringwood,
Victoria, Australia
Penguin Books Canada Limited, 2801 John Street,
Markham, Ontario, Canada L3R 1B4
Penguin Books (N.Z.) Ltd, 182–190 Wairau Road,
Auckland 10, New Zealand

First published in the United States of America by
J. B. Lippincott Company 1948
Published in Penguin Books in Great Britain 1954
Published in Penguin Books in the United States of America 1982
Reprinted 1982, 1983

LIBRARY OF CONGRESS CATALOGING IN PUBLICATION DATA
Crispin, Edmund, 1921–1978.
Love lies bleeding.
Reprint. Originally published: Philadelphia:
Lippincott, 1948.
I. Title.
PR6025.O46L68 1982   823'.914   81-20999
ISBN 0 14 00.0974 4   AACR2

Printed in the United States of America by
Offset Paperback Mfrs., Inc., Dallas, Pennsylvania
Set in Primer

TO
THE CARR CLUB

CONTENTS

LOVE LIES
BLEEDING

† 1 †
LASCIVA PUELLA

The headmaster sighed. It was, he recognized, a plaintive and unmanly noise, but for the moment he was quite unable to suppress it. He apologized.

"The heat . . ." he explained, and waved one hand limply in the direction of the windows, beyond which a good-sized lawn lay parching in the mid-morning sun. "It's the heat."

As an excuse, this was colorable enough. The day was torrid, almost tropical, and even in the tall, shady study, its curtains half drawn to prevent wood and fabric from bleaching, the atmosphere was too oppressive for comfort. But the headmaster spoke without conviction, and his visitor was not deceived.

"I'm sorry to plague you with my affairs," she said briskly, "because I realize that your time must be completely taken up with the arrangements for Speech Day. Unfortunately, I've no choice in the matter. The parents are insisting on some kind of investigation."

The headmaster nodded gloomily. He was a small, slight man of about fifty, clean-shaven, with a long, inquisitive nose, sparse black hair, and a deceptive mien of diffidence and vagueness.

"It would be the parents," he said. "So much of one's time is spent in trying to dissipate the futile alarms of parents. . . ."

"Only in this case," his visitor replied, keeping with decision to the matter in hand, "something really does seem to have *happened.*"

From the farther side of his desk, the headmaster looked at her unhappily. He invariably found Miss

Parry's efficiency a little daunting. He seemed to see, ranked indomitably behind her, all those bold, outspoken, competent, middle-aged women whose kind is peculiar to the higher levels of the English bourgeoisie, organizing charity bazaars, visiting the sick and impoverished, training callow maidservants, implacably gardening. Some freak of destiny into which he had never inquired had compelled Miss Parry to forsake this orbit in search of a living, but its atmosphere still clung about her; and no doubt her headship of the Castrevenford High School for Girls was calculated rather to confirm than to mitigate it. . . . The headmaster began to fill his pipe.

"Yes?" he said noncommittally.

"Information, Dr. Stanford. What I most need is information."

"Ah." The headmaster removed some vagrant strands of tobacco from the bowl of his pipe and nodded again, but with more deliberation and gravity. "You'll permit me to smoke?" he asked.

"I shall smoke myself," said Miss Parry decisively. She waved the proffered box firmly though not unkindly aside and produced a cigarette case from her handbag. "I prefer American brands," she explained. "Fewer chemicals in them."

The headmaster struck a match and lit the cigarette for her. "It would probably be best," he suggested, "if you were to give me the facts from the beginning."

Miss Parry blew out a long stream of smoke, rather as though it were some noxious substance that must be expelled from her mouth as quickly and as vigorously as possible.

"I need hardly tell you," she said, "that it has to do with the play."

This information struck the headmaster as being, on the whole, more cheering than he had dared to hope. For some years past, the Castrevenford High

School for Girls had cooperated with Castrevenford School itself in the production of a Speech Day play. It was a tradition fruitful of annoyances to all concerned, the only palliating circumstance being that these annoyances were predictable and ran in well-worn grooves. Mostly they consisted of clandestine embraces, during rehearsals, between the male and female members of the cast—and for such incidents the penalties and remedies were so well tested as to be almost automatic. The headmaster's spirits rose. He said:

"Then this girl is in the play? I'm afraid I haven't been able to give it much attention this year. It's *Henry V,* isn't it?"

"Yes. The choice didn't please my girls very much. Too few female parts."

"Doubtless the boys were disappointed for the same reason."

Miss Parry laughed, sincerely yet still briskly, as if to imply that humor, while essential to cultivated intercourse, must not be allowed to usurp the place of more important matters.

"Very distressing to all parties," she said. "Anyway, this particular girl is playing the part of Katharine. Her name is Brenda Boyce."

The headmaster frowned as he lit a second match and applied it to the bowl of his pipe. "Boyce? Are they local people? A boy of that name was here up to about two years ago. A rather worldly boy, as I recall."

"That would be a brother," said Miss Parry. "And you might describe the whole family as worldly. The parents are of the expensive, cocktail-party-and-chromium kind."

"I remember them." The headmaster deposited the spent match delicately in an ashtray surmounted by a silver elephant. "Quite likeable, I thought. . . . However, that's not relevant at the moment."

"The parents are relevant in a way." Miss Parry sat back and crossed her sturdy, uncompromisingly utilitarian legs. "That is to say that their sophistication offers some clue as to what this problem is *not*. Brenda, as you might expect from her upbringing, is rather a fast little baggage—she's sixteen, by the way, and due to leave at the end of this term—and a pretty child into the bargain. She is not, therefore, likely to be upset by any demonstration of—um—youthful erotism."

Here Miss Parry gazed at her host with marked severity. "Go on," said the headmaster. He was aware that Miss Parry required no encouragement from him, but conversational silences, even when motivated by the mere necessity of drawing breath, must out of ordinary courtesy be bridged somehow.

"As you know," Miss Parry proceeded, "there was a rehearsal of *Henry V* in the Hall here yesterday evening. And when Brenda got home from it at about half-past ten, she was, according to her parents, in a very peculiar state of mind."

"What do you mean exactly?"

"Evasive. On edge. Yes, and frightened, too."

They could hear the headmaster's secretary typing in the little room next door and the fitful buzzing of flies on the windowpanes. Otherwise it was very quiet.

"Of course," said Miss Parry after a moment's pause, "they asked her what was the matter. And—to be brief about it—she would give no explanation at all, either to her parents or to me, when I questioned her this morning."

"The parents telephoned you?"

"Yes. They were evidently worried—and that, Dr. Stanford, is what worries *me*. Whatever their faults, they aren't the sort of people to make a fuss about nothing."

"What did the girl herself say to you?"

"She implied that her parents were imagining things and said there was nothing to explain. But I could see she was still upset, and I'm tolerably certain she was lying. Otherwise I shouldn't have troubled you about it."

The headmaster meditated briefly, scrutinizing as he did so the familiar objects of the room: the rich blue Aubusson carpet, the reproductions of Constable and Corot on the walls, the comfortable leather-covered armchairs, and the big flat-topped desk at which he sat. He said thoughtfully:

"Yes. I see why the upbringing is relevant. You mean that even if someone *had*—ah—made a pass at this young woman——"

He paused on this mildly plebeian mode of expression, and Miss Parry completed the sentence for him.

"It would not have distressed her. Exactly. In fact, it would probably have had just the opposite effect."

"Indeed." The headmaster appeared to be brooding over this evidence of female precocity. "Then you think," he said presently, "that it's something more serious than that?"

Miss Parry assented. "In a way."

The headmaster eyed her with some apprehension; they had spoken of sexual matters before, but for the most part in general and hyperbolic terms; and at the moment directness seemed called for.

"Seduction?" he murmured uncertainly.

Miss Parry volleyed courageously. "I had thought of that," she admitted—and then leaned forward with a gesture almost of impatience. "But I'm inclined to rule it out. You'll allow me to speak frankly?"

"I should welcome it," said the headmaster gallantly.

Miss Parry smiled—a small, nervous smile so out of keeping with her habitual candor that it was a kind of revelation to him; he realized suddenly that she found such topics objectionable not out of prudery or obscurantism but because their discussion was a real derogation of some unacknowledged ideal of decency to which she subscribed. He liked and respected her for it, and he smiled back.

"There are two possibilities," she said. "A rape, which she couldn't help; or a seduction, which she regretted afterwards."

Miss Parry hesitated. "I know it's unpalatable," she went on, "to talk about a girl of sixteen in terms like that, but I hardly see how it can be avoided. . . . *If* it is a rape, then I scarcely imagine that one of your boys is responsible. . . ."

"Agreed," said the headmaster. "To my knowledge, there isn't a boy in the school who'd have the nerve."

"And as to seduction . . . well, in the first place, Brenda is a self-possessed and knowledgeable child, quite capable of taking care of herself. And in the second place——"

"Yes?"

"In the second place, I asked her outright this morning if anything of that sort *had* occurred. Her only reaction was surprise—and I'm positive it was genuine."

"I'm greatly relieved to hear it." The headmaster pulled a handkerchief from his breast pocket and dabbed perfunctorily at his forehead. "But in that case I don't understand what upset the girl—*or* why she should be so secretive about it."

Miss Parry shrugged. "No more do I. As far as I can see, sex is out of it; and although there are a good many conceivable alternatives, there's no actual evidence for any of them."

"Then how can I help you?"

"All I want is to establish, as far as possible, that nothing untoward happened during the rehearsal or

on the premises here. My responsibility ends with
that."

"I see. Well, that should be easy enough. I'll speak to
Mathieson, who's producing the play. . . . If you like,
I'll do it now. I believe he's teaching this period, so I
can easily get hold of him."

"There's no immediate hurry." Miss Parry rose and
stubbed out her cigarette. "The whole affair is probably an ignis fatuus. Perhaps if you could telephone me
later on . . . ."

"By all means." The headmaster, too, had risen. He
pointed to a statuette of Aphrodite that stood on a rose-
wood side-table by the door. "I'm very glad," he said,
"that that woman isn't responsible. When we have
trouble with the play, it's generally safe to assume
that she's at the bottom of it."

Miss Parry smiled. "The Platonic halves . . . ," she
said.

"The Platonic halves," said the headmaster firmly,
"are best kept apart until they've left school. Apart
from anything else, a little enforced abstinence makes
the eventual impact much more violent and exciting. . . ." He became belatedly aware of the duties of
hospitality: "But won't you stay to lunch?"

"Thank you, no. I must be back by the time morning
school finishes."

"A pity. But you'll be at the—ah—celebrations tomorrow?"

"Of course. Who's giving the prizes?"

"It *was* to have been Lord Washburton," said the
headmaster, "but he's fallen ill, so I've had to get a
last-minute substitute—the Oxford Professor of English, who's an acquaintance of mine. He should be
interesting—in fact, my only fear is that he may be *too*
interesting. I'm not quite sure that he's capable of the
sustained hypocrisy which the occasion demands."

"In that case I shall come to the speeches. As you know, I avoid them as a rule."

"I only wish I could," said the headmaster. "Not in this particular instance, but in general . . . well, well. I suppose these crosses help to justify my three thousand a year."

He showed Miss Parry out and returned to the correspondence that lay on his desk. A Mrs. Brodribb, it appeared, had much to say on the subject of Henry's school certificate results—a matter on which the headmaster himself was only imperfectly informed. There was to be a meeting of the Headmasters' Conference in a fortnight's time. Someone wished to endow a prize for the best yearly essay on "The Future of the British Empire." . . . The headmaster groaned aloud. There were far too many prizes already. The boys wasted too much of their time competing for them, and the masters wasted too much of their time setting and correcting them. Unluckily, the donor in this instance was too eminent to be offended; the only gleam of comfort was that with tact he might be induced to read the essays and award the prize himself.

The headmaster glanced rapidly at the remaining letters and then put them aside. The problem of that *lasciva puella,* Brenda Boyce, had aroused in him a mild curiosity—and since the matter had to be dealt with, it might as well be dealt with now. He went to a dark green metal filing cabinet and investigated its contents; they revealed the fact that Mathieson was at present teaching English to the Modern Lower Fifth. The headmaster picked up his gown and mortarboard, and carrying them under his arm, made for the door.

† 2 †
FIND OUT
MOONSHINE

" 'For I have learned,' " said Simblefield, a small, spotty, cowardly boy, " 'to look on nature not as in the hour of thoughtless youth but hearing oftentimes the still, sad music of humanity nor harsh nor grating though of ample power to chasten and subdue.' "

He paused, and an expression of pleasure appeared on his unprepossessing features. Simblefield's highest aim, in the recitation of poetry, was to get through his allotted portion without actually omitting any of the words; and this he had succeeded in doing. That there were subtleties of interpretation beyond and above this simple ambition he was, of course, vaguely aware, but in the flush of his present triumph he held them of no account.

In the silence that followed his breathless intoning, Mr. Hargrave, the school's most savage disciplinarian, could be heard in the next room booming Latin at his cowed and sycophantic form. Simblefield looked expectantly at Mr. Mathieson, who was gazing with folded arms out of the classroom windows. Being an exceptionally naive and stupid boy, Simblefield supposed that Mr. Mathieson was seeking for words adequate to commend his performance; but in this diagnosis Simblefield was mistaken, for in fact Mr. Mathieson had fallen into a transient and inchoate daydream and was momentarily unaware that Simblefield had finished. He was an untidy, heavily built man of middle age, clumsy in his movements; and he wore an ancient sports coat with leather pads sewn to the elbows, and a pair of baggy gray trousers.

The sound of fidgeting aroused him, and his reverie merged discouragingly into the austere reality of the classroom. It was a large, boxlike place, the lower reaches of its walls liberally decorated with ink and finger marks. The master's desk, ponderous and antiquated, stood on a dais beside a pitted and pock-marked wall blackboard. There were a few cheerless pictures of indefinite rustic and classical scenes. A thin film of chalk covered everything. And some twenty boys sat behind wilfully collapsible desks, occupying their brief intermission in various more or less destructive and useless ways.

Mathieson observed that Simblefield was no longer giving tongue but was, instead, gazing at him with much complacency.

"Simblefield," he said, "have you any notion at all of the meaning of this poem?"

"Oh, sir," said Simblefield feebly.

"Just what is our attitude to nature in our thought-less youth, Simblefield? You must be well qualified to answer that question."

There was some laughter of a rather insincere kind. "Potty Simblefield," said someone.

"Well, Simblefield? I'm waiting for an answer."

"Oh, sir, I don't know, sir."

"Of course you must know. Think, boy. You don't take much notice of nature, do you?"

"Oh, yes, sir."

"No, you don't, Simblefield. To you, it's simply a background for your own personality."

"Yes, sir, I see, sir," said Simblefield rather too readily.

"I have grave doubts, Simblefield, as to whether in fact you do see. But some of the others may."

There was an instant clamor.

"I understand, sir."

"Only a fool like Simblefield wouldn't understand."

"Sir, it's like when you go for a walk, sir, you don't really notice the trees."

"Sir, why do we have to read Wordsworth, sir?"

"Quiet!" said Mr. Mathieson with determination. An uneasy hush ensued. "Now, that is precisely the way in which Wordsworth did *not* look at nature."

"Wordsworth was a daft fool," someone said sotto voce.

Mr. Mathieson, after briefly considering tracing this remark to its source and deciding against it, went on:

"That is to say that for Wordsworth nature was more than a mere background."

"Sir!"

"Well?"

"Didn't Wordsworth nearly have his head cut off in the French Revolution, sir?"

"He was certainly *in* France shortly *after* the Revolution. As I was saying——"

"Sir, why do they cut people's heads off in France and hang them in England?"

"And electrocute them in America, sir?"

"And shoot them in Russia, sir?"

A further babel arose.

"They don't shoot them in Russia, you fool; they cut off their heads with an ax."

"Sir, is it true that when they hang a man, his heart goes on beating long after he's dead?"

"Oh, Bagshaw, you idiot."

"Yes, you fool, how could he be dead if his heart was beating?"

Mathieson banged on his desk.

"If anyone speaks again without permission," he said, "I shall report him to his housemaster."

This was at once effective—being, indeed, an infallible specific against any form of disorder. At Castrevenford, to be reported to one's housemaster was a serious affair.

"Now," said Mr. Mathieson, "let us return to the subject in hand. What, Simblefield, do you suppose Wordsworth to mean by 'the still, sad music of humanity'?"

"Oh, sir." Simblefield was clearly dismayed at this further demand on his meager intellectual resources. "Well, sir, I think it means . . . look here, sir, suppose a mountain or a bird or something . . . ."

Luckily for Simblefield, whose ability to camouflage his ignorance was held in well-justified contempt by the rest of the form, he was not required to finish, for it was at this moment that the headmaster entered the room.

The boys got hastily to their feet, amid a scraping of desks and banging of chairs. It was rare for the headmaster to visit a form room during school hours, and their curiosity was tempered by an apprehensive mental inventory of recent misdeeds.

"Sit down, gentlemen," the headmaster remarked benignly. "Mr. Mathieson, can you spare me a minute or two?"

"Of course, Headmaster," said Mathieson; and to the boys: "Go on reading until I come back."

The two men went out into the corridor. It was bare, echoing, with uneven wooden boards; and owing to the fact that the teaching block had not been designed for its present purpose, being actually a converted lunatic asylum (a circumstance that regularly provoked a good deal of mediocre wit), the light was insufficient. At present, however, the corridor had the merit of being comparatively cool.

"Aequam memento rebus in arduis servare mentem," said Mr. Hargrave in the adjacent room, "does not mean 'Remember to keep a month's water for the hard roads'; and only a blockhead like you, Hewitt, would credit Horace with making such an asinine remark."

The headmaster said: "How did the rehearsal go last night, Mathieson?"

"Oh . . . well enough, Headmaster. I think we shall get a reasonable performance."

"No troubles or holdups of any kind?"

"No. I don't think so."

"Ah." The headmaster appeared to be listening to the sounds that emanated from the Modern Lower Fifth—abrupt crescendos of chatter alternating antiphonally with panic-stricken outbursts of shushing. He applied his forefinger judicially to the center of his lower lip.

"This girl who's playing the part of Katharine," he resumed. "How does she strike you?"

"She acts well," said Mathieson.

"But apart from that: as a personality."

Mathieson hesitated before replying. "To be frank, Headmaster, she seems to be rather a sexy young creature."

"Yes, I'm glad to have you confirm that. The situation is that she arrived home from last night's rehearsal in a state of considerable agitation, and we can't find out what upset her."

"She was perfectly all right during the rehearsal," said Mathieson. "Almost too lively, in fact."

"Yes. Well, I'm pleased to hear it; it lessens our responsibility to some extent. . . . Do you know if she has —ah—designs on any particular boy?"

"I may be quite wrong, but I rather thought that Williams——"

"Williams? Which Williams? There are dozens."

"J.H., Headmaster. In the Modern Sixth. He's playing Henry."

"Oh, yes, of course. I think I'd better have a word with him. . . . By the way, your dress rehearsal's this evening, isn't it?"

"Yes, sir."

"I'll try and look in," said the headmaster, "if I can find the time."

So Mathieson returned to the task of instilling Wordsworthian metaphysics into the barren intellects of the Modern Lower Fifth, and the headmaster made his way to the porter's office, where he left instructions that J. H. Williams was to be summoned to his study immediately after morning school.

When Wells, the porter, entered the Modern Sixth room ten minutes before the end of the last period, he found Mr. Etherege expounding the technics of demonology and black magic.

Wells was not greatly surprised at this. Mr. Etherege was one of those leavening eccentrics who are sometimes to be found at a large public school, and he had been at Castrevenford for so long that he now legislated for himself, both as to what he taught and as to how he taught it. He had a fancy for the esoteric and remote, and among his more recent obsessions were Yoga, Notker Balbulus, an obscure eighteenth-century poet named Samuel Smitherson, the lost island of Atlantis, and the artistic significance of the blues. No boy passed through his hands without acquiring some knowledge of whatever obscure and useless subject happened to interest him at the moment.

The framers of Education Acts have little use for such dominies as Mr. Etherege; but in this, as in so many other things, they are grossly imperceptient. The fact is that every large school requires an *advocatus diaboli*—and at Castrevenford Mr. Etherege occupied this important post. He was flagrantly lacking in public spirit. He never attended important matches. He was not interested in the spiritual welfare of his boys. He lacked respect for the school as an institution. In short, he was impenitently an in-

dividualist. And if, at first sight, these characteristics
do not appear particularly commendable, you must
remember their context. In a school like Castrevenford a good deal of emphasis is necessarily laid on
public spirit, and the thing is liable to develop, if un-
regulated, into a rather dreary fetish. Mr. Etherege
helped to keep this peril at bay, and consequently the
headmaster valued him as much as his more sternly
dutiful colleagues. His divagations from the ap-
proved syllabus were the price that had to be paid,
and its evils had in any case been minimized by the
removal from his timetables of all work for important examinations.

Cautiously skirting the mirific sign of the penta-
gram which was chalked on the floor, Wells delivered
the headmaster's message to Mr. Etherege, who
passed it on, embroidered with pessimistic conjecture,
to J. H. Williams. Wells departed, and Mr. Etherege
commented briskly on the *Grand Grimoire* until an
electric bell, shrilling violently throughout the building, indicated that morning school was over; at this he
uttered a cantrip, designed, as he said, to protect J. H.
Williams from bodily harm during his interview with
the headmaster, and dismissed the class. Williams—
a dark, clever, good-looking boy of sixteen—at once
made his way through a jostling, clamorous rout of his
contemporaries to the headmaster's study, his vague
apprehensions unallayed by Mr. Etherege's promise
of supernatural protection.

He found the headmaster gazing out of his window,
with his hands clasped behind his back.

"Williams," said the headmaster without preliminary, "you must not make assignations with young
women."

A moment's reflection had persuaded him that this
was the likeliest gambit for their interview. He knew
that Williams was a candid and sensible boy, who

would deny such an accusation only if it were untrue.

Williams went red in the face. "No, sir," he said. "I'm sorry, sir."

"Be more accurate, Williams," the headmaster admonished him mildly. "If, at your age, you're sorry that you arranged to meet an attractive girl, then you ought to be examined by a doctor. . . . The phrase you should use in such circumstances is 'I apologize.' "

"Yes, sir," Williams agreed, rather helplessly.

"And where exactly *was* this rendezvous?"

"In the Science Building, sir."

"Ah. I take it, then, that the arrangement was made during last evening's rehearsal?"

"Yes, sir. The rehearsal ended at nine forty-five. So there was a quarter of an hour to spare before I needed to be back at my house."

The headmaster made a mental note that this gap must not be allowed to occur next year.

"This appointment," he said, "was it made on your own initiative?"

"Well, sir"—Williams risked an apologetic grin— "one might say it was a cooperative effort."

"Indeed." The headmaster considered for a moment. "Have you any excuses to make?"

"Well, sir, I don't know if you've actually *seen* Brenda, sir——"

The headmaster interrupted him. "Yes, that's obviously the only justification you could offer: *Vénus tout entière à son Williams attachée.* Being in the Modern Sixth, you should know your Racine."

"It's only natural at my age, sir," Williams murmured hopefully, "as you said yourself."

"Did I?" said the headmaster. "That was indiscreet of me. But if we all gave way to our natural impulses as and when we felt like it, we should soon be back at the Stone Age. . . . What exactly happened during your meeting with this young woman?"

Williams looked surprised. "Nothing, sir. I wasn't able to turn up."

"What?" the headmaster exclaimed.

"Mr. Pargiton caught me, sir, just as I was leaving the Hall. As you know, sir, we're supposed to go back to our houses immediately the rehearsal's over, even if it finishes early. . . . And of course, I was heading at the time in the opposite direction to Hogg's. Mr. Pargiton"—Williams's tone betrayed considerable resentment—"took me back and handed me over to Mr. Fry."

The headmaster reflected that Pargiton's officiousness, which was normally rather tiresome, had its uses after all.

"And you're prepared to swear," he said, "that after the rehearsal you never set eyes on the girl?"

"Yes, sir. That's the truth."

The headmaster sat down abruptly in the swivel chair behind his desk. "As I said before, you must not make assignations with young women."

"No, sir."

"Nor must you, on leaving this room, go round complaining about obscurantist repression of wholesome desires."

"No, sir, I shouldn't dream——"

"Your mind, Williams, is probably full of half-baked Freudian dogma."

"Well, actually, sir——"

"Forget it. God forbid that you should be permanently celibate. But the term lasts only twelve weeks, and if you can't abstain from the opposite sex for that length of time without suffering psychological damage, then your brain is an altogether feebler instrument than I've hitherto believed."

Williams said nothing; his logic was incapable for the moment of contending with all this.

"And in conclusion," the headmaster remarked, "kindly remember that there will be hell to pay if you attempt to meet this girl again. . . . Now go away."

And Williams took himself off, mightily pleased both at the efficacy of Mr. Etherege's spell and at the headmaster's directness and good sense. He did not suspect that the headmaster's directness and good sense had been carefully calculated so as to appeal to his own youthful mixture of idealism and cynicism. The headmaster had had considerable practice in getting the results he wanted.

Perceiving that Pargiton lingered in front of the teaching block, the headmaster sought, and found, confirmation of Williams's narrative. He then telephoned to the high school and gave Miss Parry a concise summary of what he had learned.

"I see," she said. "In that case I'll return to the attack. How long could Brenda have waited in the Science Building?"

"Until about half-past ten, I suppose, when Wells locks it up for the night."

"Good. Thank you very much."

"By the way," the headmaster added, "you might let me know what results you get."

"Of course," said Miss Parry. "I'll telephone you later on."

"Later on" proved to be about ten minutes before the beginning of afternoon school.

"Look here," said Miss Parry, "are you quite certain that boy is telling the truth?"

"I'm positive," the headmaster replied. "Why?"

"Brenda denies that she ever went anywhere near the Science Building."

"Oh, Lord. . . . Well, mayn't that simply mean she was leading Williams up the garden path?"

"It may. I don't know."

"Does she deny having arranged to meet Williams?"

"No. She wanted to at first, but I think that was only to protect the boy. She maintains that she thought better of it and went home instead."

"I see. . . . No other information?"

"Nothing. The girl's as obstinate as a donkey. . . . There's only one thing I'm sure of."

"What's that?"

"Something," said Miss Parry, "has nearly frightened her out of her mind."

THIEVES BREAK IN
AND STEAL

The site of Castrevenford School is a substantial rec-
tangle, bounded on the west by the River Castreven
and on the east by a main road. Elsewhere the line of
demarcation is vaguer: Northward the playing fields
peter out indeterminately into farming land, while to
the south there is a confusing huddle of school buildings adjacent to a disorganized cluster of houses
named Snagshill, which is a suburb both of Castrevenford and—more definitely—of the school itself.
The main teaching block—a large but comfortless
eighteenth-century erection of red brick, ivy-covered
and a kind of game reservation for mice—stands isolated on the western boundary, with a clock tower,
roofed by well-oxidized copper, surmounting it. From
it, a gentle slope, planted with elms and beeches and
riddled with rabbit warrens, runs down to the river
bank. Here the school boathouse is situated, and a
substantial landing stage. Across the river there are
fields, woods, a distant grange; and beyond them can
be seen the towers and spires of Castrevenford town,
three miles upstream.

The boardinghouses are seven in number, scattered
irregularly about the circumference of the site. At the
northeastern angle is the chapel, an uncommonly hid-
eous relic of late Victorian times, put up with such
parsimony and haste that the authorities go in hourly
fear of its subsidence or total collapse. The school
gates open on the main road. A long drive runs from
them, through an avenue of oaks, to the teaching
block—which may be most conveniently referred to

by its title of Hubbard's Building. Near the gates is the
Hall, severely boxlike and utilitarian. The Science
Building, the Scout Hut, the Armory, and the Library
are grouped together on the south side near Davenant's, which is the largest of the boardinghouses. In
it the headmaster's study is situated, since his private
house is half a mile away from the site.

The rest of the area is occupied by playing fields,
squash and fives courts, the gymnasium, the swimming pool, the tuck shop, and the carpenter's work-
shop. It is provided with a complex tracery of asphalt
paths designed specifically, in the view of the boys, to
make them walk the maximum possible distance between their houses and Hubbard's Building.

It was this scene—or at all events a part of it—that
the headmaster contemplated as he stood at his study
window, meditating the problem of Brenda Boyce. At
five minutes to two the school bell began tolling, and
the headmaster, finding his conjectures profitless, fell
to considering whether, in spite of the more conservative members of the staff, its wretched clangor should
not be permanently silenced. The thing was intended,
of course, to encourage punctuality; but it had not
been used during the war, and the resumption of its
daily tintinnabulation had resulted in no appreciable
decrease in the steady minority of latecomers. There
were too many bells at Castrevenford altogether.
There were the clock chimes, which sounded the
hours, halves, and quarters with peevish insistence;
the bells in the Science Building; the electric bell that
marked the beginning and end of each lesson; the
hand bells in the houses; the chapel bell, which had
obviously suffered some radical mishap during its
casting. . . .

By now the site was filled with ambling droves of
boys, converging on Hubbard's Building with books
and files under their arms. And among them the head-

master observed Mr. Philpotts, running across the dry grass toward Davenant's.

Mr. Philpotts was a chemistry master whose principal characteristic lay in a sort of unfocused vehemence, resulting in all probability from an overplus of natural energy. He was a small, stringy man of about fifty, with immense horn-rimmed spectacles, a long, sharp nose, and an unusual capacity for garrulous incoherence. In his present haste lay no reason for apprehension or suprise; he always ran, in preference, apparently, to walking. But unfortunately he was of a complaining disposition; the smallest upset was liable to bring him scurrying to the headmaster's study, full of ire and outraged dignity; and the headmaster, watching his approach, had little doubt that in another minute or so Mr. Philpotts would be assaulting his ear with some complicated tale of woe.

The prospect did not depress him unduly, since the wrongs and affronts which Mr. Philpotts suffered seldom demanded more than a little tact in their settlement. And so, when Mr. Philpotts knocked on the study door, it was with a cheerful voice that the headmaster invited him in.

It soon became plain, however, that Mr. Philpotts had something of more than ordinary importance to relate.

"A scandal, Headmaster," he panted. "A most dangerous and wanton act."

He was invited to sit down but declined.

"The perpetrator must be found and punished," he proceeded. "Most severely punished. Never in all my experience as an assistant master——"

"What is the matter, Philpotts?" the headmaster interposed with some severity. "Begin at the beginning, please."

"A theft," said Mr. Philpotts emphatically. "Nothing more nor less than a theft."

"What has been stolen?"

"That's exactly the point," Mr. Philpotts spluttered. "I don't know. There's no means of telling. I can't be always stocktaking. There isn't the time. And what with Common Entrance and Speech Day and the mid-term reports——"

"Then something has been taken from the chemistry laboratory?" the headmaster demanded after a moment's rapid diagnosis.

"A cupboard has been forced open," Mr. Philpotts explained with indignation. "Forced open and rifled. I warn you, Headmaster, that I cannot hold myself responsible. Many's the time I've said the locks were inadequate. Many's the time——"

"No one is attempting to blame you, Philpotts," said the headmaster smoothly. "What does this cupboard contain?"

"Acids," said Mr. Philpotts with unusual directness and pertinence. "For the most part, acids."

"A good deal of poisonous stuff, in fact?"

"Exactly. *That* is what makes the offense so serious." Mr. Philpotts inhaled violently, by way of expressing his disapproval. "You *see,* no doubt, how serious it is?"

"Certainly I see, Philpotts," said the headmaster with considerable asperity. "By some miracle, my judicial faculties are still functioning. . . . You have no idea what, if anything, is missing?"

"I presume that *something* is missing," said Mr. Philpotts tartly. "Otherwise there would seem to be little point in breaking open the cupboard. . . . The only thing I can say definitely is that no very large *quantity* of any substance has been taken."

The headmaster said: "Very well. I shall have to consider what's the best thing to do. In the meantime, will you see to it that the chemistry laboratory is kept locked whenever it's not actually in use? It's rather late in the day for such precautions, but we don't want to be caught out a second time. . . . By the way, when did you discover this?"

"Last period this morning, Headmaster. I wasn't teaching until then. I can guarantee, too, that the cupboard was all right at five o'clock yesterday afternoon, because I had occasion to put some apparatus away in it."

"All right, Philpotts," said the headmaster. "I'll let you know as soon as I've decided what steps to take."

Mr. Philpotts nodded importantly, left the room, and bounded away in the direction of the Science Building. As the headmaster returned to his window, the tolling of the school bell ceased, and such boys as were still on their way began running. A few moments later, as the clock struck two, the headmaster heard the distant trilling of the electric bell in Hubbard's Building. A flushed and desperate latecomer scampered past and in a last frantic burst of speed vanished from sight. There was peace.

But the headmaster scarcely appreciated it. A theft of poison—even a conjectured theft—was, as Mr. Philpotts had platitudinously observed, a serious matter. Moreover, it was far from easy to decide on any effective course of action. The guilty person was not necessarily a boy—indeed, the headmaster inclined, in the absence of definite evidence, to dismiss this hypothesis. But there were the groundsmen, the members of the staff, the public (who could move with relative freedom about the school premises), and, of course, Brenda Boyce, who on Williams's showing had definitely been in the Science Building on the previous evening. . . .

He bit irritably at the stem of his pipe. Though he was averse from informing the police, it was obviously his duty to do so. Very reluctantly he reached for the telephone.

It was at about this moment that Mr. Etherege left
the masters' common room with Michael Somers. And
as both of them were going in the same direction, they
fell into conversation.

Somers was the youngest member of the Castrevenford staff—a slim, tall, wiry man, good looking but for
a hint of effeminacy in the smallness and regularity
of his features. He had smooth black hair and a tenor
voice whose agreeable modulations held a suspicion
of artifice and self-consciousness. He taught English,
and with conspicuous competence, but he was not
popular with the boys, and the headmaster, who had
a certain respect for the merciless perspicuity of the
young, was inclined privately to distrust him on that
ground. Experience had taught the headmaster that
the principal, if not the only, reason for a master's
unpopularity was insincerity. Mere severity never
affected the boys' judgment unless it was associated
with hypocrisy or cant; and leniency—Somers was
notoriously lenient—was a bribe that by itself was incapable of winning their affection.

Somers's colleagues regarded him with mixed feelings; the current of his conceit, though subliminal,
was strong enough to be perceived. But Mr. Etherege,
who reputedly was devoid both of morality and of
human affections, assessed his fellow beings solely by
the criterion of their suitability as an audience for his
own utterances; and since Somers was appreciative
and attentive, Mr. Etherege held him impeccable.

"And what," Mr. Etherege demanded, "is the matter
with Love?" He was referring not to the passion that
drowned Leander but to one of his senior colleagues.

Somers looked surprised. "The matter?" he said. "I
didn't know anything was the matter with him. How
do you mean?"

Clearly this reply was disappointing to Mr. Etherege. In addition to his other eccentricities he operated as a kind of central clearinghouse for Castrevenford scandal. In some ineluctable fashion he managed to acquire the most intimate information about everyone and everything, and he was always prepared to pass it on. But now, a likely wellspring having dried up, he was slightly aggrieved. And certainly, if Somers was ignorant of Love's temperamental disorders, there was not much enlightenment to be hoped for elsewhere. Love had been Somers's housemaster at Merfield, and Somers was very much his protégé. Mr. Etherege sighed.

"I should have thought," he said reproachfully as they toiled up a flight of stone stairs, "that you would have noticed it."

"I've hardly seen him for the past week," Somers explained.

"He seems to be consumed by some inner fury," said Mr. Etherege. "He's touchy, irascible, and uncivil. Love, I freely admit, is not an exuberant man at the best of times; his innate puritanism is too strong. But this phase is quite exceptional. Obviously something has annoyed him very much."

"He tends to sulk," said Somers, "whenever things aren't exactly to his liking."

This comment struck Mr. Etherege as being too obvious and uninteresting to require affirmation—or, indeed, an answer of any kind.

"In fact," he proceeded, "the school is overburdened with mysteries at the moment. . . . By the way, how is your wrist?" He pointed to Somers's right arm, which was protected by a sling.

"Pretty well recovered, thanks. But what's all this about mysteries?"

"You've surely heard about the theft from the Science Building?"

"Oh, that. Yes. Philpotts told me when I was on my way in to school this afternoon."

"And about the high-school girl?"

"No. What high-school girl?"

"She had an assignation with J. H. Williams in the Science Building," said Mr. Etherege. "That in itself would be nothing out of the ordinary, of course. But it appears, in the first place, that Williams didn't turn up, since he was headed off by that busybody, Pargiton; and in the second place, that the girl arrived home in a state of great distress and trembling. . . . What do you make of that?"

They had come to the door of Somers's form room. A half apprehensive murmur of conversation was audible from inside. Somers shrugged and said: "Could she have had anything to do with the theft?"

"Up to the present," said Mr. Etherege, "she's refused to say a word. But it's sinister, Somers, undeniably sinister. It's exactly the sort of situation which ends in murder."

The afternoon wore away. The headmaster, having telephoned the police station, spoken to the superintendent, and received the promise of a visit immediately after tea, went on to the dictating and signing of letters and notices. At two forty-five he dismissed Galbraith, his secretary, into the next room and went to his window to watch the school disperse. On Fridays, afternoon school was bisected by the J.T.C. parade, so that the second period began at a quarter to five instead of a quarter to three. The electric bell jangled in Hubbard's Building, and the headmaster heard the murmur of released tension which followed. It grew quickly to an uproar, compounded of the scraping of desks and chairs, the banging of books, and the clatter of feet on wooden staircases,

with overtures of talk and whistling. A throng of
some five hundred boys poured out of the doorways,
the khaki of their uniforms interspersed here and
there with the blue of the Air Training Corps and
the diurnal gray of the medically unfit, clutching
files, rubbing at their belts with the sleeves of their
tunics, saluting the occasional nonmilitant master
who, his work for the moment finished, mounted his
bicycle and rode off down the drive. In the quarter-
hour break the boys dispersed to their houses, their
heavy corps boots rattling on the asphalt. Presently
the site was again deserted, save for an infrequent
group of boys or masters waiting for the parade to
begin. The sun shone fiercely, and the leaves of the
oaks threw a network of dappled shadow over the
drive. The sky was cloudless and vividly blue.

At such a time as this the headmaster was generally
visited by one or two members of his staff in search of
instruction or enlightenment, but on this particular
day he was uninterrupted and before long returned to
his desk and began rather somnolently to prepare the
address he was to give at the chapel service on the
morrow. From time to time a bellow of command or
the tramp of marching and countermarching drifted
through the open windows from the parade ground.
And the hands of the clock on the mantelpiece stood
at four when a small red sports car of exceptional
stridency and raffishness pulled up outside Davenant's and Gervase Fen, Professor of English Language and Literature in the University of Oxford, ex-
tracted himself laboriously from it.

He was a tall, lanky man, a little over forty years of
age. His face was cheerful, ruddy, and clean-shaven,
with shrewd and humorous ice-blue eyes, and he had
on a gray suit, a green tie embellished with mermaids,

and an extraordinary hat. He gave the car a laudatory pat on the bonnet, at which it suddenly backfired, and gazed about him with vague approbation until the headmaster emerged to greet him and conduct him into the study, where he slumped down into an armchair.

"Well, well," said the headmaster. "It's most kind of you to help us out like this, at the last moment; particularly as we haven't seen one another for so many years. What have you been doing with yourself?"

"Detecting," Fen replied with great complacency.

"Oh, ah. Of course. I've read the reports in the papers. There seems to have been a great deal of crime at Oxford just recently."

"Do you never read Matthew Arnold?" Fen demanded. "Oxford is proverbially the home of lost corpses."

The headmaster chuckled, rang for Galbraith, and ordered tea. "You've come at the right time," he said when the secretary had departed. "We have a couple of minor mysteries of our own."

"Oh?"

"And possibly of a criminal nature. I'm expecting the local superintendent of police after tea."

Fen raised his eyebrows. "Do explain," he said.

The headmaster explained. Warming to his subject, he passed from the episode of the cupboard to the unaccountable behavior of Brenda Boyce. Fen listened attentively, and when the headmaster had finished:

"Yes," he remarked, "I think you were wise to tell the police."

His host grimaced wryly. "I'm afraid they'll have a good deal to say about our leaving chemicals in such an accessible place."

"Can you rely on them to act discreetly?"

"Oh, yes. Stagge is a very sensible man." The headmaster paused expectantly. "Well, have you any suggestions?"

"None, my dear Horace. There are a good many possible explanations—most of them innocuous, I may say—and nothing to show which is the right one. Not enough data, in fact. What kind of advice do you want, anyway?"

"The girl," said the headmaster slowly, "isn't really my affair. Whatever upset her pretty certainly happened *after* she'd left the rehearsal. On the other hand, there is a link with the chemistry-laboratory business in the fact that she arranged to meet Williams in the Science Building."

"Could you make an announcement about this theft to the school?"

"I scarcely think it would have any effect. And besides, I have an irrational conviction that no boy was responsible. I can't explain it, I'm afraid; it's simply that in the pattern of schoolboy behavior, which I know tolerably well, this thing doesn't fit. You occasionally get a boy who steals—yes. But *what* he steals is almost invariably money or food."

For a moment they were both silent. The corps parade was over, and through the windows they could see a mob of boys streaming into Davenant's, noisily intent on tea. Fen frowned.

"About this man Philpotts——" he began, but interrupted himself to listen to some indefinite bumping and scratching sounds outside the study door. "What on earth's that?" he inquired.

"You'll see," said the headmaster a trifle grimly. He got to his feet, went to the door, and opened it. A dog came in.

"Good God," said Fen in a muffled voice.

The dog was a large, forbidding bloodhound, on whose aboriginal color and shape one or two other breeds had been more or less successfully superimposed. He stood just inside the doorway, unnervingly immobile, and fixed Fen with a malevolent and hypnotic stare.

"This," said the headmaster, "is Mr. Merrythought. . . . He's rather old," he added, hoping perhaps to distract attention from the singular inappositeness of the name. "In fact, I might almost say he was very old indeed."

"Is he"—Fen spoke with great caution, rather as Baalam's ass must have spoken after perceiving the surprise and alarm created by his first attempt—"is he yours?"

The headmaster shook his head. "He isn't anybody's, really. He belonged to a master who died, and now he just wanders about the site. He ought to be put away, really," said the headmaster, regarding Mr. Merrythought with considerable distaste. "The trouble is, you see, that he's liable to homicidal fits."

"Oh," said Fen. "Oh."

"They happen about once every three months. As a matter of fact there's one due about now."

"Indeed."

"But don't worry," the headmaster remarked cheerfully. "He likes you. He's taken quite a liking to you."

Fen did not appear much pleased by this disclosure. "I see no signs of it," he objected.

"He would have bitten you by now," the headmaster explained, "if he hadn't liked you."

At this, Mr. Merrythought lurched suddenly forward and began to advance slowly on Fen, who said, *"Now* look what you've done."

"Don't be alarmed," said the headmaster, standing well out of Mr. Merrythought's path. "He wants to make friends."

But Fen was not able to accept this assurance. "Go away," he adjured Mr. Merrythought. "Go away at once."

"You mustn't cross him," said the headmaster. "It's fatal to cross him, because then he has a fit. That's why I had to get up and let him in."

By this time Mr. Merrythought had come up to Fen, who was gazing at him with unconcealed apprehension. Still glaring balefully, Mr. Merrythought lowered his head onto Fen's knees ("There," said the headmaster) and in this posture brooded for some moments, dribbling slightly the while. Presently he went away and began trying to climb onto a table.

"Well," said the headmaster briskly, "now that he's found something to occupy him . . . you were asking about Philpotts, I think."

"Yes," said Fen, shifting his chair so as to keep Mr. Merrythought well in view. "Yes. Quite. Philpotts . . . is he a temporary master?"

"No. On the permanent staff. He's been here for years."

"I suppose you've had a lot of staff changes recently."

The headmaster gestured assent. "It's been a great nuisance," he said. "Things are more settled now, but at the time it was very trying—and one can't blame the war for all of it. People got restless and left inexplicably. . . . There was Soames, for example, who suddenly broke away after twenty years' teaching and went off to be jokes editor to a firm of matchbox manufacturers. And young Sheridan, of course—quite a brilliant creature—who was lured on to the terra incognita of the B.B.C. and became one of those recurrent people in the Third Programme; Morton went to the B.B.C., too, and took a job as an announcer. . . . I understand that he shouted so loud when introducing a variety program that he fell down on the floor in a syncope and never rallied." The headmaster appeared much moved. "A melancholy end, though I suppose . . . *oh, Lord.*"

This final ejaculation was occasioned by the activities of Mr. Merrythought, who was now attempting to
scale a wall. He kept falling back onto the floor with
a terrible impact.

"We can't have that," said the headmaster. "He'll
hurt himself seriously in a minute."

He rummaged in a drawer and eventually produced
from it a rubber bone. Mr. Merrythought seized this
and began to play a game with it. He held it in his
mouth and moved his head with great rapidity from
side to side. Then he suddenly opened his mouth. If
the bone did not catch on his teeth and fall harmlessly
onto the carpet, which it generally did, it flew off at a
tangent with considerable velocity. Mr. Merrythought
would then totter away to retrieve it, and the whole
process would begin again.

"He's almost human, isn't he?" said the headmaster.
"Though I doubt if that can honestly be regarded as a
compliment . . . ." There was a knock on the door. "Ah.
That will be our tea."

They talked of indifferent matters while they ate
and drank. Mr. Merrythought was presented with
some weak tea in the slop basin, but he only planted
his foot in it, uttered a snort of pain, and returned to
the rubber bone. Eventually the headmaster looked at
his watch and said:

"I wonder when the superintendent will arrive. In
five minutes' time I'm supposed to be talking to the
Classical Sixth about Lucretius. I suppose I shall have
to leave them to their own devices."

"I'll take the period if you like," said Fen.

The headmaster looked up hopefully. "Wouldn't you
find it very tiresome?"

"Not in the least."

"I don't like leaving them alone," the headmaster
explained, "if it can be avoided. They tend to settle
down and play bridge."

"All right," said Fen, finishing his tea, stubbing out his cigarette, and rising. "Tell me where they are, and I'll go at once."

"I'll take you over and introduce you."

"No, no, my dear Horace. There's not the slightest necessity for that; I can introduce myself."

"Well, if you insist . . . the room is the first door on the right as you go in at the main entrance. They're quite a peaceable, genteel lot of boys, you'll find. Come back here afterwards and I'll take you to my house. . . . I'm really most grateful."

"I shall enjoy myself," said Fen truthfully and made for the door. Mr. Merrythought instantly abandoned the bone and lumbered after him.

Fen was indignant. "I do believe he's going to follow me," he said. "He thinks I'm White of Selborne, I expect."

"I'll pick up his bone," said the headmaster, "and while his attention's distracted, you must slip out."

"Blackmail," Fen grumbled. "A blackmailing dog."

But he cooperated in the maneuver, and it was successful. Pursued by sounds that suggested that Mr. Merrythought's trimensual fit was imminent, he made his way to the Classical Sixth room.

† 4 †

HOLOCAUST

The High School for Girls was in Castrevenford town, with the headmistress's house adjoining it. And since Miss Parry was a woman sensible of the civilized graces, her study was a pleasant room—broad, cool, predominantly pink and white, with a delicately patterned chintz on the armchairs and Dresden vases on the mantelpiece. There were many flowers, and beyond the windows you could see, on the left, a sparkling segment of the river, with five of the pollarded willows that stood along the towpath. The late afternoon sun flared on the red brick wall enclosing the small garden, drawing the scent from the roses, lying in rich, butter-gold streaks across the lawn, where a tall gate intercepted its rays. Beyond the wall was a huddle of old houses, and beyond them the spire of St. Sepulchre's, its brazen weathercock motionless and glittering against the sky.

At five o'clock on the afternoon in question, Miss Parry was gazing at this scene, in an attempt to dispel the mental indigestion occasioned by reading thirty consecutive essays on the pontificate of Leo X, when her telephone rang. She reached for the instrument a little reluctantly. In the normal way she enjoyed responsibility, but for one reason and another the past week had been abnormally trying, and she was conscious of a growing desire for solitude and leisure. Feeling this a treachery and having a practical rather than an analytical mind, she was inclined to blame the heat. On the other hand . . . .

"Castrevenford 473," she said. "Yes, this is Miss

Parry speaking. Who is that? . . . Oh, Mrs. Boyce. . . .
Brenda hasn't arrived home? . . . I see. . . . To the best
of my knowledge she left here just after four, yes.
. . . Possibly she's gone to the shops or to a cinema.
. . . Oh, I see. Yes, that does rather alter the situation. . . . Naturally you're worried, if you particularly
asked her not to linger on the way home. . . . Yes.
. . . Yes. . . . Well, there are still a few of the older girls
in the building; I'll ask them. . . . Of course. . . . Yes. I'll
ring you back immediately. Goodbye."

The bell jangled spectrally as she replaced the receiver. After a moment's consideration she got to her
feet, left the study, walked along the short passage
that connected her house with the school buildings,
crossed the gymnasium, and entered a corridor of
studies. From one of the nearest, youthful voices could
be heard arguing. Her arrival at its door was heralded
by a furious noise suggestive of the *Deutschland*
breaking up on the Kentish Knock.

"Damn these hockey sticks," said one of the voices
with injured fervor.

"Elspeth, you shouldn't swear so."

"I shall say damn, and I shall say blast, and I shall
say bloody hell——"

"Elspeth!"

With raised eyebrows, Miss Parry opened the door.

The study appeared to be occupied chiefly by com-
estibles, textbooks, games equipment, and bedraggled
wildflowers wilting over the edges of jam jars. Its furniture was rudimentary, and its windows looked out
over the tennis courts. Crammed into it were four
sixth-form girls, wearing pleated navy-blue skirts,
black shoes and stockings, short-sleeved blouses and
ties. Officially, they were a committee meeting of the
High School Literary Society; actually, they appeared
to be doing little beyond eating. They stood petrified at
their headmistress's apocalyptic entry, like those Cor-

nish maids whom the wrath of Jehovah transmogrified in granite for dancing naked on the Sabbath Day.

Miss Parry favored them with a comprehensively omniscient and admonitory stare. She said: "Has any of you girls seen Brenda Boyce since school ended?"

There was a moment's silence until someone plucked up courage to reply. Then:

"No, Miss Parry," said Elspeth. And:

"No, Miss Parry," the others chorused respectfully.

"Did any of you see her leave for home?"

"No, Miss Parry," said Elspeth.

"No, Miss Parry," said the others.

The generalized lack of information conveyed by this liturgical responsary struck Miss Parry as profitless. She directed her attention to Janice Dalloway, the girl (she was suffering, it should be said, from a temporary access of evangelical mania) who had rebuked Elspeth's blaspheming.

"When did *you* last see Brenda?" Miss Parry demanded.

"Oh, Miss Parry, it was at the end of history, only Miss Fitt kept me behind to talk about my work, and then I came straight here, so I didn't see her when she went out of school."

"Perhaps she's in her study," a third girl volunteered.

Miss Parry, expectant of further suggestions, received none. "Very well," she said at last. "Go on with your meeting. And remember that you must be out of the building by six o'clock."

"Yes, Miss Parry," said Elspeth.

"Yes, Miss Parry," the others chanted dutifully.

"In the normal way," Miss Parry added in parting, "I like to regard your studies as inviolate—which is to say that I don't take official cognizance of what is said in them. But swearing, Elspeth, is another matter."

She paused; Elspeth went rather pale and studied the floor intently. "If I hear you using language like that again, there will be trouble."

She departed, closing the door behind her. A gust of awestricken whispering pursued her along the corridor.

The study that Brenda Boyce shared with another girl was very similar to the first, but tidier, and at present empty. Miss Parry was on the point of quitting it when she caught sight of an envelope lying on a desk by the open window. Investigating, she found it was addressed to herself and opened it.

Dear Miss Parry [she read]—

Please don't worry about me. I'm going away with someone who will make me happy. I can look after myself, so don't worry. I'll be writing to Mother and Father. Thanking you for everything you've done for me,

Yours sincerely,
Brenda Boyce

Miss Parry uttered an involuntary exclamation of annoyance and dismay; yet—oddly enough—the first thought that occurred to her was that Brenda's prose style had undergone a remarkable change. None of the usual prolonged euphuistic periods were in evidence—though this rather consciously unlettered simplicity might be due to the stress of some emotion. . . . Miss Parry hunted out a specimen of Brenda's handwriting and compared it with the handwriting of the note; they tallied exactly—but the stylistic dissimilarity remained. From the laborious flamboyance of "the visit to France, the spectacle of bare scaffolds streaming with aristocratic gore, awoke multifarious echoes in Wordsworth's rhythmicised autobiography" it was a far cry to "I'm going away with someone who will make me happy." Too far a cry, Miss Parry reflected. She put the paper and envelope carefully into a pocket and strode back to her study, little relishing the job of communicating her discovery to Brenda's parents.

In the event, however, they were contained and sensible about it—the more so as Miss Parry did not apprise them of her vague doubts regarding the authenticity of Brenda's letter. Mr. Boyce asked her to communicate immediately with the police; she had more information than they, he said, and the superintendent had better see her first.

But the superintendent, she was informed over the telephone by the sergeant in charge at the police station, was at present visiting the headmaster of Castrevenford School. Miss Parry thanked him, replaced the receiver, and, lifting it again, dialed the number of the headmaster's study.

The call came through just as the superintendent was on the point of departure. He was a tall, burly, youngish man in plain clothes whose features some freak of heredity had assembled into a perpetual expression of muted alarm, so that to be in his company was like consorting with a man dogged by assassins. Apparently he regarded the business of the cupboard as a will-o'-the-wisp, and he was rehearsing his views to Fen, who had that moment returned from his period with the Classical Sixth, when the telephone rang. It was the headmaster who answered it.

"Yes, Miss Parry," he said. "What? Disappeared? . . . Good God. . . . Yes, the superintendent's here. One moment."

He handed the instrument to Stagge, who listened in silence to Miss Parry's narrative. "Very well, ma'am," he said finally. "I'll come down immediately. We'll trace her if it's humanly possible. . . . Yes. Good-bye."

He rang off and explained the situation to the others. "So it's possible she's gone away with some man," he concluded, and glanced at the headmaster. "I don't know if one of your older boys——"

"Oh, my dear fellow," the headmaster expostulated, "that's hardly probable. When a girl of that age elopes with a man, it's generally someone much senior to herself."

"Just the same, sir, if you could make a check . . . ."

"I can't, Superintendent. At least, not until ten o'-clock. The boys are allowed to be out with their parents this evening, and they're not due back before then."

Stagge squared his shoulders and picked up his hat. "Well, I shall have to do what I can. I hope you'll let me know, sir, if anything more that's unusual happens here—anything at all, however harmless it may seem. One can never be sure what one's up against."

And with this nebulous threat he departed. The headmaster relapsed into a chair.

"This *would* happen just before Speech Day," he muttered. "Heaven help us."

"Heaven help the girl," said Fen rather grimly. "I don't believe in this elopement. It's the sentimental who elope, and according to you Brenda Boyce is anything but sentimental."

"You mean——"

"I mean that she's been either abducted or killed."

The headmaster stared incredulously. "But why, my dear Gervase? *Why?*" And when Fen shook his head and remained silent: "It's incredible. . . . I don't know what's going to happen about the play. I must tell Mathieson." He got up and went to the window, whence he was lucky enough to observe that pedagogue slowly receding on a bicycle. "Mathieson!" he called. "Mathieson!"

Mathieson braked violently, wobbled, dismounted, and led his machine back to the window. The headmaster hurriedly explained matters to him.

"Well, Headmaster," he said eventually, "the girl who's playing Isabella knows the part of Katharine and is more or less capable of taking it. That means I shall have to spend the whole of tomorrow drumming Isabella's part into someone fresh. . . . Fortunately there's very little of it."

The headmaster agreed that this was indeed fortunate; he seemed almost inclined to congratulate Shakespeare on his prescience in the matter. After a little further discussion Mathieson went away, and Fen drove the headmaster back to his house, where they bathed and dined. Over coffee the headmaster said:

"I'm afraid I shall have to neglect you this evening. I've got to go back now and interview one or two of the more importunate parents, and after that there's a Fasti meeting."

"What in God's name is a Fasti meeting?"

"It's to settle the school calendar for the rest of the term and make sure that the various arrangements don't clash."

"Are they likely to?"

"Very likely. There are sixteen different school societies, all with their meetings. There are sports fixtures and prize examinations and supernumerary chapel services. There are lectures, concerts, recitals, cinema shows. . . . Never a dull moment, I assure you."

"That's all right," said Fen. "I shall go on working at my detective novel."

"At your *what?*"

"I'm writing a detective novel."

"Indeed," the headmaster remarked noncommittally.

"It's a very good one," said Fen with great simplicity. "You see, it all begins on a dark and stormy November night in the Catskill Mountains——"

"Yes," said the headmaster, rising hastily. "Well, later, my dear fellow. I must be off now."

"And in a log cabin there's a beautiful girl sitting shivering by the fire. She's shivering, you understand, not because she's cold, but because," said Fen dramatically, "she's *afraid.*"

"I see," said the headmaster, sidling toward the door. "Well, you must tell me all about it when I've time to do it justice. In the meanwhile, make yourself at home. There's whiskey in the drawing-room sideboard." He hurried out.

Darkness was falling when he left the house, climbed into his car, and drove back to the school site, and it was still oppressively hot. But the parents proved less refractory than usual, and the Fasti meeting, though lengthy, less productive of acrimony. Shortly before a quarter to eleven it broke up, and the headmaster was just preparing to depart when Galbraith appeared. He had returned to his bachelor home shortly before four that afternoon, but now trouble had arisen over the chapel tickets, and he needed advice. Seating accommodation in the chapel was very restricted, and tickets for parents who wished to attend the Speech Day service had to be stringently rationed. Some misunderstanding had arisen between Galbraith and the chaplain, and more tickets had been issued than could possibly be honored. . . . The headmaster had had a tiring day, but he discussed ways and means with as much enthusiasm as he could muster.

He was still discussing them when, at two minutes past eleven, the telephone rang. Virginia Love's voice was so blurred with hysteria that he hardly recognized it. He listened in stupefaction to what she had to tell him.

"Very well," he said, and stumbled over the words. "This—this is a most tragic business, Mrs. Love. I don't know what to say ... my utmost sympathy. . . . I'll get in touch with a doctor and with the police. . . . Yes. . . . Yes, of course. . . . Good-bye."

He rang off, controlling himself with difficulty, and turned to Galbraith.

"It's Love," he said. "Shot."

Galbraith looked bewildered; his professional competence seemed incapable of coping with anything like this. "Shot?" he echoed foolishly. "You don't mean killed?"

"Yes. Killed."

"Suicide?"

"I don't know. His wife was too upset to say very much. But in any case——"

The telephone rang again. The headmaster took it up; listened, incredulous and appalled.

"All right," he said at last. "Stay there and don't touch anything. I'll make the necessary arrangements." He replaced the receiver. "That was Wells, speaking from Hubbard's Building. He's just found Somers in the common room. . . ."

He put out one hand to brace himself against the back of a chair. His face for a moment was livid.

"Somers is dead, too," he said. "Shot through the eye."

† 5 †
BLOODY-MAN'S-FINGER

"You arrived opportunely," said the headmaster; and Fen, sprawled in one of the leather-covered armchairs, nodded somberly. "I've no doubt Stagge will welcome your help; certainly I shall. Things are going to be very difficult. Of course, everything possible must be done, but I can't help wishing this hadn't happened on the evening before Speech Day. It's callous, no doubt——"

"No, no," Fen interrupted. "Your principal responsibility is to the school. . . . I suppose it's too late to cancel anything?"

"Far too late. The program will have to go through as arranged. I only hope we can hush things up until at least tomorrow evening. But I forsee the most appalling complications. Publicity of that sort . . . ." The headmaster gestured expressively and fell silent.

Beyond the oblongs of light from the study windows there was a darkness so thick as to seem almost palpable; yet the flowers—the roses and verbena—seemed to welcome its embrace, for their scent was sharper and more vivid than it had been during the daytime. A moth fluttered round the lamp on the desk, its wings beating a rapid, intermittent tattoo against the buff-colored parchment of the shade. Pools of shadow lay in the corners, but the light splashed glittering onto the brass andirons that stood sentinel to the unlit fire and onto the cut-glass tumbler that Fen was pensively rotating between his long, sensitive fingers.

"You sent your secretary home?" he said.

"Yes. After I'd telephoned the police. There was no point in his staying."

"Good. Then let's get down to essentials. Apart from the repercussions on the school, are you personally distressed by the deaths of these two men?"

The headmaster rose abruptly and began pacing round the room. His thin hair was dishevelled, and his eyes looked unnaturally hollow with fatigue. One hand was thrust into his pocket, and the other held a cigarette that was burning away unregarded and scattering its ash in little compact clots onto the heavy blue carpet.

"To be candid, no," he answered after an interval. "I never liked either of them very much. But that fact is irrelevant, I trust."

He halted before an old mirror in a delicate gilt frame and made a halfhearted attempt to straighten his hair. Fen continued to contemplate the dioramic reflections on his glass.

"Tell me about them," he said. "Character, history, personal ties—that sort of thing."

"As far as I can." The headmaster resumed his pacing. "Love, I think, was the more interesting character of the two. He teaches—taught, I suppose I must say—classics and history. Competent, methodical—a satisfactory man in most ways."

"Did the boys like him?"

"They respected him, I think, but he wasn't the sort of person who invites affection. He was a puritan, not altogether lacking in shrewdness. Duty was his lodestar. It would be wrong to say that he *disapproved* of pleasure, but he was inclined to regard it as a necessary medicine, to be taken at specified times, in specified doses. And for all his competence" —the headmaster abandoned this hazy diagnosis to be more specific—"he was never a successful housemaster."

"I didn't realize," said Fen, "that he was a house-master."

"Not here. At Merfield. When he left Cambridge, he came here as an assistant master. Then he went on to Merfield and got a house. And then, when he reached the age limit for housemasters, he came back here as an assistant master. That was during the war, when we badly needed staff."

"How old is he?"

"Sixty-two, I think."

"Surely most schoolmasters retire at sixty."

"Yes. But Love wasn't the sort of man to retire as long as he kept his faculties and could do his job. The Loves of this world don't retire; they die on their feet." The headmaster took a silver clock from the broad, carved mantel, emptied a key out of a vase, and began winding it. "As a matter of fact," he went on, "Love has been rather a problem to me. Since the war ended, the governors have been clamoring for a staff age limit of sixty, and by rights I ought to have got rid of him. But I persuaded the board to make an exception in his case."

"Why?"

"I had a certain admiration for him," the headmaster explained as he restored key and clock to their places. "He always seemed to me to be rather like the Albert Memorial—intrinsically graceless, but so uncompromising as to compel respect. And, of course, the soul of probity, even in the smallest and most trivial things; the sort of man who'd return a stamp to the post office if it hadn't been canceled. That may have been why he was a failure as a housemaster. Ruling a house too rigidly and meticulously is always a mistake."

"A man whom there were none to praise and very few to love," Fen remarked sadly. "But he is in his grave, and, oh, the difference to me. . . . What about his private life? Was he married?"

"Yes. His wife's a wispy, mousy little woman—all the character rubbed out of her, I suspect, by years of ministering to him."

"Anything else?"

"I can't think of anything. The man you really ought to talk to is Etherege. He knows all there is to know about everyone."

Fen emptied his glass with a single gulp and set it on the floor beside his chair. The blue curtains stirred, almost imperceptibly, in a breeze too inconsiderable to alleviate the dry, prickly heat. The moth, momentarily quiescent, was clinging to the inside of the lampshade, its outline blurred and exaggerated by the opaque parchment. The remote but persistent baying of a dog suggested that Mr. Merrythought was communing with some inward grief. It was the only sound. The building might have been draped and muffled in a pall.

And palls, Fen thought, were not inappropriate in the circumstances. He found a battered cigarette loose in his pocket, and after ascertaining that it did not belong to one of those evil and recondite brands to which the shortage occasionally condemned him, lit it.

"All right," he said. "I'll take your advice and talk to Etherege, whoever he may be. And now, what about Somers?"

The headmaster, with that protective deliberation of movement which heat compels, lowered himself into a chair, rubbed his sleeve across his forehead, and yawned.

"Lord," he said, "how tired I am . . . Somers. Yes. Quite a young man. Educated at Merfield, where he was head boy in Love's house. Love thought the world of him. I should have told you that favoritism was one of Love's few vices. The way he coddled Somers at Merfield aroused a good deal of resentment."

He yawned again and apologized. "Somers taught English," he went on. "Clever, and a shade conceited. Not popular. He came here a year ago, from the army."

"Married?"

"No. He has—had—has—rooms in a rather nice Palladian house in Castrevenford town; it's supposed to have been designed by Nicholas Revett. I don't blame him for preferring to live away from the school," the headmaster added rather inconsequently. "I always used to if possible . . . however."

"Any relatives? Any close friends?"

"Neither. Parents dead, no brothers or sisters. And as to friends—no, I don't believe he was intimate with anyone here. Once again, Etherege would be the man to ask. Anything else?"

"No, thanks." Fen blew a smoke ring and watched it expand, opalescent, against the lamp. "Not until I've seen the bodies, anyway." He brooded for a while. "I hope," he said at last, "that the superintendent isn't going to raise difficulties about allowing me in on this."

"I shouldn't imagine so." The headmaster looked up at the clock and saw that the time was twenty-five minutes past eleven. "In any case, we shall soon know."

The superintendent arrived five minutes later. He wore uniform; and an intensification of the habitual expression of alarm on his features suggested that he was oppressed by the magnitude of the disaster. Fen suspected that, like Buridan's ass, he could not decide what to tackle first. With him were a doctor—an undersized man with bloodshot eyes, neatly bearded and unexpectedly rancorous in utterance—a sergeant, carrying a worn black gladstone bag, and a constable.

Outside, an ambulance was parked, and its white-coated attendants were wandering about, spectrally illuminated by its sidelights, until their services should be required.

The social formalities were hurriedly consummated, and Stagge addressed himself to Fen.

"Murder's a bit outside my usual province," he admitted. "If it *is* murder, that is. So if you'd like to lend a hand, sir, your experience would be most valuable." He smiled engagingly, and the admixture of mirth which this gave to his normal mien produced a singularly bizarre and ghastly effect.

Fen murmured his gratification in suitable terms.

"Splendid," said the headmaster, heroically stifling a yawn. "You can well understand, Stagge, how distressed I am. Personal feelings apart, this tragedy comes at a very unlucky time for the school. It will be impossible, of course, to keep these deaths a secret, but nonetheless——"

"You would wish me to act as unobtrusively as possible." Stagge raised his forefinger, apparently in order to focus their attention upon his perspicacity and tact. "I appreciate your position, Dr. Stanford, and I'll do my best. If we're lucky, the newspapers may not get hold of it till after Speech Day. But I'm afraid, on the other hand, that there are bound to be rumors . . . ."

"Unavoidable," the headmaster agreed. "It's just got to be faced. Fortunately we have many more applications for entry to the school than we can possibly deal with. There'll be a falling-off when the news is published, and some foolish people will take their sons away, but I've no doubt it will still be possible to keep the numbers up to the maximum." He became abruptly aware that the occasion was not particularly well suited to a recital of his own problems and stopped short.

"Let's get at the bodies, then," said the doctor vampirically, "or we shall be up all night."

Stagge nodded, rousing himself. He glanced nervously at Fen. "I thought, sir, that we might go and look at Mr. Somers first; then go on to Mr. Love's house."

"Good," said Fen. "Let's make a move, then." His words broke the temporary paralysis, and after a little shuffling for precedence, they all trooped out into the darkness.

The headmaster led the way with a torch that he had taken from a drawer of his desk, and during the three minutes' walk to Hubbard's Building no word was spoken. The breeze brushed weakly against their faces, tantalizing them with the prospect of a coolness that never came. A layer of cloud obscured all but a handful of stars. Leaving the turf, their shoes rattled with startling vehemence on the asphalt, and they all breathed laboriously, as though the heavy, tepid air were deficient in oxygen. Presently the ivy-covered bulk of the teaching block loomed above them, and they passed inside.

Dim, infrequent lights were burning. They crossed a bare, stone-paved entrance hall and climbed a broad flight of wooden stairs whose treads were hollowed by generations of hard use. The windowpanes, made mirrors by the blackness beyond them and the illumination within, reflected their silent procession, and their footsteps awoke harsh echoes. The building seemed tranced into stillness as by a magician's wand. They entered a long corridor, bare, shadowy, and deserted. The numbered doors on either side bore the marks of merciless kicking on their lower panels, and near one of them lay a forlorn single sheet of exercise paper, heavily scored over in red ink and with the dun imprint of a footmark on one corner. At the end of the corridor they came to a door that was more solid and opulent than those of the classrooms. A line of yellow light shone under it. The headmaster pushed it open, and they entered the masters' common room.

It was a large, tall room, symmetrically rectangular. A well-filled green baize notice board was fixed to the wall near the single door. Several tiers of small lockers, painted black and bearing their owners' names on small strips of pasteboard thrust into brass slots, were at the far end. They saw half-empty mahogany bookcases, a worn, mud-colored, ash-impregnated carpet, a long line of hooks with one or two gowns that had turned green with extreme age. A large table occupied the center, littered with ink pots, cross-nibbed pens, ashtrays, and bulky envelopes. Smaller tables flanked it. There were three chairs that were comfortable and a large number that were not. The hessian curtains were undrawn and the windows wide open. And on the floor, looking up at the small flies that crawled on the ceiling, lay the body of Michael Somers.

Yet their first and strongest impression was not of that, but of the heat. It beat against them in a scorching wave, and they saw that it came from a large electric fire standing about halfway down the room. Wells, the porter, stumbled hurriedly to his feet, the sweat running down his face like rain. He mumbled something, but for the moment no one paid any attention to him. After the first overwhelming shock of the heat, they had eyes for nothing but the body.

It was lying supine by a small table, with an overturned chair beside it. Clearly Somers had fallen back against the table and slid down it, for his head was propped against one of the legs, and his arms were outflung as if he had tried to save himself. Blood had streamed down the left side of his face onto the carpet, and where his left eye had been there was a riven, pulp-encrusted hole at which a bluebottle was feeding.

They looked, and, sickened, turned away again. The headmaster said rather shakily: "Why in God's name have you got that fire on, Wells?"

"It was like that, sir," Wells stammered, "when I found him. And you told me not to touch anything."

He wiped the sweat from his face with a limp and soaking handkerchief. Even the bald crown of his head was a hectic, fever-stricken crimson, and his thin, stooping body seemed on the point of collapse. He felt for a back of a chair, his damp palm slipped on the polished wood, and he staggered momentarily.

Fen loosened his tie and unbuttoned his collar. He stood at a window and watched while the sergeant, under Stagge's direction, photographed the body and its surroundings. Then the doctor began his examination. Stagge, meanwhile, had approached the electric fire and was regarding it dubiously. After a moment's consideration he went to the wall switch to which it was attached and flicked it off with a pencil. The bars of the fire faded from scarlet through orange to ocher and then became black. Stagge turned to Fen.

"An extraordinary thing, sir," he said, "using a fire on a broiling evening like this." He hesitated. "I've heard that such methods have been used to warm a corpse and so create uncertainty about the time of death."

Fen was fanning himself with his pocketbook, an activity which, he found, generated far more warmth than it dispelled; he desisted abruptly. "Yes," he said. "But in this instance the fire's several feet away from the body. And since it's portable, I'm afraid that theory will have to be ruled out." Preoccupied, he moved to the small table against which Somers's body was lying.

"It looks to me," Stagge observed with a diffidence unsuited to so self-evident a proposition, "as if this was where he was working."

They gazed at the table in silence. A blotting pad lay on it, its white surface covered with mirror-images of black-ink writing. They could make out the words "satisfactory," "very fair," "a marked improvement since the beginning of term," and innumerable repetitions of the initials "M.S." A pile of small, printed report forms was on the blotter, and scattered around it were several envelopes similar to those on the central table. Each one bore the name of a form, with a list of initials of masters below it, and contained further report forms. For the rest, there was an ashtray with one or two cigarette stubs, a large circular well of blue-black ink, a mark book, an open bottle of black ink, a long, broad strip of black cloth with the ends knotted together, and a pen.

Stagge turned to the headmaster. "These are mid-term reports, I take it?"

"Yes, Superintendent." The headmaster had followed Fen's example in loosening his tie; he looked raffish yet weary. "Form masters and visiting masters were due to have finished them by five this afternoon; then they were to have gone to housemasters and finally to me."

"Mr. Somers was behind schedule, then?"

"Yes. I was aware of the fact." The headmaster pointed to the strip of cloth on the table. "That, of course, is a sling. Somers sprained his wrist a few days ago, just before the reports were put out, and wasn't able to do any writing until it got better. However, he told me yesterday afternoon that he would have them done by the morning of Speech Day, and that was early enough." He smiled faintly. "I always arrange for the *terminus ad quem* to be a little earlier than is strictly necessary, since even schoolmasters are fallible."

"Couldn't one of the other masters have acted as his amanuensis?" Fen asked.

The headmaster spoke rather uncertainly. "Yes, I suppose so. But probably he didn't want to burden anyone else with the job. This is a very busy stage of the term, and even filling in 'satisfactory' two hundred times takes longer than you'd imagine. What's more, Somers was a form master and had to deal with all the various headings for his form, in addition."

"Ah." Fen was pensive. "When the reports are finished, do the housemasters collect them?"

"No. Wells does that. He divides them up into houses and passes them on to the appropriate men."

Fen looked at Wells. "Apparently," he remarked, "you've taken some of them away already. There don't seem to be many here."

"Yes, sir," said Wells. "All the ones Mr. Somers had finished, or hadn't anything to do with, are in my office. But I haven't taken any since Mr. Somers come in here this evening."

There was a momentary silence, and the sergeant, snatching zealously at his opportunity, said: "Fingerprints, Superintendent?"

Stagge gestured haplessly. "Leave that for the moment," he said. "There are bound to be prints of everyone on the staff all over this room." He tapped on the table. "I take it, then, that Mr. Somers was working here when someone interrupted him. He got up, knocked over the chair, faced *away* from the table and *towards* the door, and was shot. . . ." He paused, gloomily considering this hollow and unenlightening reconstruction, then observed that the doctor had finished his first brief examination of the body. "Well?" he demanded.

The doctor dusted his knees and wiped his eyes. "Exactly what you'd expect," he said. "He was shot at a distance of something like six feet with—I *think*—a .38."

"Six feet," Stagge muttered. He paced out the distance to where the murderer had presumably stood, and having arrived there, looked about him rather vaguely in search of inspiration; but apparently none was forthcoming, for he made no further remark.

"He must have a thick skull," the doctor went on, nodding toward the body, "because the bullet's lodged in his brain. . . . Death was instantaneous, of course."

"Time of death?" Stagge asked.

"Anything between half an hour ago and an hour and a half."

Stagge consulted his watch. "And it's twenty minutes to midnight now. Between ten and eleven, in fact. Anything else?"

"Nothing," said the doctor uncompromisingly. "Can he be taken out to the ambulance?"

Stagge shook his head. "Not for a moment. I must go through his pockets, and the sergeant must take his fingerprints. After that you can have him."

He bent down and removed the contents of Somers's pockets, laying them on the central table. At first glance there seemed nothing unusual about them: keys, money, a wallet—containing bank notes, an identity card, and a driving license—a pencil, a handkerchief, a half-filled tortoiseshell cigarette case, and a utility petrol lighter. . . .

"But what on earth is he doing with that?" Fen inquired.

"That" was a large sheet of spotless white blotting paper folded into eight, which had been in Somers's breast pocket. Stagge turned it over carefully in his hands.

"Well," he said, "I don't see anything specially odd about a man carrying blotting paper. I dare say. . . ."

But Fen had taken the sheet away from him and was comparing it with the pad on the table. "Same kind," he observed, "same color, same size." He glanced round the room. "And there are several identical pads, all with clean blotting paper." Turning to Wells, he said: "Are you responsible for renewing the blotting paper in these pads?"

"Yes, sir. I do it on the first day of every month, regular."

"Wells is a stickler for routine," the headmaster put in.

"And this," said Fen thoughtfully, "is June first."

Wells nodded eagerly; with the switching off of the electric fire, something of his animation had returned. "I changed the blotting paper earlier this evening, sir."

"I dare say," the headmaster remarked rather deprecatorily, "that Somers wanted some and just pinched it. People do that sort of thing, you know."

But Fen seemed dissatisfied with this explanation. To Wells he said: "Where do you keep the fresh blotting paper?"

"In a cupboard in my office, sir."

"And where does it come from in the first place?"

"Well, sir, from the school stationery shop."

"And is the same sort of blotting paper sold to the boys and the masters when they happen to want it?"

"Yes, sir, I believe so."

"When you replace it, do you put a specific amount in each pad?"

"Yes, sir. Three large sheets, folded double."

"Good," said Fen. "Have a look at all the pads in this room, then—including the one Somers was using—and see if there's a sheet missing from any of them."

Glad of occupation, Wells began to bustle about. Stagge said:

"I don't quite see what you're getting at, Professor Fen."

"Was ist, ist vernünftig," said Fen cheerfully. "All facts are valuable, Superintendent."

Stagge's self-confidence visibly waned at this evasive response, and he was silent, watching the sergeant at his disagreeable task. He had cleaned Somers's fingers with benzoline and pressed them onto an inked metal plate; now he was transferring the prints to a sheet of white paper. Finishing the job, he straightened up, red with effort, and said:

"What about his wristwatch, sir? You'll be wanting that?"

Stagge grunted. "I'm glad you reminded me," he said and bent down to unstrap it. The headmaster, watching this operation, broke in with:

"He's wearing it the wrong way round."

Fen looked at him with interest. "The wrong way round?"

"He always wore it on the *inside* of his wrist, as I believe the Americans do. It isn't like that now."

Stagge had the watch at his ear, holding it delicately by the edge of the strap. "Anyway, it isn't going," he said, and examined it. "The hands are at five to nine."

"Is it broken?" Fen asked.

"Not that I can see."

"What about opening the back, then?"

For answer Stagge went to the sergeant's gladstone bag, took from it a jar of gray powder, and with a camel's-hair brush dusted this onto the glass and silver of the watch. He stared for a moment, blew off the powder, and picked up the sheet of paper with Somers's fingerprints on it. For two or three minutes he was absorbed in the comparison, which he made with the help of a pocket lens.

"Somers's own prints are on it," he said at last, "and no one else's. Which is what you'd expect." He prised off the back of the watch and studied its mechanism. "Broken, all right," he commented. "And deliberately broken, I'd say."

"To give a wrong impression of the time of death?" the headmaster ventured.

"Five to nine," Stagge pointed out. "Not a very sensible choice. And the glass isn't smashed."

Wells had returned from his inspection of the blotting pads and was hovering inquisitively at the edge of their little group. "I saw Mr. Somers at ten o'clock, sir," he said. "Alive and well."

"Ah," said Stagge. "We'll have a word about that in a minute."

The doctor, who had been dosing himself impatiently with snuff during this interchange, said: "Can he be taken away now?"

"All right," Stagge agreed. "But don't *you* go away, Willans," he added hastily. "We've got another body to look at yet."

"I'll wait outside," said the doctor, who was perceptibly bored. He left the room, and presently the men from the ambulance appeared with a stretcher and carried the body away. They were all relieved to see the last of it, and Fen took some pleasure in crushing the bluebottle, which, deprived of its obscene banquet, was crawling incapably about on the floor.

"Now, Wells," he said, "what about those blotting pads?"

"Not a sheet missing from any of them, sir."

This intelligence pleased Fen; he was about to make some comment on it when Wells added: "But as regards the watch, sir, I can tell you something about that. Mr. Somers mentioned to me when I last saw him that it was out of order."

Fen looked more gratified than ever. "A delightful problem," he murmured.

"Problem, sir?" said Stagge.

"Consider, Superintendent," Fen adjured him dreamily. "Someone has according to you deliberately shattered the works of that watch. Now, that someone *might* have been Somers; but if so, he wouldn't strap the watch back on his wrist in what to him was an unaccustomed position."

"We're assuming, sir," said Stagge, "that it was the murderer who broke the watch."

"Are you? But from what Somers told Wells it would appear *that the watch was broken before the murderer ever came on the scene.* The murderer, consequently, was not under the necessity of breaking it. He might reset the hands—yes. But to do that he'd scarcely *remove* the watch. It's a curious, contradictory business, and the explanation. . . ."

Fen paused, and a curious glitter appeared in his eyes; but when after a moment he spoke, it was only to say, in the mildest of tones: "I think Wells is our star witness. Can we hear what he knows about it all?"

"I'd like to suggest," the headmaster interposed, "that we sit down. The heat. . . ."

They accepted the proposal with alacrity, Stagge motioning the sergeant and the constable to do the same. "Now, Wells," he said.

Wells, a little flustered at being pushed thus incontinently into the limelight, gained time by prolongedly blowing his nose. "I'm not quite sure, sir, what it is you want to know."

"Everything," said Stagge peremptorily.

Wells smiled feebly and pocketed his handkerchief. "Well, sir," he began, "it's like this: Every weekday evening I'm over in this building, working in my office, between ten and eleven."

"Where is your office?"

"Just inside the east door, sir."

"That's the door we came in by," the headmaster explained. "And by the way, when Wells says *every* evening, he means exactly that. His regularity's a standing joke."

"Only way to be sure of getting things done, sir," said Wells, with a smugness that earned him Fen's heartfelt disapproval. "Anyway, at eleven o'clock, in the normal way, I shut the windows and lock up the building and go home. This particular evening I arrived here about a quarter to ten, so as to empty the ashtrays and deal with the blotting paper. Mr. Etherege was in here, finishing his reports. I chatted to him for a bit, and somewhere round five to ten Mr. Somers turned up."

"Did he seem his usual self?"

"Yes, Superintendent; I didn't notice anything out of the way."

"And he was alone?"

"Yes, sir. Mr. Etherege chaffed him with having left his reports to the last moment, and they counted up the number he still had to do, and Mr. Somers said he'd be able to finish them by eleven."

"Just one question," Fen interrupted. "Why on earth didn't he take the reports home and deal with them there?"

"It's strictly forbidden to remove them from this room," said the headmaster. "About thirty-five men have to fill them in during less than a week, and if each one took them home with him, there'd be chaos."

"I see. Go on, Wells."

"Mr. Somers, sir, he said to me: 'My watch is broken, Wells, so you'll have to let me know when it's eleven; but don't disturb me before then.' And he settled down to work, at that very table."

"Was it placed as it is now?" Stagge asked.

"Yes, sir, except it's got knocked a bit askew with him falling against it. . . . Anyway, I went out of here with Mr. Etherege and left Mr. Somers on his own. Mr. Etherege walked down to my office with me, and then he went off. I got down to my work. Then at eleven o'clock"—Wells licked his dry lips—"I came up here and found him like you saw."

Stagge frowned. "You must have heard a shot, though."

"No, sir. I heard nothing."

Stagge looked rather blank at this. "I take it," he said
to the headmaster, "that the nearest building would
be Davenant's."

"Yes, Superintendent. It isn't particularly near,
mind you; I don't know if one would hear a shot. Anyway, I've been in my study all evening, with the windows open, and I heard nothing."

Fen had been examining the windows of the common room; there were two symmetrical sets of them
opposite to one another in the longer walls. "I suppose," he said, "that these windows on the west look
out over the river. Is there a public footpath?"

"Not on this side, sir," Stagge replied. "And the one
on the other side isn't much frequented."

"And these other windows . . . ."

"They look out on a little inner courtyard."

"Ah." Fen seemed a trifle bored, as though he were
asking these questions rather from duty than from
inclination. "Well, I think a test is indicated, to see
whether a revolver shot here is audible in Wells's
office; one sometimes gets acoustical freaks in old
buildings like this. On the other hand, it's possible
that a silencer was used."

"Not only possible, but likely," said the headmaster.
They turned unanimously to stare at him. "There is—
or perhaps I should say there was—a silencer in the
J.T.C. armory."

"An odd thing, surely, for a school to possess," Fen
commented.

"In fact, it belonged to Somers," the headmaster explained. "He picked it up while he was in the army,
somewhere in France or Germany, and handed it over
to Sergeant Shelley as a kind of memento. I remember
hearing about the thing, but I don't think I ever set
eyes on it myself."

Stagge brought out a notebook and wrote something

hurriedly on a virgin page. "I'll make inquiries. It'll be worth finding out, too, if any of the pistols are missing from the armory. . . . Now." He closed the notebook. "As regards access to this room. . . ."

"There's only one outer door from which you can arrive here," said the headmaster. "And that, of course, is the one we came in by. Hubbard's Building is inconveniently divided into three watertight compartments, each with its own outer door."

Stagge addressed himself to Wells. "I think you said that your office is just inside the door."

"Yes, sir."

"Did anyone go in or out while you were working there between ten and eleven?"

"Not a soul, sir. I had my door open because of the heat, so I could see as well as hear."

"M'm," said Stagge. "In that case, the murderer reached this room in some other fashion. There's no doubt," he added parenthetically, "that he was *in this room;* Somers couldn't, for instance, have been shot through the windows. . . ."

"The murderer might have been hidden in the building before Wells settled down in his office," the headmaster suggested, "and not have left until Wells came up here to mount guard."

"That's possible, of course—though it'd be a needless risk if there were any way of getting in and out of the building unobserved. Would the windows of the downstairs classrooms be open?" Wells nodded assent. "That would be one method, then," Stagge went on. "I must have a look at those windows— though not, I think, until daylight. . . . Well, we have a few facts: Somers was shot with a .38 revolver, some time between ten or eleven, by someone who was either concealed in the building or got in through one of the downstairs windows." He scratched his nose, rather dubiously, with the end of a pencil. "I wish we could narrow down the time a bit."

"There's one obvious way of doing so," said Fen.

"Oh? What's that, sir?"

"Somers was writing reports," Fen remarked, yawning grossly. "To judge from Wells's account, Etherege must know exactly how many he still had to write when he began the job at ten o'clock. By examining the forms and getting someone whose writing is similar in size and type to duplicate Somers's efforts under the same conditions, we can find out approximately how long he spent working at the reports. In any event, we can get a *minimum.*"

Stagge snapped his fingers. "Damn good idea, sir. I'll see that that's done."

"I'll even venture a prophecy as to the result," said Fen, yawning again. "I think you'll find that that minimum represents close on an hour's work."

Stagge stared. "You mean he was killed just before Wells found him?"

"I propose to be tiresome," said Fen, "and not satisfy your curiosity. My idea's only tentative, and I'd rather wait for confirmation—or otherwise."

"Well, we must humor you, I suppose." Stagge's jocosity was perceptibly tempered with regret. "Wells, have a look at those reports and find out if Somers finished his job."

They sat watching while the porter examined the reports. Eventually he said: "Yes, they're all completed, sir."

"I'm afraid I must confiscate the lot," Stagge told the headmaster. "I'll let you have them back, of course, at the earliest possible moment." He glanced inquiringly about him. "I rather think, you know, that we ought to be making for Mr. Love's house. . . . Lord, all this business over again. What a night!"

"I've just been thinking"—Fen spoke with his eyes

closed—"that I shouldn't much like to stand up in this room and shoot a man with the lights on and the curtains open. . . . Wells, were the curtains open when you were in here at ten o'clock?"

"They were, sir. And still open when I found Mr. Somers's body."

"M'm. That doesn't prove or disprove anything very valuable. Oh, one other thing: Was there much likelihood of Somers's being disturbed at his solitary vigil?"

"Very little, sir. It's rare for any master to come here at that time of night."

"And there are lavatories," said Fen surprisingly. They all gazed at him in bewilderment. "Well," he continued rather peevishly, "there *are* lavatories in the building, I suppose?"

"Just outside the door," Wells informed him hastily. "First on the right."

"And in that case," said Stagge, getting to his feet, "I think we'd better all make a move, or Mrs. Love will be wondering what's become of us." He collected the report envelopes into a pile and thrust them underneath his arm. "I'm afraid, Dr. Stanford, that we shall have to keep this room locked for the time being."

"Oh, my dear fellow, how inconvenient. Masters will be wanting to come in and fetch things from their lockers."

"We'll make some arrangements about that," Stagge assured him. "By the way, sir, what line are you going to take with the staff? I don't see that the news can be kept from them for very long."

The headmaster looked worried. "I think, if you see no objection, that I'll try to get them all together before chapel tomorrow, tell them what's happened, and impress on them the need to keep quiet about it. They'll be sensible enough, I fancy."

"No details, please, sir. The bare facts only."

"My dear Stagge, of course."

They all bestirred themselves and left the room, the superintendent (having closed and latched all the windows) locking the door after them and pocketing the key. Wells led the way downstairs.

"And incidentally, Stagge," said the headmaster, "is there any news of that girl? All this has been such a shock that I'd almost forgotten about her."

"Nothing so far, sir," Stagge answered. "I've made the routine inquiries—railway stations and so forth—but without result. I can tell you, all this business is straining our local resources quite a bit. I may have to ask the chief constable to call in Scotland Yard."

He glanced at Fen as he spoke, but Fen had not heard. He was thinking of Brenda Boyce and of the reasons that made it certain that she, too, was dead.

† 6 †
LOVE LIES BLEEDING

They came out into the darkness and were met by the doctor. Wells remained behind to lock up the building, and the headmaster excused himself from accompanying them to Love's house.

"I've a feeling," he said, "that my condolences to Mrs. Love wouldn't mix well with your own investigations. Besides, I'm tired, and I don't really see that I can be any help."

"Very well, sir," Stagge agreed. "And as to the morning——"

"The chapel service is at ten, but I'll be in my study by nine. You can get hold of me there and then, and of course I shall be glad to hear what progress you've made. For the rest"—the headmaster was lighting a cigarette, and the match flame threw his cheekbones into relief and evoked fugitive shadows about his eyes —"for the rest, it's going to be a difficult day. I shall be extremely busy, but if you should happen to want me urgently. . . ." He blew out the match, and the obscurity seemed more oppressive after its small illumination.

"We'll be as discreet as possible, sir," Stagge promised. "I generally turn up at Speech Day in any case, so my being about won't surprise people."

"Good night, then. . . . Oh, Gervase, I'll leave the front door open for you, and there'll be whiskey and sandwiches in the drawing room. Good night again. And good luck."

He climbed into his car and drove away. The police car and the ambulance, followed by Fen in Lily Chris-

tine III, headed for Love's house. It was a longer journey than Fen had expected, and he calculated that a
fast walker would need at the very least a quarter of
an hour to accomplish it. The little party reassembled
at the gate.

"I can't think where we are," Fen complained. "I've
simply been pursuing your taillight."

"We're on the far side of Snagshill, sir," Stagge informed him; and with this sparse intelligence he had
for the moment to be content, since the darkness
defied all attempts at orientation. They trooped up the
path to the front door, and Stagge rang the bell. The
house appeared to be a medium-sized, unremarkable
bypass-type villa of flesh-colored brick. Presently the
door was opened by a diminutive, astigmatic elderly
woman whose cheeks bore the sticky marks of recent
weeping, and whose lusterless gray hair straggled un-
tamably over her ears and forehead. She blinked at
them uncertainly.

"Is it the police?" she said. "I thought you were
never coming."

She stood aside as they entered the hall. It was
little more than a passageway, prolific of lino-
leum, gum boots, antlers, umbrellas, and ancient
raincoats, its atmosphere compounded in equal pro-
portions of coffee and floor polish. The single electric
bulb shone wanly, and there were yellowed visiting
cards on a tarnished silver tray. As for the woman
herself, the headmaster's "wispy, mousy" described
her very adequately, Fen thought; but he was relieved, if also a little surprised, to see that she
showed no signs of hysteria. This fact, indeed, led
him to suspect that her lifelong subordination to her
husband might not have been entirely to her taste.
She was distressed, certainly; yet one received no impression that an indispensable prop had been struck
away from her.

As Stagge explained, in halting, hyperbolic phrases, the reason for their delay, her eyes widened.

"Michael!" she exclaimed. "What a ghastly, ghastly thing. . . . And my husband was devoted to him. Oh, dear, it's a night of disasters." She became suddenly voluble. "At first it was all right, being alone with Andrew, I mean, and then I began to get frightened because no one came, and you'll think this is silly, I know, but I started wondering if it was all a horrible dream, the way you do when things don't happen as you expect. . . ." She checked herself and flushed, like one discovered in a contemptible action. "Oh, but you'll be wanting to see him."

"If you please, Mrs. Love," said Stagge awkwardly.

"I won't go in with you," she said. "You won't need me. And I don't want—I don't——"

She choked on the words, inhaling in long, ragged gasps. The doctor, proffering consolation of a brisk, professional kind, led her to a chair. After a moment's embarrassed and unhappy silence the others went on to a door at the end of the hall, glad of the excuse to escape.

The room in which they found themselves a moment later was clearly Love's study. In an unpretentious fashion it was luxurious. The volumes on the bookshelves were grouped according to size—an over-decorative habit that Fen irrationally abhorred. There were filing cabinets, a desk, two capacious and sybaritic armchairs. French windows gave on to the back garden, with closed curtains of what looked remarkably like Point d'Alençon lace. On a brass tray of Indian design, which rested on trestles beside the door, stood an untouched tray of coffee and biscuits, with two clean cups. The flexible chromium reading lamp momentarily suggested a laboratory, and the suggestion was reinforced by a pervasive air of surgical spotlessness which was oddly at variance with what they had seen in the hall. The arrangement of the various objects on the desk, Fen noted, betrayed the hand of an almost fanatical precision.

Then they looked at Love, slumped forward in one of the armchairs, with his back to the French windows.

He had died as swiftly as Somers, though not, perhaps, so horribly. Lank gray hair had fallen across his high, bony forehead. One hand hung limply over his knee, while the other was tightly clenched in a reflex spasm. His lean, broad chest lay over the left arm of the chair, and his head sagged, stretching the sinews of a thin brown neck. A book was open on his lap, and Fen moved closer to examine it. *Pilkington's French Grammar: The Use of the Subjunctive* (I). Then a smear of blood. The trappings of death, Fen reflected, were only too often ignominious. To be hounded into eternity, like Pitt, voracious of pork pies, or with a mind preoccupied, in the last instant, with the French subjunctive . . . ."

"He can't have known anything about it," Stagge was saying. "Shot from behind, from the French windows. His head must have been an easy target, above the back of the chair." Without moving the body, he crouched down to look into its face. "There's an exit wound through the cheek." He straightened up, stared about the room, and after an instant walked rapidly to the desk. "And here, I fancy, is the bullet, embedded in the wood." Producing a penknife, he began to prise it out.

The doctor joined them, announcing that he had left Mrs. Love in the parlor. The ritual of the common room was reenacted. Photographs were taken; likely surfaces, including the handles and frames of the French windows, were tested for fingerprints; the doctor, examining the body, announced that a .38 had again been used, that Love had been dead between one and a half and three hours, and that there were no complications that he could see; and Love's pockets failed to provide anything of interest.

"This business is as featureless as the other wasn't," Stagge grumbled. "The basic data are the same, of course: He was shot from the same size gun, from the same distance, between ten and eleven. Apart from that. . . ."

He waved one hand acerbly and vanished into the garden, where he spent some minutes prowling about with an electric torch. Fen, becoming dolorously aware of his own inanition, set himself rather dutifully than optimistically to investigate the contents of the desk. Presently Stagge returned, perceptibly uninspirited.

"There's an asphalt path," he reported, "running from the French windows round the house to the front gate. And the ground's as hard as rock. No cigarette stubs. No footprints. No fragments of clothing caught on projecting nails. *Nothing.*"

"There's something here, though," said Fen, looking up from a pile of papers which he had taken from a drawer. "And it may help us towards the motive. Read this."

He held out a plain sheet of notepaper with a few lines of neat handwriting on it. Stagge reads the words aloud.

" 'This is to put on record the fact that two of my colleagues at Castrevenford School are associated together in what can only be described as a deliberate fraud, which. . . .' " Stagge snorted in disappointment. "And there it stops. But you're quite right, sir. There's no doubt this is important."

"The really interesting thing about it," said Fen, "is that he's half crossed out the word 'colleagues.' "

"So he has. That's curious. And it's odd he didn't finish it. I suppose he was either interrupted or else decided the statement didn't serve any useful purpose."

"Ah," said Fen obscurely. "Lend me your lens a moment, will you?"

He examined the handwriting, comparing it with other examples of Love's calligraphy which he had found in the desk. "It's authentic, all right," he remarked, "and to judge from the condition of the ink, written not later than this morning." He handed the lens and the paper to Stagge and seemed about to make some further comment when he caught sight of a stack of corrected essays on the desk. He picked up the top one and contemplated it thoughtfully.

"Listen to what this boy has written," he said. " 'The phrase "ἀρχόμενος ὡσεὶ ἐτῶν τριάκοντα" used in St. Luke's gospel is ambiguous.' And this is Love's marginal correction: 'The word *ambiguous* can only properly be used of something which has *two* possible meanings, not of something which has more than two; substitute *vague* or *indefinite*.' "

Stagge looked very blank. "I don't see what you're getting at, sir."

Fen replaced the essay. "No?" he said cheerfully. "It's quite relevant, I think. . . . Well, what now?"

Stagge consulted his watch. "Half-past one. I don't see that there's much more we can do apart from talking to Mrs. Love. Is she fit enough to answer questions, Doctor?"

"Yes, I think so," said the doctor. "She's had a nasty shock, but I doubt if she's bowled over with grief. I knew Love slightly, and he was domineering in an insidious, underhand sort of way. His wife may look characterless, but I suspect that secretly she resented her serfdom."

"Could she have shot him?" Stagge asked curiously.

"Psychologically, you mean? I don't see why not."

"Except that she didn't," said Fen; and spoke with

such tactless certainty that the superintendent showed signs of irritation.

"That remains to be seen," he stated curtly. "Doctor, you'd better get him out to the ambulance while we're talking to her."

The parlor, in marked contrast to the study, was a shabby, untidy room, as characteristic of the wife as the other had been of the husband. Its only remarkable feature was a spirited depiction over the fireplace, in a large gilt frame, of Lot's wife being transmogrified into a pillar of salt, with the Cities of the Plain burning tumultuously in the background and Lot himself looking on rather as though the metamorphosis were some interesting technical process specially exhibited for his enjoyment. Beneath this overwhelming canvas, like votive offerings at the shrine of some pagan deity, a profusion of unfinished attempts at sewing, knitting, darning, and embroidery lay scattered on the chairs and tables. Even to the uninstructed eye it was evident that Mrs. Love's housekeeping was of the most primitive and desperate kind, and Fen, meditating on the incessant small stresses that must result from the marriage of a chronically tidy man with a chronically untidy woman, was no longer surprised at the lack of serious grief in Mrs. Love's reactions to the evening's event.

Her volubility had returned, and although she sat twisting a tear-sodden handkerchief in her hands, an unhealthy gleam of excitement lurked in her eyes. Stagge, embarked on a prolegomenon of discreetly consolatory phrases, found himself cut short.

"Who did it, Mr. Stagge?" she exclaimed. "Did he kill himself? What happened?"

Stagge disguised an obscure sense of outrage as best he might. "We don't think your husband killed himself, Mrs. Love, since we found no weapon in the room. As to what happened, we were hoping you would be able to help us there."

He paused, and from the hall they heard the tramp of feet and the murmur of voices. Mrs. Love said:

"But how can I help you, Mr. Stagge? I know nothing about it, nothing; the whole thing has been a complete surprise to me; I should say a most terrible shock. And dear Michael, too, such a nice boy. I remember him well at Merfield; my husband had a house there, you know—Peterfield it was called, though I think the system they have here of naming houses after housemasters is much better. Anyway, dear Michael was head boy for a year before he left, or was it a year and a term——"

"Yes, ma'am," Stagge broke in hurriedly. "We know something about that. But as to this evening——"

"It was the coffee," Mrs. Love said unexpectedly.

"I beg your pardon, ma'am?"

"I'd run out of coffee, a most unusual thing for me; I'm sure I don't know how it happened, unless Mrs. Fiske, that's my charlady, has been using it; servants are so difficult nowadays one never knows what they're doing when one's back is turned; but anyway, I knew Andrew wouldn't drink tea or cocoa; he's exceedingly particular about things like that and never touches alcohol of course, so I thought to myself——"

"Just one moment, Mrs. Love: Let's get everything in order. Exactly when did you last see your husband alive?"

She appeared surprised at the question. "Why, at dinner, of course. After dinner Andrew always worked alone in his study until a quarter to eleven exactly, and he made it a rule that he wasn't on any account to be disturbed, so inconvenient because people who didn't know his habits realized he was in, and

I had to explain that he couldn't see them, and often they went away offended."

Fen, awaiting a hiatus, saw his opportunity. "But of course," he said, "the other masters would be aware of all this."

"Oh, yes, it was something of a joke among them. They always said they could set their watches by Andrew, and it was as near true as made no difference; sometimes I used to chaff him about it, tell him he musn't get into a rut, but he'd never alter his ways, and naturally I had to fit in with them, and not being temperamentally a punctual person, I've always found it difficult; still, you can't have everything, can you?"

To this proposition Stagge very heartily agreed, less because he was impressed by its sapience than because he foresaw that the interview would last until dawn if he did not take every available chance of getting a word in. "And what happened after dinner?" he said.

"Why, Andrew worked alone in his study, and I sat in here writing letters; it's a job I hate; I always leave them till the last possible moment and beyond, though Andrew makes a point of answering his the very day they arrive, which is the only way really, because otherwise they prey on one's mind."

"And did anyone call during the evening?"

"Oh, no, Mr. Stagge. Didn't I tell you about Andrew being so regular in his habits? You see, he always——"

"Yes," said Stagge hastily. "You did tell me. I quite understand. Now, did you hear anything unusual during the evening?"

"Well," said Mrs. Love, after pausing, unprecedentedly, for reflection, "there was a weird play on the wireless, very intelligent, I expect, but not the sort of thing I like; they do broadcast such extraordinary things sometimes; I dare say Andrew would have made something of it; I always felt with him that I had so much to live up to in a way it was a strain."

"No doubt," Stagge remarked rather tactlessly. "No doubt it was a strain. And you didn't leave the house at all?"

"But I did. I went out to post my letters."

"At what time, ma'am?"

"I can tell you that because I always have to have my eye on the clock, and I remember thinking that there was just time enough to post them if I hurried, and then they'd go by the early morning post, and although it's tiresome the pillar box being so far away, I felt I *ought* to put myself out because two of the letters I should have written *weeks* ago, and although one post earlier probably wouldn't make much difference, one feels in a case like that that one has to do what one can."

Stagge suppressed a sigh of impatience. "But you still haven't told us, ma'am, what time you *did* go out."

"Oh, haven't I? It was at twenty-five minutes past ten. I left the kettle on for our nightcap, you see——"

"And when did you return?"

"At twenty to eleven, Mr. Stagge. And it was then I found there was no coffee left; I use the kind you just mix with milk or water, and the tin was quite empty; I'm sure it was Mrs. Fiske; I shall speak to her about it; and I knew Andrew would be annoyed, because he likes his coffee at a quarter to eleven punctual to the minute, but it couldn't be helped; I ran to Mrs. Philpotts's house to borrow some; it was the best thing I could think of, and what with her chatter (some people seem to be able to talk for hours without taking breath; I don't know how they do it, I'm sure), anyway, it was eleven by the time I got the coffee ready and took it in to Andrew and—and"—her garrulity suddenly expired—"and found him."

She dabbed at her eyes with the handkerchief. It

was not a feigned emotion, Fen thought, but it stemmed from the nerves rather than from the affections.

"One thing more, ma'am," said Stagge, taking advantage of her quiescence. "Do you know of anyone who might have wished your husband harm?"

A welter of explanation followed, but divested of its encrusting irrelevances, it came to very little and offered no useful suggestion of motive. And since the question had been a purely formal one, Stagge decided that no useful purpose could be served by their remaining longer. He got to his feet, eyeing Fen eloquently, and Fen, who by this time was partially comatose, obediently followed his example. Stagge said:

"You've been very helpful, Mrs. Love," and his face reddened slightly at this harmless demonstration of hypocrisy. "We'll leave you now, and you must get some rest."

"Are you going—are you going to take him away?"

"With your permission, yes." Stagge hesitated. "I don't know if you've any friend you'd like to have with you for the night. . . ."

"Oh, no." She spoke with curious emphasis. "I shall be all right. This will be the first time I've been on my own for nearly forty years. I shall be all right."

At the gate they met the sergeant, the constable, and the doctor.

"I've got him inside," said the latter, nodding toward a louring black shape interpretable as the ambulance. "And if you ask me, it's about time we all went to bed."

Stagge was absently flashing his torch on and off. "Yes," he said slowly, "I think it is. Well, I don't know if I've done everything I should have done. As I said earlier, this sort of thing's new to me."

"In my opinion," Fen remarked, "you've handled the case admirably—and in very unusual and trying circumstances, too."

Stagge was plainly cheered by this testimonial. "Well," he said more briskly, "what do you think about it all?"

"Love may have been shot while his wife was out of the house, but if a silencer was used. . . ."

"It's likely, isn't it," Stagge said, "that he was killed before a quarter to eleven, the time when she regularly took him his coffee. That's to say, it's likely if the murderer knew of that particular habit. There were two cups on the tray, so I take it she had hers with him in the study. . . . Well, I'll sleep on it, sir, and see you in the morning."

They said good night, and after Fen had obtained directions for reaching the headmaster's house, parted, silent and tired. And Fen shivered a little as he climbed into his car, for the turn of the night was approaching—the time, he reflected, when sick men most often die. He was very thoughtful as he drove home through the darkness.

† 7 †

SATURNALIA

Speech Day dawned bright and clear—an uncommon eventuality for which the headmaster was devoutly thankful; at least he would be spared the nuisance of hurriedly substituting an indoor program for an outdoor one. Over breakfast, in the sunny morning room, Fen narrated the circumstances of Love's demise, and the headmaster listened gloomily.

"What with tiredness and worry," he said, "I was quite light-headed last night. Now I feel like a drunkard on the morning after—only too conscious of the sordidness of it all. I must remember to write to Gabbitas this morning for a couple of substitutes." He poured out more coffee. "Heavens, how I detest change! I sometimes think that change, and change alone, is the source of all misery. No doubt Eden was quite static and lethargic."

"All progress involves change," Fen remarked rather tediously. He was never at his best at breakfast.

"Then all change is evil," said the headmaster dogmatically. "On the material plane, anyway. Nature demands—for some inscrutable reason—an equilibrium. Destroy one equilibrium, and you're in misery during the transition to another. A man owns a bicycle and feels content. Then he begins to want a car and is miserable—the old equilibrium between himself and his possessions being destroyed—until he gets it. So it goes on."

"I'm inclined to think," said Fen, "that neither opposing nor advocating change makes much difference to the sum total of human misery. History suggests that it stays constant in quantity, if not in kind. Science rids us of plague but endows us with the atom bomb. Humanitarianism rids us of sweated labor but offers us the horrors of political agitation in its place. There's a choice of evils, but that's all."

"Pessimist," said the headmaster. "Ah, well, this is scarcely the time for philosophies of history. Have you any ideas about these murders?"

"Some strong suspicions. But we haven't collected all the necessary data yet."

"I see." The headmaster finished his coffee and thrust an aged cherrywood pipe into his mouth. "Well, I shall go and robe myself now. Are you going to wear your ceremonial trappings all day?"

"Good God, no. It'll be far too hot. I'll wear them for the actual speeches, and that's all. . . . By the way, have you a school list I could borrow?"

"There's one on the hall table," said the headmaster as he made for the door. "You can keep that."

He departed upstairs, and Fen, having found the list, settled down on the terrace in the sunlight to examine it, while the birds sang lustily in the high beeches and the last wisps of early mist vanished from beneath the hedges. The list was in the form of a small booklet bound in yellow paper. The bulk of it consisted of catalogs of boys, but to these he paid scant attention, concentrating instead on the first three pages, which contained a roster of the names, addresses, and telephone numbers of the masters, followed by a similar catalog of the other employees of the school—to be specific, the adjutant of the J.T.C., his assistant, the bursar, the librarian, the headmaster's secretary, the matron of the sanatorium, the medical officer, the proprietor of the school shop, the head groundsman, the porter, the carpenter. Fen noted that domestic staffs were not included, but that, fortunately, was not important.

He took out a pencil and traced runic signs in the margin.

Presently the headmaster reappeared, resplendent in the crimson and scarlet robe of an Oxford Doctor of Civil Law, and they drove to the school site and the study in Davenant's. On the way the headmaster explained the day's program.

"The chapel service, at ten, is quite a short one. Then at a quarter to eleven there's a mass gymnastic display in the playing fields, accompanied by the corps band. Nothing after that till the afternoon; the boys lunch with their parents, mostly, and the staff tends to drift down to The Boar in Castrevenford and drink gin. Speeches and prize-giving at two-thirty—and since we can never get everyone into the Hall, the cricket match between the First Eleven and the Old Boys begins at the same time, to give the outcasts something to look at. At four, or as near as possible, there's a gigantic garden party at my house, with tea in relays. After dinner there's a play—or there will be if Mathieson can manage it without Brenda Boyce. And tomorrow—God be praised—a whole holiday."

The site was still more or less deserted under the sun as they drove up the oak-lined drive, for on this morning the boys breakfasted late. One or two, however, were already strolling about, wearing dark blue suits and carnations or roses in their button-holes—this last a traditional ostentation permitted to even the smallest and most insignificant new-comer on Speech Day. They saluted the headmaster as he passed, and in gazing earnestly at the sky with a view to prophesying the weather he narrowly missed immolating one of them. Wells was visible, hurrying distantly on some obscure administrative errand. Mr. Merrythought, inscrutably misanthropic, was scratching himself tentatively beneath a tree. And from the windows of Davenant's, as they arrived there, came a sanguine uproar of shouting and whistling.

The headmaster at once plunged into conference with Galbraith, with a view to assembling the staff in one of the classrooms before chapel, and soon Galbraith retired to his room for a prolonged bout of telephoning. At a quarter past nine Stagge arrived. Dark rings round his eyes suggested that he had slept little, but he spoke with an attempt at animation. He said:

"I've posted a plainclothes constable outside the masters' common room, sir. He's got the key, so if anyone wants anything out of there, they've only got to ask. I needn't add that an eye will be kept on them while they're getting it. Perhaps you'd inform the masters about the arrangement when you see them."

"By all means, Superintendent. I hope they'll all be there."

"So do I," said Stagge rather grimly. "And that's another way in which you can help me. I should like to know whether they *are* all there—and if not, why not. Is anyone likely to be absent?"

"Not if my secretary can get in touch with them all. There's no one ill, and it's an unwritten law that all masters shall be present on Speech Day. Before I came here, they tended to sneak off to London in order to avoid the parents, but I've stopped that." Stagge nodded his satisfaction. "And have there been any—ah— further developments?" the headmaster inquired.

"Very few, sir. I've examined the two bullets, and although they'll have to go to a ballistics expert for a further check, I've no doubt, myself, that they came from the same gun. What we have to do now is to find out where that gun came from and where it's gone."

"The river," Fen suggested.

"I'm afraid it may be that, sir. Still . . . ."

"What are your plans for the day, then?" the headmaster asked.

"We've a good deal to get through, sir. There are the two postmortems—of course, we can't do more than wait for the results of them. Then Mr. Somers's rooms and the common room will have to be thoroughly searched. We shall have to look into the provenance of the weapon—that is," Stagge charitably interpreted, "where it came from. We shall have to find out how long Somers took writing those reports. And—heaviest job of all—we've got to discover where everyone was between ten and eleven last evening. I'm putting three men on to that, and it might be as well, sir, if you were to inform the masters that they're likely to be interrogated discreetly during the day. Anyone who has anything to hide will be prepared for that, so it gives nothing away and can't do any harm."

"My dear Superintendent, I very much appreciate your unobtrusive methods."

"Provided unobtrusiveness doesn't interfere with our efficiency, sir, you shall have it. And now, if you've a moment to spare, you may be able to help me."

"In what way?"

"I believe, sir, that you were here in your study last evening up to the time I arrived."

"That's so. From eight thirty onwards."

"Did you leave the room at any time, sir?"

"No. Not even for a moment."

"And you heard nothing unusual?"

"Again, no."

"Did you at any time hear a car or a motorcycle moving about the site?" Fen asked.

The headmaster reflected for a moment. "That's more difficult, but I don't think so. . . . Wait, though," he added resipiscently, "I'm not sure whether Galbraith came in his car. . . . No, he didn't. I remember now. And all the people at the Fasti meeting were on foot, I'm certain."

"Very good, sir," said Stagge. "Now, this Fasti meeting: At what time did it begin?"

"Nine thirty. Whenever housemasters are concerned we have to have our meetings rather late, as in the evenings they have things to look after in their houses."

"And the meeting ended when?"

"Just before ten forty-five. People were leaving when Galbraith arrived."

"I see." Stagge produced his notebook. "Now, sir, can you give me a list of the people who were at the meeting? Just the names."

The headmaster frowned as he lit his pipe. "Philpotts, for cricket. Weems, for music. Saltmarsh, for the corps. Mathieson, for the Cinema Club. Du Cann, for outside lecturers. Peterkin, for examinations. Stout—the chaplain—for religious services. Morton, for swimming. Lumb, for rowing. . . . I think that's the lot."

"Thank you, sir. Was anyone missing who ought to have been there?"

"No one. A full attendance."

"And they all left together?"

"In a bunch, Superintendent. Of course, they probably separated when they got outside. But I was too pleased at being rid of them to notice."

"And after that, you were alone with your secretary until you received the news?"

"Exactly."

"Were there any other official functions going on at this time?"

"No. A good many unofficial ones, though. The evening before Speech Day is always an evening of parties."

"Ah." Stagge shut his notebook and returned it to his pocket. "That may help us a good deal. We shall try, you see, to get a list of all those who have no alibi for any part of the relevant period—ten to eleven. And when we've discovered how long Mr. Somers worked at his reports, we shall be able to narrow the list down still further."

The headmaster said: "Are you, then, assuming that these murders cannot have been an—ah—outside job?"

"We're assuming nothing, sir," Stagge answered, so stiffly and officially as to forbid further inquiry, "until we have more facts to go on. Oh, one other thing: I should like your personal opinion as to the reliability, or otherwise, of your school porter, Wells, and of Mr. Etherege."

The headmaster was surprised. "They're both quite trustworthy, I should say. Wells has been with the school for over twenty years; he's a fussy man, but the soul of honesty. As to Etherege, he's a more complex case. He takes a devouring interest in his fellow beings, and I've never known his scandal to be inaccurate. I trust him, I think, on the rather vague grounds that he enjoys thinking and reading and talking too much to indulge in any action which isn't essential to keeping him alive and clothed and fed. I don't know if I make myself clear. . . ."

But he was not destined to be enlightened on the matter, for at this moment: "The clans are gathering," Fen announced from his post at the window. They went to join him.

A group of masters was assembled outside Hubbard's Building, and more were arriving at every moment. The white hoods of the Bachelors, the red of the Masters, the buttonholes—pinpoints of color at this distance—and the more exotic gaudiness of one or two Doctors were splashed vividly against the liver-colored brick and green ivy. They seemed reluctant to leave the sunlight. And the rest of the site was crescently animated. Cars were being parked on an exiguous gravel half-moon or along the sides of the avenue.

Boys were emerging in increasing numbers to greet, guide, and control their apprehensive kin. Mr. Philpotts was running across the First Eleven pitch, his gown flying behind him like a banner. And everywhere there were parents—parents mouselike, parents aggressive, parents ostentatious, parents modest, parents subdued, parents animated: a growing rout lured together under the radiant porcelain sky—and for what? the headmaster wondered. It was improbable that they enjoyed themselves. It was improbable, even, that their offspring enjoyed themselves. And yet there was a glamor about it all which stirred the blood, and the headmaster himself, as he contemplated the spectacle, was not immune.

"It's nearly a quarter to," he said cheerfully, "so I must go. Are you coming with me, Superintendent?"

"No, sir, I don't think so. It's hardly necessary for me to be there."

"Very well. But from now on, remember, I shall be up to my ears in it." He spoke almost with gusto.

"I'll get on quietly with my job, sir," Stagge assured him, "and if anything important should happen, I'll find a way of letting you know."

"What about you, Gervase? Are you coming?"

"I might as well," said Fen. "See you in ten minutes," he added to Stagge.

"Galbraith!" the headmaster called. The secretary appeared inquiringly in his doorway. "Come with me and take a tally of the devils, so that we can be sure they're all there."

"I got into touch with everyone, sir."

"Good. But come just the same." The headmaster went to a bowl of roses, selected a fine bud, broke off the stalk, and pressed it upon Stagge. "Protective coloring," he told him. "Now you can pretend to be a parent." He picked up his mortarboard and clapped it rakishly onto his head. "Are we ready? Then let's go."

He strode energetically across the site toward Hubbard's Building, with Fen and Galbraith on either side of him like pilot fish escorting a shark. Boys saluted; fathers lifted their hats; mothers nodded and smiled. The headmaster responded to them all with a discreet affability. Fen, though he had been persuaded to abandon his tie with the mermaids, still presented a distinguished and festive appearance. "They'll think you're Lord Washburton," the headmaster remarked.

And "So I ought to be," said Fen. The staff, observing their employer's approach, moved inside the building. And the three men followed them as the clock in its copper-roofed tower struck the three quarters.

They were assembled in the room where Fen had made a pretense of pedagogy on the previous day—some thirty men of all ages, seated on the tops of desks or on the windowsills, interested, curious, argumentative. Fen lounged in the doorway with Galbraith. The headmaster, subduing his ferial spirits to the exigencies of his announcement, made his way to the dais.

"Gentlemen," he said, and they fell silent. "I'm sorry to have been obliged to call this brief emergency meeting, but there is, as you will hear, good reason for it. You will have noticed that neither Love nor Somers is amongst us. It is my painful duty to tell you that—that they are dead, and in circumstances which point to murder."

There was a movement of astonishment and dismay, but no one spoke. The headmaster, glancing quickly at their faces, went on:

"Somers met his end last evening in the masters' common room. For that reason the room is at present locked, but a plainclothes constable is on duty there who will admit you if you require anything urgently. I feel sure you will appreciate the necessity of this temporary inconvenience and will cooperate with the police in the matter."

He paused. A dead stillness held the room in trance. The only movement came from Galbraith, who, being a small man, was obliged to stand on tiptoe to count those present.

"The police have also asked me," the headmaster proceeded, "to warn you that you may be interrogated during the day. They are being kind enough to act discreetly, and in view of this I must ask you to speak of this matter, for the time being, to *no one,* and among yourselves as little as possible. You will easily see how ruinous any rumor of these events would be to our day's program. We must safeguard the interests of the school, and there can be no callousness in avoiding conversation and conjecture on the subject during the few hours before the news breaks. Please behave during the day as if nothing had happened, whatever your personal feelings may be.

"That is all, gentlemen. You will naturally be curious as to the details of the affair, but I am not allowed to say more than I have. By this evening, no doubt, it will all be public property. In the meantime let us have as happy and successful a day as we can."

He gestured dismissal, and after a moment's hesitation Peterkin, the second master, moved forward. "I'm sure I'm speaking for all my colleagues when I say that we shall do our utmost to—to carry out your wishes."

A murmur of concurrence was followed by a brief, uncertain hush. Then they filed out, slowly and mutely. Fen would have given much to see into their minds. He went to join the headmaster.

"Everyone here, sir," Galbraith reported.

"Good," said the headmaster. "I'm glad *that's* over . . . and now, chapel."

They emerged from Hubbard's Building, in the

wake of a furtively murmuring band of dominies, as the bell began tolling. The many groups lingering on the site veered toward it, and an ambling, disorganized procession began. To Stagge—his lapel lifted so that his prominent nose might more effectively take in the scent of the yellow rose in his buttonhole—the substance of the meeting was conveyed. Galbraith left them and hurried back to the study in Davenant's.

"What now?" Fen demanded.

"I think," said Stagge, "that I'll have a look at the common room, while everyone's out of the way."

"I shall go to the service, then, and meet you afterwards."

"Very well, sir. Later on I'm going to investigate Mr. Somers's rooms. I don't know if you'd like to come with me. . . ."

"I'll be there," Fen promised.

He walked to the chapel with the headmaster, who immediately disappeared through the vestry door, and waited, contemplating the crowded approaches, until the cessation of the bell warned everyone to go inside. Fen had no ticket, but he persuaded Wells to allow him into one of the galleries and stood at the back throughout the service, observing with faint amusement an inordinate degree of surreptitious whispering in the masters' stalls. The choir processed in red and white, with the chaplain and the headmaster bringing up the rear; prayers were read; hymns were sung and canticles chanted, in voices of electrifying volume and timbre; the headmaster expatiated on such few topics as are simultaneously appropriate to prize-givings and the Christian religion; and Parry's "Jerusalem" brought the proceedings to a noisily idealistic close.

Fen slipped out a little before the end, and lighting a cigarette, walked back across the empty site to Hubbard's Building. Through a gap in the beech trees he could see the river, with a single swan dipping its beak and head into the water with the luxurious deliberation of an epicure placing a spoon in a coffee cup. Oblongs of radiant emerald among the dry grass of the playing fields marked the cricket pitches, and the heat was refracted fiercely from the asphalt paths. Mr. Merrythought was stretched at full length under a tree; a sparrow watched him with the cheerful insouciance of a street Arab. Thousands of feet up, a skylark sang in adoration of the sun. Light flashed, swift and dazzling, from the windscreens and polished metal of the long line of parked cars. Turning as he came to the porch of Hubbard's Building, Fen saw the crowds emerging from the chapel and spreading out like a jet of multicolored steam from a narrow orifice. The clock chimed the half-hour.

Stagge, grimy and flushed with effort, was still in the common room; his work, he admitted morosely, had met with no success, and he still had the downstairs classrooms to examine. Fen commiserated mildly, refrained from offering to help, and went outside again. On leaving chapel, the boys had abandoned their relatives and hurried back to their houses to change. The headmaster was drifting sociably from group to importunate group. Old Boys of three months' standing strolled aggressively about with pipes in their mouths, unsuccessfully attempting to conceal their automatic subservience to erstwhile form masters and housemasters. Presently the return of the boys, clad now in white vests, blue shorts, and running shoes, made it clear that the display was about to begin. The corps band arrived, their well-polished instruments glittering in the sun, and assembled by the cricket pavilion. An audience of parents, masters, Old Boys, and domestic staff gathered at the edge of the field. The boys disposed themselves in orderly ranks on the turf. Major Percival, adjutant to the corps and gymnastics instructor, climbed a stepladder with a large gray megaphone in his hand and surveyed them complacently. The clock struck a quarter to eleven. "Attention!" said Major Percival through his megaphone and was instantaneously obeyed. Sergeant Shelley lifted his baton. Mr. Merrythought fell into a spasm of premonitory barking. Conversation flickered, faded, died. The band, squinting down their noses at the music clipped to their instruments, launched into a Sousa march.

For twenty minutes—while the band played marches, waltzes, and potpourris, and Major Percival bellowed words of command—the school waved its arms and legs, stood on its head, bent and unbent, turned somersaults, marched and countermarched—all with a clockwork precision that drew murmurs of admiration from its progenitors and a qualified approval from its temporal pastors. Certainly they made a colorful and attractive spectacle, Fen thought—and then told himself regretfully that he ought to be more usefully occupied than in gazing at colorful and attractive spectacles. Loose ends must be tidied up; the case had been exceptionally straightforward and obvious so far (the problem of motive apart), but it might be useful to have confirmation on one or two points. He looked about him, perceived a middle-aged master standing alone some few yards off, and went up to him. "I wonder," he said, "if you'd mind pointing out Mr. Etherege to me?"

"I am Etherege," said the middle-aged master. He took Fen's hand and then dropped it suddenly, as though it were a nettle. "I'm very pleased to meet you," he went on. "Your boy is doing splendidly. I have great hopes for him."

"No, no," said Fen. "I'm not a parent."

"Indeed?" said Mr. Etherege civilly and shook hands again, in the same perfunctory fashion as before. He had neat dark hair, thin at the crown, and wore horn-rimmed spectacles. Despite the disreputable hacking coat and gray flannel trousers which he wore beneath his gown, he was overwhelmingly urbane, with the air of an impoverished but unrepentant aristocrat. Fen introduced himself, and Mr. Etherege, apparently on the point of shaking hands a third time, thought better of it and gestured, instead, at the school's gyrations.

"Are you enjoying this?" he asked.

"Tolerably well," said Fen. "It has the unexacting, boneless charm of a ballet."

"It represents Discipline," said Mr. Etherege, whose question had clearly been less a demand for information than a pretext for some discussion of his own. "And to the uninstructed mind, Uniformity." His abstract nouns were audibly furnished with capital letters. "But the latter notion is fallacious."

"No doubt," said Fen. He perceived that this incipient homily required punctuation rather than argument.

"Fallacious," Mr. Etherege proceeded, "because the attempt to produce Uniformity inevitably accentuates Eccentricity. It makes Eccentricity, as it were, *safe*. It is only when a boy is thrown on his own devices, in business or at the university, that he tends to become typed. Man is a gregarious animal. At school Gregariousness is compulsory and inescapable and thus encourages its opposite. But in the world at large, a man who desires the company of his fellows is compelled to associate himself with some broadly defined Category—the *sportif,* the artistic, the studious, and whatnot—and in so doing has the sharp edges of the Individuality rubbed away. It is only in a place like this that you can be sure of finding freaks."

"Ah," said Fen.

"In fact, much of the criticism of the public schools

is based on a childish psychological Error—to wit, that the adolescent mind is receptive rather than critical. This is simply untrue. The customary left-wing objections to a preponderance of schoolmasters of the conservative persuasion are therefore foolish. In these matters the senior boys always take the view diametrically opposed to that of their instructors. To install socialist masters would inevitably result in a nationwide revival of Conservatism."

Mr. Etherege paused upon this magniloquent prognosis, and Fen grasped the opportunity of changing the topic. "Interesting," he observed not untruthfully. "Love, then, must have encouraged libertinism, and Somers—what did he encourage?"

"Somers lacked personality," said Mr. Etherege, "with the result that he neither encouraged nor discouraged anything."

"And he also, I take it, lacked money."

"His salary was three hundred and seventy pounds a year," Mr. Etherege stated tranquilly, "and the balance in his bank account, when he died, must have been about a hundred and fifty pounds. Therefore it's inconceivable that he was murdered for profit. He had made no will, so that what little he had will go to a very well-to-do aunt in Middlesbrough who is his nearest relation. He had no particular friends and no particular enemies, so that murder from personal motives is almost equally inconceivable."

"What about women?"

"His sexual life," said Mr. Etherege didactically, "was confined to one young woman named Sonia Delaney, who works as a mannequin at a West End store, and whom he visited once or twice each holidays. The arrangement was a purely commercial one, and I see no possibility of any complications there."

"Then you're at a loss to suggest any motive for his murder?"

"I am at a loss," Mr. Etherege admitted dolefully. His expression reminded Fen of a cricketer who has missed a particularly easy catch.

"And as regards Love?"

"Love," said Mr. Etherege with something like venom, "was an automaton, not a human being." It was clear that Mr. Etherege was peeved at Love's failure to supply grist to his highly efficient mill. "He and his wife were temperamentally incompatible; she might have killed him."

"In fact, she did not."

"No? Then most probably he was interfering with some harmless vice, and its practitioner turned on him."

"Sonia Delaney?"

Mr. Etherege shook his head. "He knew about her."

"And raised no objection? I thought Somers was his protégé."

"Love was a puritan but not undiscriminating." Mr. Etherege, whose face during the last few moments had been wrinkled with discomfort, now produced a large handkerchief and blew into it with such violence as to suggest that he was attempting to emulate the effect of Roland's horn at Roncevaux. "Hay fever," he explained. "What was I saying?"

"You were saying that Love's puritanism was not indiscriminate."

"Exactly. It was a *commercial* puritanism, so to speak—concerned above all with money. Love no doubt objected to Somers having a mistress; but he would have objected far more if, for example, Somers had been attempting to cheat the Inland Revenue Department."

The band was by now playing the vapid strains of the "Merry Widow" waltz. "A commercial puritanism," Fen thought; that fitted well enough with Love's statement about a fraud. Otherwise Mr. Etherege had not so far been conspicuously helpful, for all his astoundingly detailed knowledge. The problem of motive would have to be tackled from some other standpoint.

"Do you mind," Fen said, "if I ask you one or two more questions?"

Mr. Etherege simultaneously sneezed and uttered assent. The resultant sound caused a momentary consternation among their immediate neighbors. "That's better," he said, plying his handkerchief vigorously. "That's cleared it. Yes, ask anything you like. I've already been approached on the matter of the reports. If you're wanting to know anything about them, I can tell you quite definitely that when I left the common room at ten last evening Somers had ninety-seven to write."

"Your information seems extraordinarily exact."

"It is," said Mr. Etherege rather smugly. "In this particular instance there is, of course, a good reason for that. Immediately following the first period yesterday afternoon I asked Somers when he was likely to finish his reports (you must understand that I knew he would be late with them, on account of his wrist). He said he proposed to begin them at ten that evening and hand them over to Wells at eleven. I completed my own reports earlier in the evening, and as it seemed to me that he would have his work cut out to do the job in the stated time, I counted the number he had to fill in. As I say, it was ninety-seven."

"And can you say *which* ninety-seven?"

Mr. Etherege sneezed again. "Oh, yes," he observed when he had recovered. "For the good reason that Wells took the remainder down to his office at ten."

"Useful," Fen commented. "Tell me more. Was Wells's regularity, in renewing the blotting paper and sitting in his office between ten and eleven, generally known?"

"Most certainly."

"And Love's chronometric habits?"

"Likewise a recurrent and tedious joke."

"Good. Have you noticed anything odd about Love's behavior recently?"

"Yes. I mentioned it to Somers only yesterday. He seemed to be brooding over some injury." A look of occupational frustration appeared on Mr. Etherege's urbane countenance. "But what the injury was," he added morosely, "I don't know. Nor, apparently, did Somers."

"How did Somers come to sprain his wrist?"

"He fell off his bicycle," said Mr. Etherege, "about a week ago."

"Did anyone see this happen?"

"About five hundred people, I should say. It happened in front of Hubbard's Building just as we were all coming out of early school. He was trying to avoid some idiot boy who wasn't looking where he was going. A very nasty sprain, I may add; I saw it myself."

"Did Somers always use black ink?"

"Ever since I've known him he's used it."

"Ah," said Fen pensively. "And in that case——"

He was interrupted by a round of applause. The display was at an end. Major Percival climbed down from his stepladder. The band trudged away to rid itself of its instruments, the boys returned to their houses to change, and the spectators, for the most part infirm of purpose, began wandering slowly and vaguely about.

"Is there anything more?" Mr. Etherege asked, pinching the bridge of his nose to stifle a threatened sneeze. "Because I see two parents bearing down on me."

"Nothing, thanks. You've been most helpful."

Mr. Etherege released his nose, sneezed instantly, and contemplated the approaching couple with visible dismay. "I cannot imagine," he said, "why so ill-favored a pair should feel it incumbent upon them to breed . . . excuse me." He went up to the male partner and took him limply by the hand. "Very pleased to meet you," he said. "Your boy is doing splendidly. I have great hopes for him."

Fen left him, went in pursuit of Sergeant Shelley, who was heading for the armory, and caught him up almost at its door. He made himself known, and Shelley saluted him with respect. Shelley was an old professional soldier who had been obliged to leave the regular army because of gastric trouble. Though he carried himself rigidly, he looked far from well. He had rheumy blue eyes, close-cropped hair, a pale face, a small moustache, and (Fen was interested to notice) a pronounced Cockney accent. And he possessed that habit of pertinence and economy of words which a military career often induces.

"I should like, if I may, to ask you a few questions," Fen said without preliminary. "Have you heard any rumor of what happened last night?"

"A bare outline, sir, from Wells."

"Admirable. Then I needn't take up your time with explanations. A .38 revolver was used in both cases, and we want to know if by any chance it came from the armory."

"I thought of that, sir, and I was just going to look. I 'aven't 'ad a chance to do it up to now."

"Let's go inside, then."

The sergeant took a key from his pocket and unlocked the door. The armory was no more than a low, oblong wooden hut, extremely stuffy, and so inadequately furnished with windows that even on this brilliant morning it was necessary to switch on the electric light. There was a pervasive smell of oil. A very large number of antiquated rifles stood in racks along the walls. At the far end, other equipment—

belts, haversacks, water bottles—lay in heaps. An im-
prisoned fly buzzed vehemently against one of the
dusty panes, and Shelley's boots were loud on the uneven planks of the floor.

He went immediately to a sizable cupboard and
opened it, Fen noting that it was kept unlocked.

"The ammunition's kept 'ere, sir," he said. "Mostly
blanks, o' course. But there ought to be three Colt .38s
and some cartridges to go with 'em."

His examination of the cupboard lasted only a few
moments. "You were quite right, sir," he said. "One of
'em's gone." He dragged out a cardboard box with a
green label and opened it. "An' this box o' cartridges
ought to be full; only it ain't."

"What about the silencer?" Fen asked.

Shelley looked blank for an instant; then: "Oh, I get
you, sir. The one Mr. Somers gave me. I'd almost forgotten about it." He rummaged again in the cupboard.
"That's gorn, too," he said presently.

"Surely it's rather risky to leave that cupboard unlocked?"

"Well, not really, sir. I'm always 'ere when the boys
come in to fetch their rifles, and when they put 'em
back again. And the rest of the time the armory's shut
up."

"How many keys are there?"

"There's me own, sir, and there's one that's kept in
the orderly room, and Wells 'as one—'e 'as all the keys
—and the 'eadmaster 'as one which is kept in 'is secretary's room."

"And I suppose that in the normal way no unauthor-
ized person would be able to get hold of any of those
keys—that's to say that the places where they're kept
would be locked up when no one was there."

"That's so, sir."

"During the past week or so, has this place been left
open and unattended at any time?"

Shelley hesitated and flushed slightly. "Well, sir, I'm afraid it 'as. Yesterday afternoon it was, during the parade. I opened up as usual for the boys to get their rifles, and then I 'ad a bit of a spasm of my stomach trouble, and Major Saltmarsh—that's our O.C.—excused me from parade. And I felt so bad I went and sat down for a bit in the orderly room without lockin' up first. . . . I shouldn't 'a' done it, I know. Do you think that's when the pistol was taken, sir?"

"Possibly," said Fen. "But I shouldn't worry too much about your own responsibility. The murders would have happened in any case, whether you'd locked up or not." He examined the two small windows. "No one came in through these, anyway. It's obvious they haven't been opened for months."

They went out again into the sunlight, and Fen, taking leave of Shelley, walked toward Hubbard's Building. He reflected that he had taken no precautions in the matter of preserving fingerprints, but since he knew who had stolen the gun, that was unimportant. For the rest, the interview had proved and disproved nothing.

A general movement away from the site was in progress. Cars were being started and driven down to Castrevenford town. In Hubbard's Building Fen found Stagge concluding his fruitless task and acquainted him with the substance of what he had learned from Shelley and Etherege. The superintendent did not seem much enlivened thereby.

"The fact is, sir, that we're marking time," he said, "until these alibis are dealt with. I've finished here, so I'm going into town now to look at Somers's rooms and his bank account. I've also got a man at the station making that experiment with the reports, and I want to see what results he's got."

"I'll come, if I may," said Fen. "And there's one

thing I particularly want to know: Has there been any news of Brenda Boyce?"

Stagge made negative signs. "Nothing, sir. We've made all the routine inquiries and searched in all the likely places, but she seems to have disappeared off the face of the earth. The plain fact is that we just haven't got sufficient men to deal with all this. I'm seeing the chief constable for lunch, and I'm pretty certain he'll want to call in Scotland Yard."

They drove to Castrevenford in Stagge's car. Castrevenford is a substantial and flourishing Warwickshire market town, unusually fortunate in its architecture and almost completely lacking in slums. The farmers of the district are prosperous, and Castrevenford shares their prosperity. It has historical associations of a mild, provincial kind; battles were fought nearby during the Civil War, and a discreet proportion of the famous—commemorated in inoffensive statuary—have been born there. The main road bypasses it, and so it is comparatively quiet. On this splendid day of early June it looked mellow and hospitable.

The car drew up in front of the narrow Palladian house in which Somers had lived, and, accompanied by the landlady, Fen and Stagge went up to his rooms. They found nothing helpful, though Fen took a fleeting interest in a book called *The Fourth Forger,* which Somers had apparently been reading recently; it dealt largely with the fabrication of Shakespeare manuscripts. The private papers were unenlightening, consisting as they did chiefly of modest bills and receipts. Of private correspondence there seemed to be none, and the landlady deposed that to the best of her knowledge he had never received any. He had certainly been a friendless man, Fen reflected—perhaps by inclination eremitical.

They spent no more than ten minutes there before

going on to the bank. The manager, who was a personal friend of Stagge's, made no difficulties about allowing them to examine Love's and Somers's accounts. The former offered little of interest; in money affairs Love had evidently been as meticulously regular as in everything else. Somers's balance was only forty-eight pounds—but on the previous day he had unprecedentedly withdrawn a hundred pounds in one-pound notes. An interview with the clerk who had transacted the business had no useful result, since Somers had given no indication as to the purpose for which he required the money.

"Interesting, that," said Stagge as they left the bank. "We didn't find any such sum on him or in his rooms. What's become of it, I wonder? Did the murderer steal it?"

But Fen, though he was unwontedly sober and thoughtful, made no suggestion. They went on to the police station, and the news of the third murder reached them scarcely five minutes after they had arrived there.

† 8 †
THE DEATH
OF A WITCH

At this point our narrative is suddenly enriched by the presence of one Peter Plumstead, a clerk on holiday from an insurance office in London. Mr. Plumstead was enjoying a fortnight's walking tour. He had taken his holiday early in part because, being unmarried, he had only himself to consider, and in part because of a shaky if understandable theory that something had gone wrong with the progression of the English seasons, and that he was therefore more likely to get fine weather in early June than in the dog days. At the start of his travels a day of almost incessant rain had weakened his faith in this hypothesis, but since then he had been abundantly justified, and he sang gaily as he traversed the lanes and fields. He was a young man, earnest but kindly, with rather large green eyes and stiff, intractable brown hair; and he wore the clothes appropriate to his recreation: shorts, stout shoes, and open-necked shirt, with a haversack and a stout ashplant.

"Give to me the life I love," sang Mr. Plumstead; "let the something go by me, tum-te-tum-te-tum-tum-tum, and the something nigh me."

Warwickshire, he had concluded, was a more interesting and beautiful county than Leicestershire. In the first instance he had taken a train to Leicester and was now working his way back to London by way of Warwickshire, Oxfordshire, Bucks, and Middlesex. At Leicester he had dutifully contemplated the Jewry wall; at Nuneaton, Astley Castle; at Warwick, Lord Leycester's Hospital; and at Stratford he had both vi-

sited the Festival Theatre and perused *As You Like It*
at a secluded spot on the bank of the Avon. Thus it
came about that at eleven o'clock on the morning of
Speech Day—a festivity of whose existence he was,
however, unaware—he found himself walking along
a quiet lane within four miles of Castrevenford
School.

"Bed in the bush with stars to see," sang Mr. Plumstead, "bread I dip in the river, something something
a man like me, there's the life forever."

He was in high spirits. There were cowslips in the
fields and bluebells in the woods. The hedges were
white with may, and he had seen blossom on the plum
trees. He glimpsed violets half-concealed in the grass
that flourished on the banks of the lanes and picked a
handful to cram into a buttonhole. The birds caroled
lustily, and on the woods that crowned the low and
distant hills the light flowed down like hot gold. The
sky overarched the scene, a vivid blue bowl with the
sun set like some fabulous fire opal in its center.

It was a few minutes after eleven when Mr. Plumstead came to the cottage. It stood on the right side of
the lane and was Elizabethan, he thought, or even
earlier. The thatch was in a ruinous condition, and the
chimneys stood askew. The square panes of the small
windows were grimy and misanthropic, the garden a
wilderness in which even the outlines of the beds
were no longer discernible. At the rear the cottage was
hemmed in by dismal-looking larches. A gross and
evil-smelling duck looked out upon the world through
the bars of the rickety gate. Mr. Plumstead, who had
already that morning walked eight miles without a
pause, halted and returned its truculent gaze. And
when this palled, as it very quickly did, he resumed
his inspection of the cottage.

The presence of the duck was the only evidence of
habitation he had seen so far; the windows were ap-

parently curtainless, and no smoke rose from the chimneys in the still, hot air.

But presently, while he looked, an old woman appeared behind one of the windows. She did not seem to be paying any attention to Mr. Plumstead, but thanks to the coating of dirt on the glass and the obscurity of the room within, it was difficult to be sure. She was talking, perhaps. To herself? No, there was a shadowy outline somewhere beyond her which might be a man or a woman. Mr. Plumstead, indefensibly inquisitive, stood on tiptoe, the better to peer over the straggling, unpruned thicket hedge. But now both figures were moving out of his range of vision; they were gone. Mr. Plumstead stepped back onto the dusty road.

And then he heard the scream.

It was in no sense a melodramatic scream. Mr. Plumstead described it afterward as a choking, half-muted wail, very thin and very brief, and for a moment he doubted whether it were human at all. He stood hesitant. It seems likely that had he moved at once he might have been able to save everyone a good deal of subsequent trouble and danger—might even have earned a small immortality among lovers of great poetry. But the fear of making a fool of himself held him temporarily in check. Several seconds passed before he brought himself to open the gate and enter the weed-infested garden.

The duck backed apprehensively along the path, like a courtier quitting the presence of royalty, and, when Mr. Plumstead quickened his pace, turned and fled into a nearby clump of foxtail grass, where it set up a surly quacking. Mr. Plumstead knocked nervously on the door, but there was no movement from inside the cottage. After a short pause he tried the door and found it open. A taproom smell drifted to his nostrils. He peered into the shadowy passage.

"Hullo!" he called. "Is there anyone there?"

Apparently there was not; the occupants of the house, like the haunted Listeners in De la Mare's poem, made no reply.

"Hullo!" said Mr. Plumstead more loudly.

But the silence remained absolute. Not a footfall, not a breath, not the click of a latch.

Mr. Plumstead, suppressing a sudden panicky instinct to retreat, entered the cottage. His foot skidded on an empty gin bottle, and the effort of saving himself from a fall did nothing to soothe his disordered nerves. The bottle rolled away and struck against a wall. Mr. Plumstead paused to get his bearings.

The cottage was as neglected inside as out. Its furniture was rudimentary and its atmosphere stifling. Mr. Plumstead calculated that the first door on the right must lead into the room where he had seen the old woman. He opened it and entered a kind of living room.

Dust was omnipotent here. There was a single, frayed easy chair, its seat bulging with defective springs. A table with one leg slightly shorter than the others supported a loaf from which the bread had apparently been torn in handfuls, a dirty glass, and a cracked plate covered with bacon rind and congealed fat. A heap of empty bottles lay in a corner, and one, half full of rum, was on the mantelpiece beside an unlighted candle held upright by its own grease. The walls were paneled in oak. On the broad hearth, which looked as old as the house itself, the ashes and cinders of a long-dead fire were overlaid by a malodorous collection of garbage in which potato peelings predominated. The June sunlight struggled wan and diluted through the panes of the one small window, and much of the room was deep in shadow. For this reason Mr. Plumstead did not perceive the body of the old woman until he was on the point of falling over it.

"Lord," he muttered. And then, more self-consciously: "Damn it all. . . ."

Even in youth she could scarcely have been beautiful, and age had not improved her. Her face—or what could be seen of it under the blood—was incredibly lined, her nose was curved like a crossbill's beak, and her gray hair was matted with filth. She wore a stained and ragged black crepe dress and a pair of ancient carpet slippers, still mud-encrusted, though there had been no rain for at least a week. And beside her on the floor was a twisted, heavy iron poker.

But if Mr. Plumstead assimilated these details at all, he did not linger over them. He stared—with a nausea that rose until it clutched, hot and bitter, at his throat—at the hole in the old woman's head, at the obscene mingling of gray hair and gray brains and blood and splintered bone.

The shock held him aghast and motionless, talking disjointedly to himself. And so he never heard or suspected the swift, stealthy movement behind him—knew nothing until consciousness was shattered into a motley constellation of stars through which he reeled downward into an aching void. He felt the cushioned impact as he fell across the old woman's body; he felt, or perhaps only imagined feeling, fingers about his right wrist. Then the beating of his heart swelled to a hammering like drums, and blackness engulfed him.

He discovered afterward that he was unconscious for little more than five minutes. For a townee, Mr. Plumstead had considerable physical stamina and resilience, and the blow on the back of his head may have been ill-aimed. His first action on recovering consciousness was to roll hurriedly clear of his macabre mattress. Then he got slowly and cautiously to his feet. Apart from himself and the old woman, the room was empty. Mr. Plumstead, lusting for air and light, left it and went out of the front door. The sunshine dazzled his eyes. He clung to the doorpost, and with the duck as an impassive or perhaps vaguely hostile audience, vomited prolongedly onto a clump of wall-flowers.

After that he felt very much better—so much better as to be capable of summoning assistance. To go back, he thought, would not be desirable; the cottage was the first human habitation he had passed in two miles. So he trudged on along the lane, tenderly fingering the bruise on his head, and with a step considerably less sprightly than it had been ten minutes previously.

In about a quarter of a mile he came to an assemblage of buildings almost large enough to justify the name of a village, and at the first of these there were telephone wires. It was a cottage scarcely larger than that which he had just left, but later in date and a great deal more seemly in aspect. Mr. Plumstead halted at its gate, which gave on a neat and colorful front garden. Then he hastily cleared his throat to call attention to his proximity.

The young woman who was lying on a rug on the lawn looked up with something of a scowl. She was blond and pretty, and she wore sandals and quite the scantiest two-piece bathing suit that Mr. Plumstead had ever imagined possible. At the moment, however, he was too distressed to offer mental homage to the shapeliness of her suntanned limbs. "Er," he remarked inconclusively; and at this the young woman removed her sunglasses and gazed at him in surprise.

"Can I do anything for you?" she said.

"Telephone," mumbled Mr. Plumstead, reddening. "Wondered if I could use your telephone . . . you see, there's been a murder."

The young woman scrambled precipitately to her feet. "A *what?*" she demanded.

"A murder," said Mr. Plumstead, much harassed.
"Must phone the police."

"But who? Where?"

"At the cottage down the road. An old lady."

"Do you mean Mrs. Bly?"

"I don't know," said Mr. Plumstead helplessly. "Is
that her name? I was passing the cottage when I heard
a scream, so I went to see what was up, and . . . and
there she was."

The young woman scrutinized him shrewdly for a
moment. "All right," she said. "Come inside."

Mr. Plumstead followed her obediently. Modesty
suggested to him that he should avert his eyes—the
young woman's costume was decidedly exiguous—but
she was so agreeably unselfconscious that he ignored
its prompting. The telephone was in a small, sunlit
hall.

"Dial O," said the young woman, "and . . . ." Her tone
changed. "Good Lord, what have you done to your
head?"

"Someone knocked me out," Mr. Plumstead admitted ruefully. "Is it bleeding?"

"A bit. I'll get some iodex. You telephone."

"Where am I?" said Mr. Plumstead. "I mean, what's
the name of this place and this road?"

"The village is Ravensward, and this is Maiden
Lane," said the young woman. "I don't know what
Mrs. Bly's cottage is called. I don't think it's got a
name. . . . Wait here when you've phoned. I'll be down
in a minute."

She ran up the stairs. Mr. Plumstead, dialing O, conveyed the substance of his discovery to the Castrevenford police.

When the young woman returned with a jar
of iodex, she had changed her bathing suit for a
sleeveless white muslin frock. Mr. Plumstead noted
that while better satisfying the demands of modesty,

this had enhanced rather than diminished her beauty. She said, "Would you like some beer?" and on Mr. Plumstead's gratefully indicating that he would, fetched four pint bottles and two glasses and carried them out to the rug on the lawn. Here they settled down, and she examined the bruise on his head.

"It's not too bad," she said presently. "You pour out the beer, and I'll rub on some iodex."

Her fingers were cool and efficient; it was seldom, Mr. Plumstead reflected, that life provided so agreeably traditional a consummation to an adventure. When she had finished, he said:

"You've been awfully kind. . . . By the way, I ought to have told you that my name's Peter Plumstead."

"Mine's Daphne Savage." She drank her beer appreciatively; then, putting down the glass: "And I'm simply itching to hear all about it."

Mr. Plumstead told her; being an honest young man, he did not—though he would have liked to—attempt to minimize his own rather ignominiously passive role in the proceedings. When the recital was over, Daphne was silent for a moment; then:

"Why do you think you were knocked out?" she asked.

"I *imagine* because whoever it was wanted to make sure he wasn't seen getting away."

"But you saw him through the window. Wouldn't you recognize him again?"

Mr. Plumstead shook his head. "It was only a shadow. I couldn't even swear it was a man." He hesitated. "Can you think why anyone would do a horrible thing like that?"

"No, I can't, unless Mrs. Bly had some money hidden in the house. I don't know very much about her, you see. This is my aunt's cottage, and I'm just here for a fortnight's holiday. Mrs. Bly was rather a ghastly old witch, but to be killed like that. . . ." In spite of the heat, Daphne shivered a little.

Soon they were talking of other things. It transpired that Daphne was a stenographer in a City office, so they had at least a background in common. They were discussing the relative merits of various eating houses, and had each of them broached a second bottle of beer, when Stagge's car drew up at the gate.

On arrival at the police station Fen and Stagge had found a certain amount of information awaiting them.

First in interest came the experiment with the reports. An educated, rather somber-looking young constable had carried it out. He said:

"As you ordered, sir, I spoke to Mr. Etherege, and he gave me a list of the reports which Mr. Somers still had to do at ten o'clock last evening. I borrowed some blank forms from the headmaster's secretary and copied Mr. Somers's remarks as fast as I could. It took me fifty-five minutes."

"Pretty well what you prophesied, sir," said Stagge to Fen.

Fen nodded. "You write quickly?" he asked the constable.

"Yes, sir. More quickly than most people."

"There's our minimum, then," said Stagge. "And it's going to be very helpful when we get those alibi reports."

The rest of their information was of a more negative kind. The postmortem on Somers had revealed nothing out of the way, and a ballistics expert had confirmed Stagge's opinion that both bullets came from the same gun. Stagge was engaged in drawing some heavily qualified inferences from this latter fact when Mr. Plumstead's call came through.

There was nothing for it, of course, but to set forth to the scene of this third disaster. Stagge drove, with Fen sitting beside him and the sergeant with his equipment in the back. The doctor followed in his own car.

"This just about puts the lid on it," said Stagge. "Three murders and a disappearance, all in twenty-four hours. Though as far as I can gather, this thing isn't the same class of crime as the others." He snorted with vexation. "Not that that helps," he added, "unless it means we can get it cleared up on the spot. And I'm not optimistic enough to expect that."

At Daphne's cottage they picked up Mr. Plumstead, and Stagge had some difficulty, after Fen had observed the beer and been introduced to the girl, in getting him back again into the car. Then they drove on to Mrs. Bly's cottage.

All was as Mr. Plumstead had left it, and the routine of investigation need not be described again. Mr. Plumstead gave Stagge a detailed account of his own part in the affair and submitted to have his finger-prints taken—in order, as Stagge remarked, to distinguish them from those of any other stranger who might have been in the place. The doctor's report was brief and to the point: Mrs. Bly had been hit once, presumably with the poker, and had died instantly. Fen, having ascertained that the all-shrouding dust bore no recognizable foot marks, wandered off alone into the other rooms of the cottage. Their squalor, being indescribable, will not be described. One thing, however, was noteworthy: In the kitchen a new iron cooking stove had been very recently installed, and the process had apparently involved the partial demolition of the old fireplace.

Subsequently Fen went out into the front garden, where he made overtures of friendship to the duck. He was still engaged in this profitless task when Stagge emerged and suggested that they should stroll a few yards up the lane.

When they were out of earshot of the others: "Well?" Fen demanded.

"Plumstead's prints," said Stagge, "are the only ones on that poker."

"Which hand?"

"The right."

"He's left-handed."

"Yes. I noticed that."

"And they shouldn't be the *only* prints on the poker. What about the old woman's?"

They had reached the car. Stagge halted and put one foot on the running board. The lane here was tarred, and the tar, melting in bubbles, made it sticky underfoot.

"Oh, the poker's been wiped all right," Stagge answered. "The question is—who wiped it? Plumstead or someone else?"

Fen considered. "You might outline the case against Plumstead," he said mildly.

"The case is that having killed the old woman, he wiped the poker clear of prints and then put his own *right-hand* prints back on it, relying on our assuming that to be a plant. The bump on his head would be self-inflicted; it isn't a very serious one."

"But wouldn't that be oversubtle? This lane isn't much frequented, I imagine. Having killed her, the sensible thing to do would be to simply remove the traces of his presence and walk away. I understand that he's a stranger here, so there'd be nothing on earth to connect him with the crime."

Stagge drummed his fingers on the hot metal of the car. "I agree, of course. There's no proof that Plumstead's story isn't true; it hangs together well enough, and I must admit that he doesn't look like a homicidal maniac to me."

"You postulate a maniac, then?"

"Not necessarily. I was speaking loosely. The old woman may have been a miser and have had something worth stealing."

"It's all very hypothetical," said Fen. "Were there no clues other than the fingerprints?"

"None that I could see." Stagge hesitated. "Do you think there's any connection between this murder and the others?"

"*Apparently* not. But until we get some line on motive it's impossible to be sure. I don't like all this lack of motive; it's unnatural. The trouble is not so much that we can't fit the puzzle together, as that we haven't got all the pieces." There was a short silence. "Well, what are your plans?"

Stagge looked at his watch. "It's twenty past twelve. . . . I shall take Plumstead down to the station to dictate and sign a statement and ask him to stay on in Castrevenford for the time being; as he's on holiday, that oughtn't to inconvenience him. Then I've got to see the chief constable. This afternoon—" Stagge sighed profoundly—"well, I'm not sure as yet. I've got more to do than I can really cope with."

"Let me know as soon as you get the alibi reports."

"Of course, sir. Shall I drop you at the school on the way back into town?"

"Thanks, but I'll stay here and snoop about. Luckily, my lunch isn't till half-past one. Are we far from the school?"

"About three miles."

"Ah. I wonder if I can get a car to take me back there. I ought to have brought my own."

"If you like, sir, I'll send up a taxi from Castrevenford."

"Good," said Fen. "Quarter past one at the village pub, whatever it's called."

"The Beacon . . . oh, there's one other thing, sir. I

found this in one of Mrs. Bly's pockets. Would it be valuable, do you suppose?"

He handed the object over. It was a miniature, painted on silver and with a very simple frame, much tarnished, of the same metal. The head, set against a bright blue background, was of a young man, wearing a slashed black tunic with a broad collar. The hair was dark brown, and the eyes were set rather widely apart, with prominent lids. Apart from the small moustache, the sitter was clean-shaven. His nose was rounded at the tip, and his lips were very shapely. To the left of the head, against the background, was the inscription AE SVAE 29.

Fen gazed at it with considerable interest.

"I'm far from being an expert on these things," he said, "but I should imagine it probably *is* valuable. It's Elizabethan, of course, and conceivably by Hilliard. As the cottage is Elizabethan, too, I dare say Mrs. Bly found it there."

"Ah." Stagge took the miniature and put it carefully away. "And if she'd found any other things of the same kind, theft might be our motive. Very well, sir. I'll look after it. And now we must make a move."

He returned to the cottage. And Fen, after a moment's thought, walked back along the lane to visit Daphne Savage.

LOVE'S LABOUR'S WON

Fen might have said about crime what Lewis Carroll said about children: "I'm *not* omnivorous—like a pig." He preferred its delicatessen to its bread and butter. If, therefore, Mrs. Bly had been killed by some vagrant, out of mere cupidity, he was only too willing to leave the investigation to Stagge.

But the affair could not so easily be dismissed; it involved—if Plumstead were speaking the truth—subtleties beyond the mental scope of a tramp, and moreover its temporal and geographical coincidence with the other deaths was enough to arouse suspicion. A link might exist somewhere, and it would not be wasting time to attempt to ferret it out.

Through a cloud of dust thrown up by the wheels of Stagge's car Fen came to the gate of Daphne's cottage. She had settled down again on the rug on the front lawn, but she looked up with a smile of greeting as he approached.

"You'd like some beer," she stated unarguably, and Fen at once conceived a high opinion of her intelligence. Without waiting for a reply she got up and hurried into the cottage, returning thence with some bottles and a pint glass.

"You're most hospitable," said Fen, who by now was sprawling on the ground, chewing the stem of a long grass.

"I'm most curious," Daphne answered. She sat down and poured the beer. "I want to know what's been happening."

Fen smiled at her. She looked very cool and fresh in

the white frock. Her ash-blond hair, done in a long bob, swung against her shoulders as she moved, and the widely spaced green eyes were full of humor and good spirits. She handed him the glass, and he drank deeply.

"There are few young women," he observed dreamily, "who know that one wants beer, and that one wants *good* beer, and that one wants it in a pint glass. I·envy the man who marries you."

She laughed. "I've got corresponding disadvantages," she said and added hesitantly: "You must forgive me, but I didn't quite grasp who you were. Are you a policeman?"

"Heaven forbid. I'm a professor."

"Of what?"

"English."

She sat up abruptly. "You're not Gervase Fen?"

"Certainly I am."

Daphne grinned. "Then I've heard a lot about you. We have a mutual friend."

"Oh? Who's that?"

"A girl called Sally Carstairs."

"Good heavens!" Fen exclaimed. "I haven't set eyes on her since she inherited all that money from Miss Snaith. What is she doing? Is she married?"

"No, not married. She's got a flat in town."

Fen reflected. "It must be nearly ten years now. . . . Lord, how old I'm getting! Next time you see her, tell her it's extremely wicked and ungrateful of her not to have kept in touch with me."

"She has a conscience about it," Daphne assured him. "And she's always talking about the toy shop and Miss Tardy and Richard Cadogan and all the rest of it."

Fen sighed. "I was irresponsible and carefree in those days," he said. "I've sobered up a lot since then and become nostalgic, which is a sign of diminished vitality . . . well, well. My love to her when you next meet."

"Of course. But what are you doing in this part of the world?"

"Giving away the prizes," Fen explained, "at Castrevenford School."

"And you just heard about this business of Mrs. Bly and felt you must be in on it?"

"Yes," said Fen, lying discreetly. "In itself it's a crude and brutal crime, but—as Holmes would have said—it presents certain points of interest."

Daphne wriggled to a more comfortable position and smoothed down her skirt. "Do tell me," she said. "That is, unless you're anxious not to give things away."

Fen gave her a brief outline of the facts. She listened attentively, a little frown of concentration puckering her face.

"I suppose," she ventured, "that Mr. Plumstead's story is true? When I saw him pass in the police car, I wondered. . . ."

"Personally, I believe it is." Fen offered her a cigarette.

"No, thanks, I've had to give up smoking since the budget. . . . But what I don't see is why *anyone* should kill her *at all.*"

"That's our problem, too." Fen lit a cigarette for himself and threw the spent match onto a flowerbed. "I was wondering if you could help."

She shook her head. "I know very little about Mrs. Bly. You see, this is my aunt's cottage, and I'm just here on holiday."

"Ah," said Fen, "I didn't realize that." He drained his glass. "But you might know of some local person who could give me information. Your aunt, for instance."

"She's away for the day. I really think the pub's your

best bet. I know Mr. Beresford—that's the landlord—
quite well, and if I introduce you. . . ."

Fen scrambled to his feet with an alacrity that nul-
lified his diagnosis of waning vitality.

"Good," he said. "That has the additional advantage
that I'll be able to stand you a drink. Is it far?"

"No, only a few yards." Daphne emulated his movement, but with a good deal more grace. "But look here,
there's one thing I want to know."

"Yes?"

"What are the police *doing* with Mr. Plumstead?"

"Only getting him to dictate a statement."

"He isn't—he didn't say if he was coming back here
at all?" Daphne spoke rather too casually for conviction.

"If he has any sense," said Fen, "he'll come back the
first instant he can. They're going to ask him to stay
in Castrevenford for a bit."

"But he won't be able to."

"Why ever not?"

"Because all the hotels and boardinghouses are
packed out with parents."

"Then I'll advise him to come and stay at the pub
here."

"I really think," said Daphne earnestly, "that it's his
only chance."

"I'll see that he doesn't miss it," Fen promised.
"What do you think of him, by the way?"

Daphne was already making for the gate. "He seems
all right," she replied airily.

The hamlet of Ravensward had never grown sufficiently to require a church of its own. It was a peace-
ful agglomeration of small buildings, scarcely any of
them later in date than 1800. There was a small trian-
gular green and a little stream, now reduced to a

trickle, which ran under a narrow humped bridge. Some cheerful, grimy boys were optimistically fishing it on their way home from school. Otherwise no one seemed to be out of doors.

The Beacon stood next door to a little shop that sold soap and string and boiled sweets and hair-pins and envelopes. It had a steeply sloping gabled roof and tall chimneys and was timber-framed, its facade an agreeable pattern of black and white. There was a lounge bar, but it was obviously very little used. The public bar, which Fen and Daphne entered, was low built, dark and cool, with old wooden settles, well scrubbed, and dented pewter tankards hung in rows. It was pleasantly free from facetious placards and, apart from the landlord himself, was empty.

Mr. Beresford proved to be a grave, elderly man with a complexion like a pippin. He welcomed Daphne and was ceremonially introduced to Fen; plainly anonymity was not encouraged at the Beacon. Fen ordered pints of bitter for Mr. Beresford and himself, and a half-pint for Daphne.

"Professor Fen wants to know about Mrs. Bly, Mr. Beresford," said Daphne.

"Do 'e, now?" Mr. Beresford replied judicially. He scrutinized Fen closely for a moment, as if to ascertain that this wish was not prompted by any kind of frivolity, and appeared satisfied by what he saw. "Well, seeing as 'e's a friend 'o yours, Miss Savage. . . ."

He came out from behind a bar, and they all carried their drinks to a table by a window. No one spoke while they were settling down; the surroundings made it unthinkable to do more than one thing at a time. Mr. Beresford gravely proposed the health of his customers; they responded suitably; everyone drank.

Then Mr. Beresford set down his tankard, produced a pipe, thrust tobacco into its bowl with a calloused thumb, and said: "Well. . . ."

There was a question in Daphne's eyes, and Fen nodded.

"I don't know if you've heard the news, Mr. Beresford," Daphne said. "About Mrs. Bly, I mean."

"News, Miss Savage? What news might that be? She come 'ome again this morning—*that* I knows."

"She's been murdered, Mr. Beresford."

They waited while Mr. Beresford assimilated this intelligence. It was clearly not a part of his code to display strong emotion, whatever the circumstances. After a very considerable hiatus he said:

"Murdered, you tell me? Ah. That's bad. Very bad. Very bad indeed."

Upon this judgment, which though scarcely novel was spoken so impressively as to invest the word "bad" with the overtones of a whole ethical philosophy—upon this judgment he paused expectantly; and Daphne, taking her cue, narrated briefly the circumstances of Mrs. Bly's demise. Mr. Beresford heard her out with close attention.

"It's bad," he repeated when she had finished. "Shocking bad." He seemed bewitched by the monosyllable, as if it were a rune. "And this gen'l'man"—he nodded toward Fen—"'e'm one o' the police?"

"He's working with them, yes," said Daphne. "And I told him that if anyone in Ravensward could help him, you could."

With a swift, decisive movement Mr. Beresford placed his pipe in his mouth and lit it. *"Bad,"* he murmured, and made liquid noises inside the stem. Fen, who though appreciative of the leisurely tempo of rustic intercourse was mindful of his afternoon's engagements, made a discreet effort to accelerate matters.

"General information is what I need," he remarked briskly. "About friends and relatives and habits and so forth."

"Ah," said Mr. Beresford, nodding. "Well, you shall hear what I'm able to tell you, sir." He continued nodding, apparently in order to keep them silent while he arranged his thoughts. Then he took a draught of beer.

"She was a foreigner," he began abruptly. "Not been 'ere in the village more'n fifteen year."

Fen inclined his head, to indicate his thorough understanding of this fact.

"Nor she didn't mix much wi' the natives, neither. Some on 'em"—Mr. Beresford spoke in tones of enlightened scorn—"some on 'em said she were a witch. But oi don't 'ave no truck wi' talk like that. There may 'a' been witches *once*—that oi don't deny. But science 'as got rid on 'em—ain't that so, sir?"

Fen agreed—rather dubiously, however—that that was so. "So she had no friends?" he suggested.

"Not 'ere she didn't. And oi'll tell you more, sir." Mr. Beresford leaned forward confidentially and tapped his forefinger on the table. *"She drank."*

He sat back again to focus the effect of this revelation on his audience.

"Drank," he repeated impressively. "Now, oi'm a drinkin' man meself, sir, but there's drinkin' *and* drinkin'. " He made the sound commonly transcribed as "pfui!" "An' oi don't know about you, sir, but oi don't trust folks as drinks alone under their own rooftree. T'ain't natural, to my way o' thinkin'."

Fen made the deprecatory sounds that were expected of him. "And no relatives?" he said. "No husband?"

"As to an 'usband, oi never laid eyes on 'im," Mr. Beresford responded. "They *do* say as 'e upped and left 'er when she went on the drink, but that's no more 'n talk. Don't you rely on it, sir. All oi'm sayin' now is

that 'e never showed up 'ere." Mr. Beresford paused to
drink, holding up a hand to check comment. "But as
to relatives, she 'ad a son, that oi knows. A *married*
son. And off she'd go to visit 'im, whiles, though what
'is wife 'd think of 'er dirty ways . . . ."

He shook his head at the visions of domestic tension
conjured up by this reflection. Fen said:

"And where does this son live? Somewhere in the
neighborhood?"

"Ah. That oi'm not sure on. Not nearby, though; oi
think 'tis in one o' them big cities." Mr. Beresford
brooded. " 'Tis funny you should be askin' me about
'im," he commented after a moment.

"Oh? Oh? Why?"

"There were another gen'l'man—let me see, now,
today's Saturday, so it would 'a' been on Thursday 'e
come in 'ere—anyway, 'e wants to know about Mother
Bly and what's become on 'er, and oi tells 'im she's
gone off to see 'er son, and 'e wants to know where this
son lives, only, as oi say, oi can't satisfy no one about
that." A shade of aggrievedness became apparent in
Mr. Beresford's manner. "Oi 'adn't much use for 'im—
this chap as was askin' questions. 'Adn't even the decency to order 'alf a pint. One o' them teetotals, I dare
say."

A possibility occurred to Fen. "He wasn't by any
chance from the school?"

"Well, sir, 'e might 'a' been. They masters come 'ere,
whiles, for a pint or two, it not bein' far. Only oi'd not
seen this one afore."

"Could you describe him?"

" 'E were elderly," said Mr. Beresford, "and thin and
strongish, with gray 'air."

Though vague enough, it would do for Love, Fen
reflected; and if it *had* been he, then a definite connection was established between the death of Mrs. Bly
and the murders at the school—a connection that so

far he had had no other ground than instinct for suspecting.

"And fair put about, 'e were," Mr. Beresford proceeded, "when 'e found oi 'ad no idea where this son
might live. Ah. Clicked 'is tongue an' shook 'is 'ead like
he were on 'ot bricks. 'E asks me, do I know when
Mother Bly be comin' back 'ere to Ravensward, an' oi
tells him, today. An' that cools 'im down a bit, an' away
'e goes without so much as a good mornin' to me. Ah."

Mr. Beresford paused to cool his retrospective indignation with a pull at his tankard, and Fen said:

"Then Mrs. Bly has been away recently?"

"Amn't oi tellin' you that?" Mr. Beresford eyed Fen
sorrowfully, commiserating, it seemed, the tardiness
of his understanding. "She'm away visiting 'er son
since—let's see now—We'n'sday, it were. Ah. That's it,
We'n'sday. We'n'sday morning she were waitin' for
the bus to Castrevenford. 'Off again, Mother Bly?' oi
says to her. 'Just till Saturday, Mr. Beresford,' she answers, 'just till Saturday.' An' sure enough, back she
comes, this very mornin'."

Which meant, Fen reflected, that her son's home
could not be at any very great distance. It occurred to
him to inquire about her sources of income.

"She 'as the old-age pension, o' course," said Mr.
Beresford. "And 'er son, I think 'e give 'er somethin',
whiles. Must 'a' done. Where'd she get the money for
'er drinkin', otherwise?"

"Did she own anything valuable, do you know? Anything that would be worth stealing?"

Mr. Beresford slowly shook his head. "Oi doubts it,
sir. Drink were all she thought on. She'd 'a' bartered
'er own soul for drink."

"Still, I noticed when I was in the cottage that a new
stove had been installed in the kitchen."

Mr. Beresford seemed abashed at having his assertion so promptly refuted. "True 'nough," he muttered.

"That's strange, that is. *Queer.*" He pronounced the word with such minatory emphasis that they were positively startled; it seemed an epitome of all the eccentricities that had been practiced since the world began. "But Mr. Taverner," Mr. Beresford added, " 'e'll know 'bout that."

"Mr. Taverner?"

" 'Twere 'im as put stove in."

"Mr. Taverner's the local plumber and carpenter," Daphne explained.

"Ah. That's so, Miss Savage. 'E'll be in 'ere at one, so you can talk to 'im yourself. Ah." Mr. Beresford brooded. "Now, that's interesting, that is."

Fen repressed an earnest desire to ask what was interesting and waited until Mr. Beresford should think fit to offer enlightenment of his own accord. This he did after some premonitory sucking at his pipe, which had long since gone out; he said:

"You was askin', sir, if Mother Bly 'ad anythin' worth the stealing." Fidgeting somewhat, Fen agreed. "Well, sir, it's just come to me as there were some old things Mr. Taverner found when 'e were puttin' stove in. Ah. 'Idden in the fireplace, they was. An old picture, oi think oi 'eard, and summat else. Now, oi don't know as anyone 'd be wanting to steal an old picture — and 'twere only a liddle tiny thing, by all accounts —but oi'm just tellin' you, sir, in case it might be important."

"An old picture," Fen thought—probably the miniature that had been found in Mrs. Bly's pocket—and if that, then conceivably. . . .

"I suppose Mr. Taverner will be able to tell me what else there was," he said.

"Surely, sir. I wouldn't 'a' mentioned it, only. . . ."

"I'm very glad you did mention it, Mr. Beresford." A curious premonition was stealing over Fen—the sense of being on the brink of some unimaginably exciting discovery; and looking back on it afterward, he was astounded to realize that he had had at this stage no inkling of what it might be. He meditated. Mr. Beresford had supplied some information which might prove useful: that Mrs. Bly had been away, from Wednesday until this morning; that Love (if it were Love) had been inquiring about her; that she would have, in the normal way, nothing to justify a robbery, but that some "old things" had been found when the stove was installed. . . . Certainly Mr. Taverner must be questioned. And there was another line of inquiry which might yield results.

"Mr. Beresford," he said, "do you happen to know a master from the school named Somers?"

"Ah, that oi do, sir," Mr. Beresford replied readily. "Oi might almost say 'e was one o' my regulars. A very nice young gen'l'man, only quiet. Comes 'ere alone, mostly."

"And did he have any connection with Mrs. Bly?"

"Not as oi knows on, sir. Oi never 'eard 'im talk on 'er."

"I see." Fen was momentarily disappointed. "Has he been in here at all this week?"

Mr. Beresford emptied his tankard and wiped his mouth with the back of his hand. "Let me see, now. Let me see. . . . 'E were 'ere Monday evenin' and again Tuesday evenin', but oi 'aven't seen 'im since. Monday 'e were talking to Mr. Taverner. And Tuesday, 'e were that lively, I 'ad to mention it to 'im. 'Why, Mr. Somers,' oi says, 'you're on top o' the world tonight. 'Ave you been left a fortune?' An' 'e said: 'Something like that, Mr. Beresford,' 'e says, 'something like that,' an' 'e grins."

Mr. Beresford himself grinned, illustratively. But for what followed they were completely unprepared. Mr. Beresford raised one hand, brought it down on the table with an explosive impact, and said: "Wait, now!"

in tones of such violence and urgency that Daphne
upset the remainder of her beer. Mr. Beresford apologized, but hurriedly; his impassive features were as
nearly excited as they could ever be. While Daphne
scrubbed at her dress with a handkerchief, and Fen
shifted hastily away from a Niagara of beer which
was pouring over the edge of the table, Mr. Beresford
took no other action than to raise his forefinger impressively, in token of some inspiration that had visited him.

"Charlie Rumbles," he breathed at his distracted
audience. "Charlie Rumbles."

At first, and not unnaturally, they took this to be a
comment on the digestive processes of some local wor-
thy and stared at Mr. Beresford in surprise; but they
were soon disabused of the notion.

" 'E saw 'im," Mr. Beresford proceeded, pronomi-
nally obscure. " 'E saw 'im leave 'er cottage."

Fen ventured to ask for elucidation.

"Charlie Rumbles, it were." Mr. Beresford was cool-
ing off rapidly and seemed, indeed, rather confused
and ashamed at his outburst. "You 'aven't spoiled your
pretty frock, I 'ope, Miss Savage?"

"No, no," said Daphne gallantly. "Tell us what
Charlie Rumbles saw, Mr. Beresford." She scrubbed
more fiercely than ever.

Mr. Beresford, however, was by now mindful of his
responsibilities. He fetched a cloth from the bar and
mopped the table with it. Only when this operation
was complete, and Fen had ordered a second round of
drinks, did he return to the matter in hand.

"What you was askin', sir, was if Mr. Somers ever 'ad
aught to do with Mother Bly. An' oi said no, 'aving
forgotten about Charlie. Y'see, Charlie, 'e'm a bit
'ollow up 'ere." Mr. Beresford tapped his forehead sig-
nificantly. "Can't always rely on 'im. So when 'e tells
me, just afore closin' time Tuesday, as he's seen Mr.

Somers leavin' Mother Bly's cottage earlier on—well, oi didn't pay much attention. Oi thought to meself, 'e's imagining things. And that's 'ow oi came to forget."

He drank deeply, with a penitential air. For the moment Fen made no reply, for he was considering the sequence of events elicited in the last few minutes. Mr. Taverner discovers some "old things" in Mrs. Bly's cottage; Mr. Taverner talks to Somers; Somers visits Mrs. Bly and is subsequently much elated. Fen glanced at the clock over the bar and saw that the hands were close on the hour.

"And you're expecting Mr. Taverner?" he asked.

"Prompt at one, sir. Any minute, now. And 'e'll be able to 'elp you, take my word for it. 'E's a edicated man, is Mr. Taverner, and a famous preacher."

"A preacher?"

"Lay preacher, sir. 'E's preached all over county. But 'e ain't no 'oly Jesus, mind you," Mr. Beresford added—a recommendation that struck Fen as quaint. " 'Cept on Sundays, 'e likes 'is pint same as the next man."

Mr. Beresford paused to listen; footsteps were approaching the bar door, and as the latch was lifted, the clock whirred and struck one. The door opened, and Mr. Taverner, followed by a diffident, shambling, overgrown youth, entered the room.

Apart from his carpenter's clothes, which were stained with paint and impregnated with sawdust, Mr. Taverner resembled a superior butler. His face was fleshy, of an ocher hue, with pouches beneath the eyes; and his body was shaped like a pear. A Johnsonian portentousness emanated from him. The wooden floor creaked beneath his substantial weight. A chisel projected from his breast pocket. He wished the company good morning in a mellow, rotund parsonical voice. Then he moved with a measured and dignified tread to the bar, where he received, and paid

Love's Labour's Won

for, the pint of bitter which Mr. Beresford drew for
him, leaving the overgrown youth to order his own
drink. A subdued colloquy followed, and at its conclusion Mr. Taverner approached Fen and Daphne with
the same impressive, tanklike motion. To Daphne he
bowed, and then addressed himself to Fen.

"I believe, sir," he said, "that I am to have the pleasure of your acquaintance."

Fen rose, shook him gravely by the hand, and invited him to be seated; at which Mr. Taverner approached an empty chair, grasped it firmly by the
back, shook it—apparently in order to satisfy himself
that its joints were firm—and having shifted it to a
place out of the sun, lowered himself onto it with staid
deliberation. He then slaked his thirst and placed the
tankard on the table. The overgrown youth, who had
obtained a half-pint of mild, sat down to his left and
a little behind him. He seemed to be some kind of an
assistant, and in his attitude to Mr. Taverner there
was something of awe; just so, Fen thought, must a
medieval apprentice have regarded his master. Mr.
Beresford, pursuing some unguessable errand, had
disappeared into the farthest recesses of the bar.

Mr. Taverner cleared his throat. "In the midst of
life," he observed, "we are in death." His gaze was
fixed speculatively on Fen, as though measuring him
for a coffin, and he paused to allow time for his text to
be assimilated. "Naturally, sir, I am greatly shocked to
hear of Mrs. Bly's violent demise. It would hardly be
exaggerating to say that I am overwhelmed." Fen
thought that he had seldom seen anyone more resistant to overwhelming than Mr. Taverner. "And I am
sure that my assistant, Mr. Tye"—here he turned a
cold, appraising eye upon the overgrown youth—"is as
grieved as I am myself."

"Yes, Mr. Taverner," said Mr. Tye obsequiously.

"That being so," Mr. Taverner went on, "I shall be

delighted to offer you my fullest cooperation in apprehending the murderer." He glanced quickly about him, as though envisaging a pitched battle on the spot, and waved one hand in a sternly militant gesture. "So also will Mr. Tye."

"Yes, Mr. Taverner," said Mr. Tye.

"It's extremely kind of you," said Fen. "If you wouldn't mind answering one or two questions . . . ."

"My conversation," said Mr. Taverner with elephantine jocosity, "shall be yea, yea, and nay, nay. The gambit, sir, is yours."

"I'm chiefly interested in this new stove which you installed recently in Mrs. Bly's cottage."

"Ah, yes. I'm bound to confess, sir, that the nature of the commission surprised me; and that at first I was reluctant to undertake it. Isn't that so, Mr. Tye?"

"Yes, Mr. Taverner," said Mr. Tye.

"For the mercenary but unavoidable reason that I anticipated difficulty in obtaining payment for my services. However, I did, in fact, undertake it, and I was, in fact, paid." Mr. Taverner jingled the money in his pocket, presumably by way of confirming this last statement. "The previous stove, of the oil-burning variety, was damaged beyond all repair, and although Mrs. Bly had—shall we say—abandoned the great majority of civilized practices, cooking facilities were still needful to her."

"And I understand," Fen interposed rather fretfully, "that you found——"

Mr. Taverner raised his hand. "All in good time, sir. I am coming to that. In order to install the new stove, it was necessary for me to level the kitchen hearth. Mr. Tye will agree, I think, that this labor was not superfluous."

"No, Mr. Taverner," said Mr. Tye. "I mean, yes, Mr. Taverner."

Mr. Taverner bestowed on him a pitying glance but

refrained from comment. "I was obliged, in fact, to remove a number of bricks from the hearth. And what did I find? A *cache,* sir, a *cache."*

He drank deeply and with evident enjoyment. "A dry cavity," he resumed, "lined with mortar. Romantic, was it not?" Here Mr. Taverner smiled in what he evidently supposed to be a whimsical and indulgent fashion. "But alas, there was no buried treasure—nothing, that is, except a locket and some bundles of old yellowed papers. Naturally, I acquainted Mrs. Bly with my discovery."

"Yes, yes," said Fen, whose impatience was rapidly developing into a frenzy. "But as to these papers——"

"Acquainted her, I say, with my discovery." Mr. Taverner frowned reproof of Fen's unseemly precipitation, and Daphne laid a cool and soothing hand on Fen's arm. "She was, I fear, disappointed. I think you will find that Mr. Tye received the same impression."

"Yes, Mr. Taverner," said Mr. Tye hurriedly.

"She hoped, you understand, for something of value, something which she could sell. Well, there was, of course, the locket, which I told her might realize a few pounds, being of silver. 'And what about the papers, Mr. Taverner?' she asked. 'Shall I be able to sell them?' Naturally, sir, I laughed at her. 'No one wants old papers, Mrs. Bly,' I told her. 'The letters you may as well burn. But for the other packet you might get a pound or two from a museum.' You will scarcely guess, sir, what she answered." Fen made an uninterpretable noise. "She said: 'A hundred pounds, Mr. Taverner, that's what I'll ask for them. And if I don't get it, I'll burn 'em along with the others.' " Fen uttered a small, pitiful sound. "We had a good laugh over that, sir."

Fen grinned mirthlessly; he was clutching the arms of his chair so tightly that his knuckles were white.

"Can you describe these papers at all, Mr. Taverner?"

"Undeniably they were old. Very old. Yellow, as I said, and eaten away at the edges. Am I right, Mr. Tye?"

"Yes, Mr. Taverner," said Mr. Tye automatically.

"Both packets were in the same handwriting, very crabbed and faded, and with some strange misspellings. One of them, as I told you, consisted of private letters. The other seemed to be some kind of poetry, though I confess I could make little of it, beyond the title."

Fen leaned forward. "And that was?"

"Love's Labour's Won," said Mr. Taverner.

Fen looked as though he had seen a ghost—as, in a sense, he had. The incredible had happened. He made swift calculations: Stratford was fourteen miles away, not much more than an hour's ride . . . and still it was unbelievable.

Even Mr. Taverner was startled at the effect he had made. His mouth dropped open; he gaped oafishly, his ambassadorial dignity gone. Mr. Tye, to whom this momentary stasis was wholly incomprehensible, stared bemusedly at both of them. Daphne became motionless, sensing a crux but uncertain of its nature. And for half a minute they were all completely silent.

Fen was the first to recover himself, a consummation that he achieved by several times repeating to himself the words "This thing is impossible." That it was in fact by no means impossible he dared not allow himself to think; if it *were* true, and the letters—the *letters*—had been burned. . . . He shivered like one smitten with an ague. Of course it explained the murders; the stake involved was gigantic.

He found that without knowing it he had been holding his breath, and expelled it with an audible gasp.

Then he drained his tankard to the last drop, and when he looked up again, normalcy was restored. Mr. Taverner had ceased to gape; Mr. Tye had relapsed again into uncritical acquiescence; and Daphne looked merely puzzled. Sunlight winked on the bottles and glasses behind the bar, and a bee was droning fretfully on the windowpane. Fen said:

"You've been very helpful, Mr. Taverner. Very helpful"—a statement that, had Mr. Taverner only known it, represented an iron self-control; Fen's principal emotion with regard to Mr. Taverner was a desire to take him by the neck and throttle him.

"You flatter me, sir," said Mr. Taverner, unwittingly accurate. "You flatter me."

Distantly, Fen heard a car approaching—his taxi, in all probability. There was only one more question he needed to ask, and to that he already knew the answer.

"Mr. Taverner, did you last Monday evening mention to Mr. Somers, from the school, the facts about these papers which you've just given me?"

Mr. Taverner looked surprised. "I did, sir. He was most interested."

The car had drawn up at the door. Fen got to his feet.

"Yes," he said. "Yes, I expect he would have been. It may interest you to know, Mr. Taverner, that you are indirectly responsible for three murders and directly responsible for the destruction of property worth, at a conservative estimate, about a million pounds. And I suggest that in future you refrain from offering people inexpert advice about the value of their property and confine yourself to pulpits and screwdrivers. Good morning."

In a paralyzed hush he stalked out of the inn. He was at the door of his taxi when Daphne caught him up.

"Golly!" she exclaimed. "What was all that about?"

Though still simmering with fury, Fen managed to

smile. "Sorry," he said, "I oughtn't to have let you in for that."

"I don't mind. But what was it *about?* What's *Love's Labour's Won?"*

"It's a lost play by Shakespeare," Fen told her, "which hasn't been heard of since 1598. Luckily I don't think it can have been burned, though at present it's certainly in the possession of a murderer. . . . Forgive me if I hurry away." He climbed into the taxi. "I'll remember to suggest that your Mr. Plumstead comes and stays here."

The taxi moved off, and Daphne was left staring blankly after it.

† 10 †
MEDITATIONS AMONG THE TOMBS

The luncheon at the headmaster's house was a large and ceremonial affair. Miss Parry was there, and the bursar and one or two housemasters and the secretary of the Old Boys' Society and the mayor of Castrevenford and the entire board of governors. When Fen arrived, they were consuming sherry and martinis in the drawing room, about whose windows Mr. Merrythought was prowling like the wraith of Catherine Earnshaw in *Wuthering Heights.* Fen had barely time to be introduced before the gong sounded.

The meal, though larded with a rather specious gaiety, was not entirely successful. The chairman of the governors, a garrulous, self-important little man, clearly regarded it as an occasion for anecdotes and never ceased telling them from the soup to the coffee. Their point was invariably tenuous and so not immediately comprehensible, and he was generally obliged to explain it. Matters were not improved when on two occasions Fen and the headmaster, in an attempt to abolish these exegetical appendixes, laughed prematurely. But beyond the chairman's conversational reach the tropes of sociability proceeded smoothly, and Fen was occasionally relieved from the need of being jocular by Miss Parry, who sat on his left.

"I sometimes think," she said, "that there is a certain pathos about an occasion like this."

Fen examined the faces of his fellow guests for evidences of pathos, but without success.

"Not about the luncheon," Miss Parry explained

rather severely, "but about Speech Day in general."
Fen made noises of civil incomprehension. "I refer, of
course, to the parent-child relationship. This aspara-
gus is tinned."

Fen tasted it and assented. "But about the parent-
child relationship," he prompted.

"I believe that many of the boys have a lurking fear
that their parents will disgrace them in some fashion." Miss Parry emptied her glass and gazed fixedly
at a maidservant, who hastened to refill it. "And the
parents, of course, are aware of this. The fathers come
here anxious to look intelligent, amiable, and prosperous; the mothers put on their best frocks and hope that
their sons' friends will think them young-looking, attractive, well turned out. . . ." Champagne was one of
the few things capable of provoking Miss Parry to
sentimentality; she sighed. "Those with the money-
bags win, of course."

Fen nodded. "When I was a boy, I had some such
feeling. I was greatly ashamed of it then, and I am
still. It does, I agree, produce an undertow of pathos."

"But curiously enough, not with girls," said Miss
Parry. She reached for a second roll and tore it briskly
in two. "Except, of course, as regards the fathers'
looks, about which nothing can be done in any case. A
girl with a handsome father is in a fortunate position,
but everyone recognizes that it's due to an act of God,
and so there's very little ill feeling."

"And while we're on the subject of these young
women's preferences"—Fen lowered his voice and
spoke rather cautiously—"what is your opinion about
the disappearance of Brenda Boyce?"

Miss Parry hesitated for a moment; then, looking
straight in front of her: "So you've heard about that,"
she said.

Fen sensed something inimical in her tone; no doubt
she regarded the whole affair as a reflection on her

own competence and hence disliked the fact of its being bruited abroad.

"Very tiresome for you," he observed tactfully. "But, of course, you did everything you could."

She thawed a little. "Professor Fen, I'm convinced that the letter which she left is a fake."

"Yes?"

"The handwriting is hers, but the style is not. It should have been gaudy and elaborate. I'm convinced that the letter was dictated to her."

"Under duress?"

"Possibly." There was a catch in Miss Parry's voice. "In any case it could very easily have been placed on the desk through the study window."

This was no more than confirmation, Fen reflected, of what he already suspected. The murderer had, of course, made a mistake; the letter was a needless and risky elaboration. He should have killed the girl and left it at that. . . .

A momentary nausea overwhelmed him, and the champagne that he drank to relieve it had the opposite effect. How had it happened? A blow or a shot from behind? Or had she known it was coming? Had she sobbed, pleaded? Or clenched her teeth silently and closed her eyes? Or fought or tried to run away? She was sixteen. *Sixteen*. And—the thought occurred to him for the first time—her death was needless if only the murderer had chosen to change his plans, to take a little more risk himself. She might have been lunching at this moment with her parents, full of deliciously nervous anticipation of the evening's performance. . . .

Moral indignation was an emotion that Fen distrusted; he made an effort and quelled it.

After the meal he found time to ring up Stagge at the police station.

"Motive," he said curtly. "I think I have it. The

death of Mrs. Bly and the deaths here are undoubtedly connected."

"Well, *that's* an advance, sir," said Stagge, markedly respectful. "How do you work that out?"

"No time to tell you now, I'm afraid. I have to go off to the speeches. Can you meet me afterwards—about four?"

"Well, sir, if you're sure the delay won't help our man . . . ."

"No, I don't see how it can. The one thing I'm waiting for now is the alibi reports."

"They should be ready by then, sir."

"Good. Have you still got Plumstead with you?"

"Yes, sir. But there's a difficulty about finding anywhere for him to sleep tonight."

"Tell him to go to the pub at Ravensward. That young woman—Daphne Savage——"

"Yes, sir," Stagge interrupted percipiently. "I thought that myself. I'll tell him."

"You no longer seriously suspect him of killing Mrs. Bly?"

"Not really, sir, no."

"You're wise. He didn't. Good-bye for now."

Fen rang off and went upstairs to don the robes of a Doctor of Philosophy. Presently the whole party set off for the school site.

It was close on half-past two when they arrived, and the crowds of parents and boys in the sunshine outside the Hall were beginning to move into the building, their faces wearing the limp, uneasy expressions of those who are obliged to endure boredom and discomfort for appearances' sake; only those fathers who had stayed prolongedly in the Castrevenford bars showed any signs of cheerfulness. A substantial party had settled down to watch the cricket, which had already begun, and Fen cast a regretful glance at the sundappled pattern of white flannels against green turf

as he was led through a side entrance into an annex
of the Hall. The clock on Hubbard's Building struck
the half hour. Fen, the headmaster, and the governors
moved amid a *slentando* hum of conversation onto
the stage.

The Hall was as unadorned inside as out; besides, it
looked somehow insubstantial, as though built of ply-
wood, and its walls seemed as if they might burst
apart with the pressure of the mass of humanity at
present packed into it. The atmosphere was stifling;
people were fanning themselves with their printed
programs. In the front two rows of hard wooden chairs
sat the masters, robed, gowned, their attitudes varying
from indulgent ennui to virtual coma. Behind them,
in the body of the Hall, was a great concourse of per-
spiring parents. And into the gallery—the hands of
whose clock were paralyzed at five minutes past
eleven, and had been as long as anyone could remember—all the boys had been somehow crammed, with
the exception of the prize-winners, who were being
got into line in one of the corridors that bounded the
length of the Hall by two officious monitors. There
was whispering, fidgeting, shuffling of feet. Someone
was struggling to open a defective window. Through
the glass doors beneath the balcony disembodied
faces were peering.

Fen, the headmaster, and the chairman of the governors settled down on the platform behind a long
table laden with books. To the left of it sat Saltmarsh,
among whose other duties was the purchase and general organization of prizes, holding several typewrit-
ten pages clipped together. In a semicircle of chairs at
the back of the platform sat the governors, dignified
but nugatory. There was a burst of preparatory cough-
ing. The chairman of the governors got up to make his
speech.

He spoke lengthily, vaguely, facetiously, senten-

tiously. When, after what seemed an eternity, he sat
down amid relieved applause, the headmaster rose to
summarize the academic and athletic achievements
of the school during the past year and to express con-
ventionally pious hopes and aspirations for its future.
In conclusion he introduced Fen, who spoke wittily
and unimprovingly for exactly five minutes—a fact
that endeared him instantly to every member of his
cramped and sweating audience. Then he gave away
the prizes. Saltmarsh read out the names one by one
and gave the book or books to Fen, who handed them
to the appropriate boy and shook him earnestly by the
hand, while everyone clapped, in metronomic
spasms. One boy, overcome by the heat and the solem-
nity of the occasion, fainted away and had to be carried out ("Someone always faints," said the headmaster resignedly). Finally Weems, the music master, sat
down at the piano and accompanied the school song,
which the boys bellowed with the exuberance of re-
prieved assassins, while the parents, ignorant of the
words, stood looking sternly respectful and moving
their mouths in rather an improbable fashion. Thus
the speeches came to an end.

Fen left his robes in an anteroom, and after shaking
off the chairman of the governors and assuring the
headmaster that he would attend the garden party a
little later on, emerged into the open air. Stagge was
waiting for him with a briefcase in his hand, his features wearing the harassed, withdrawn look of one
who is trying to add up sums in his head. By common
consent the two men walked across the dry grass toward Davenant's and the headmaster's study, and
then they were out of earshot of the crowds, who were
either lingering to watch the cricket or drifting slowly
away in the direction of the headmaster's house.

"Well, sir," said Stagge, "I had lunch with the chief constable. He's telephoned to Scotland Yard, and they're sending some men down early tomorrow morning. I shall be relieved, I confess."

Fen spoke slowly. "I doubt, you know, if by that time there'll be anything much for them to do."

The superintendent looked up sharply. "Then this new information of yours——"

"It's not that I'm thinking so much." Fen was staring rather absently about him. "Let's sit down, somewhere in the open, and talk."

Near them was a bench embowered in laurels. They occupied it and lit cigarettes. Fen waved away a wasp that was hovering inquisitively about his nose.

"This is it, then," he said. "The motive for all these murders is a Shakespeare manuscript, and *possibly* some Shakespeare letters."

Stagge looked puzzled rather than surprised. "Manuscript, sir? Something valuable?"

"Enormously valuable. Worth, I should say, a million pounds."

"A million?" Stagge laughed, openly incredulous. "You're joking, sir."

"Far from it. I mean exactly what I say. If letters are involved as well, the sum would probably be in the neighborhood of two million."

The superintendent, watching Fen's face and seeing no evidence of a hoax there, became grave. "Perhaps you'd explain, sir. I'm not well up in these things. Can't get on with Shakespeare, to tell you the honest truth."

Fen pulled off a laurel leaf from the bush behind him and began shredding it slowly into segments along the veins.

"Well," he said after a moment's consideration, "it's like this. There are only four certain examples of Shakespeare's handwriting in existence, all of them signatures: three on the will and one on a piece of evidence given in a lawsuit in 1612."

Stagge shifted uneasily. "But how about the plays, sir?"

"There are no original manuscripts, only printed copies—the Quartos and the Folios and so forth. And one of those fetches a good many thousands in the sale room."

Stagge nodded. "I see, sir. So a complete play in Shakespeare's own handwriting——"

"Exactly. The idea's almost fabulous. I believe that in America there are people who'd give a million for it. And that's not all. That's only point number one."

Stagge gazed intently at the tip of his cigarette. "Go on, sir."

"The name of this particular play is *Love's Labour's Won.*"

"Ah, yes, sir. I fancy I was made to read it at school. About some men who settle down to study for a year and are put off it by some girls." Stagge shook his head, critically. "Didn't seem to come to much in the end."

"Whether or not it comes to much," said Fen, who as a matter of fact was rather of the same opinion, "the play *you're* speaking of is *Love's Labour's Lost*—quite a different kettle of fish. And by the way, there's a spider on your collar."

"A money spider," Stagge observed, transferring it delicately to a blade of grass. "Though to judge from what you're saying, it oughtn't to be me it's walking over. About this other play——"

"No one has read it or heard of it," said Fen, "since 1598, when Shakespeare was thirty-four."

Stagge appeared dubious. "Surely, sir, a play by Shakespeare couldn't just vanish."

Fen aimed the ash from his cigarette at the money

spider, which was sitting quiescent on the blade of grass, brooding over its experience.

"It could vanish very easily," he remarked. "Lots of Elizabethan plays have vanished—Jonson's and Nashe's *Isle of Dogs,* for example. And but for one thing, we should never have known *Love's Labour's Won* existed at all."

"What's that, sir?"

"In 1598," said Fen, "a student called Francis Meres published a book named *Palladis Tamia,* with a chapter in it entitled 'A Comparative Discourse of Our English Poets with the Greek, Latin, and French Poets.' In that chapter he talks about Shakespeare, whom he idolized, and gives a list of his works. Possibly not a complete list, but that's not the point. *'For Comedy,' "* Fen quoted, *" 'witness his* Gentlemen of Verona, *his* Errors, *his* Love's Labour's Lost, *his* Love's Labour's Won, *his* Midsummer Night's Dream, *and his* Merchant of Venice.' There it is, you see. The fact that Meres doesn't mention *Much Ado about Nothing,* which is generally thought to have been written before 1598, has led some critics to suppose that *Much Ado* is just another name for *Love's Labour's Won.* But that's only a guess. No one really knows."

"Lord," Stagge murmured, impressed despite himself with the difficulties of Shakespeare scholarship. "Lord. I never dreamed it was as complicated as all that. . . ." He roused himself abruptly. "But anyway, sir, the fact that it's a *new* play—one no one's ever read—would increase its value, wouldn't it?"

"Very much so. And finally there are the letters, *if* they still exist. Except for formal dedications, we haven't got *any* letters of Shakespeare's, printed or otherwise. You see what that means."

Stagge nodded slowly. "Fame, sir," he said presently. "Fancy a poet—a *poet*—being so famous four hundred years after he's dead that his handwriting will bring in millions." He paused, then: "I should have been a pair of ragged claws," he stated unexpectedly, "scuttling across the floors of silent seas. That's a lobster, I take it, or a crab. Do you think the chap that wrote that'll be worth the same money in four hundred years' time?"

Fen chuckled. "I didn't know you were a devotee of Mr. Eliot, Superintendent."

"Not me, sir. It's my daughter. Fifteen years old, a bit precocious, and a rare one for these modern poets. I found that bit in one of her books. Queer stuff. I can't say I disliked it, only I couldn't quite understand it, so to speak. I felt there was something there, but it was too slippery to get a grip on. However"—Stagge waved one hand in hurried dismissal of this literary digression—"to return to business. Granted the value of these manuscripts, would you mind telling me, sir, how you came to hear about them?"

Fen narrated the gist of his conversations with Mr. Beresford and Mr. Taverner.

"The sequence of events is obvious enough," he said in conclusion. "Taverner discovers the manuscripts and the miniature. Taverner tells Somers about them. Somers visits Mrs. Bly and is pleased. Mrs. Bly goes away to stay with her son, no one knows where. Love (if it was Love) inquires after her without success. Then the three murders."

"The implication being that Somers had bought these manuscripts."

"Yes. Hence, incidentally, his reading of *The Fourth Forger*. But I shouldn't say 'had bought.' Was going to buy. Remember, he visited Mrs. Bly on Tuesday evening, but he didn't get that hundred pounds out of his bank till yesterday midday."

"A hundred pounds. Yes. I think that's what you said the old woman was going to ask for the manuscript.

But I suppose Somers might have taken it away on Tuesday and promised to pay her when he could get to the bank and when she came back from visiting her son."

Fen grunted uncivilly. "I don't visualize Mrs. Bly as having quite such a trustful nature as that. Besides, if Somers already had the manuscript, there'd be no point in anyone's killing Mrs. Bly this morning. No, my theory is that the manuscript never reached Somers's hands."

"I see," said Stagge reflectively. "Someone murdered Somers to stop *him* getting it and then murdered Mrs. Bly and stole it. Whoever it was *had* to murder her, because otherwise she'd let out that Somers had been trying to buy it, and the murderer would be connected with Somers's death, too. . . ." He frowned and snapped his fingers. "That's no good, though. It's as full of holes as a sieve. In the first place, why couldn't this hypothetical chap simply outbid Somers? Why do any murdering at all?"

"He mightn't have had the money. Or Somers may have got Mrs. Bly to sign a paper agreeing to sell."

"A conditional contract," said Stagge rather surlily, "isn't legally binding."

"But, my dear Superintendent, *Mrs. Bly* was scarcely the person to know that."

"All right, sir. All right. I grant you one of those two possibilities. But our difficulties don't end there. To put the matter bluntly—why not a burglary?"

Fen lit a fresh cigarette, pushing the stub of the old one tidily out of sight among the roots of the laurel.

"Ah," he said. "I agree that's more awkward. But it isn't unanswerable. You see——"

He stopped, for something of importance had evidently occurred to Stagge. "Well?" he asked.

"I'm answering my own question, sir," said Stagge a little ruefully. "There *has* been a burglary at that cottage—we found a window had been forced, though whether it was this morning or some time when Mrs. Bly was away. . . ."

"There you are." After several attempts Fen had succeeded in blowing a smoke ring. "Look, isn't that beautiful . . . ? No, my point is this: that Mrs. Bly, realizing after Somers's visit that she possessed something valuable, *either* hid it where it couldn't be found *or* took it away with her. I think the latter is the more likely of the two."

"Very well, sir. So far, so good. Somers finds out about the manuscript. Someone else also finds out about it. That someone attempts a burglary but doesn't get what he wants. So he kills Somers because he can't outbid him or for some other reason. And he kills Mrs. Bly because—because——"

"Because he can't either pay for the manuscript or find out, without her assistance, where it is."

"Yes, sir. It fits, as well as these things ever do fit." They fell silent. From the cricket pitch they heard the click of leather against willow, and a moment later a listless round of clapping. Apparently someone had hit a boundary—or perhaps been caught out; audience reaction is identical in both cases.

"The only thing I don't quite grasp, sir," said Stagge carefully, "is where Love comes into it."

"Well, there's that unfinished statement of his: 'what can only be described as a fraud.' When people say that something can only be described as something, they mean that most other people wouldn't so describe it at all. It seems to me that Love must have been referring to an action which was legally innocent but morally dubious."

"Such as buying a manuscript worth a million pounds for a hundred because the seller was too uneducated to know its value."

"Such as that. I fancy that somehow or other Love

came to hear of this proposed transaction and made up his mind to tell Mrs. Bly of the real value of what she possessed. Hence his inquiries for her at the *Beacon.*"

"And hence his death," said Stagge. "A fortune like that is enough to tempt anyone to murder, and if Love was proposing to put a spoke in the wheel. . . ." He hesitated. "There's a snag, though. It was *Somers* who was going to buy the manuscript, and Somers couldn't have killed Love. He couldn't have killed him before ten, on the medical evidence. And of the hour between ten, when he was last seen alive, and eleven, when he was found dead, he spent at least fifty-five minutes writing reports. It's physically impossible for him to have gone right the way over to Love's house, killed him, and got back again to the common room, in only five minutes."

"You must remember," said Fen mildly, "that Love refers to *two* colleagues who are involved in this so-called fraud."

"Ah, yes. That had slipped my memory for the moment." But Stagge was still puzzled. "But look here, sir, if Somers was in cahoots with someone, that makes it odder still. It upsets all these motives we've been working out so carefully for Mrs. Bly's murder and Somers's own. Mrs. Bly wouldn't need to be murdered if these two had the money between them to buy the manuscript—as we know they had. And Somers——"

"A double cross, perhaps," Fen suggested.

"Perhaps," said Stagge doubtfully. It was clear that, like Fen, he was tiring of this particular aspect of their problem. "Anyway, there are certain steps I shall have to take, in view of this new information. One is to search that cottage from end to end and another is to see if we can't definitely identify Love as the man who was asking at the *Beacon* for Mrs. Bly."

He took out a handkerchief and wiped his brick-red forehead. "There's only one thing more, sir. These manuscripts—is it possible that they're forged?"

"I've been wondering about that," said Fen. "It's an interesting point, for various reasons. On the whole I'm inclined to think not. You see, there are two possibilities. One is that they're a modern forgery, which means that both Taverner and Mrs. Bly are involved in the fraud. But that, quite frankly, seems to me impossible. A village carpenter and a drunken witch forging a plausible Shakespeare manuscript—no, no."

"They might be only the agents."

"True. But then look at the money side of it. Three people are involved—and many weeks' laborious work on the part of the forger. And what do they ask for the thing? A pitiful hundred pounds."

"We've only Taverner's word for that."

"Not at all. It was a hundred pounds that Somers withdrew from the bank. No. Having met Taverner, I'm tolerably certain he was telling the truth, and that he did find the things where he said he did. There remains the possibility that at some time in the past some joker with a perverted sense of humor put them there to deceive whoever might find them."

"Oh, come now, sir," Stagge protested. "The thing about practical jokers is that they like to be there when their jokes take effect."

"I agree it's unlikely. I agree it doesn't ring true. All I'm saying is that it's not inconceivable. The thing that chiefly militates against the theory is that miniature, which is genuinely Elizabethan. It's too much to support that that would be hidden away just to give local color to a forgery."

Stagge had taken the miniature from his pocket and was regarding it pensively. "Do you think, sir, that it's"—he lowered his voice reverently—"*him?*"

"It very well might be," said Fen.

"Not much like the other pictures of him I've seen, though."

"No. He's younger in that, of course, than in the Stratford bust and the Droeshout engraving, where he looks like nothing in the world but a pig. Besides, I don't believe the Stratford bust is anything *like* Shakespeare; it couldn't conceivably have written *Lear.*" Fen sat up energetically. "Not forgeries, my dear Stagge. I'm certain of it. Think how near Stratford we are."

He relapsed again. "Those letters," he murmured nostalgically. "They might have explained everything in the sonnets. . . . Did that fiend of a woman really burn them, I wonder? And who was living in that cottage in the last ten years of the sixteenth century? The parish registers might help. A beautiful girl, I like to think, for when he got tired of Anne. A fancy lady. He would have been twenty-nine in 1593. . . ."

But Stagge declined to embark on this sea of hazy conjecture. "There's one thing I ought to mention, sir, about the question of forgery or otherwise. I've been picking up a good deal of odd information about various people during the day, and one of the things I happened to learn was that Galbraith—that's the headmaster's secretary—makes a hobby of old manuscripts and knows a lot about them."

Fen was interested. "Does he, indeed? I wonder if Somers spoke to him about this one? He wouldn't want to spend a hundred pounds on a worthless heap of paper. I'll ask Galbraith when I see him. . . . But what I'd much rather know is who lived in that cottage."

"What *I* want to know," said Stagge grimly, "is who committed these murders."

"Have you got the alibi reports yet?"

"Here in this briefcase."

"Then what," Fen asked, "are we waiting for?"

† 11 †

REASONING
BUT TO ERR

Stagge opened the briefcase and took a sheaf of neatly written notes from it.

"Not entirely satisfactory, sir," he observed. "We've eliminated a good many people, of course, but we've still got four—well, say three and a half—to choose from."

"A half?" Fen queried blankly. "You don't mean a boy, I take it?"

"No, no, sir. Only there's one person who could have killed Love, but not Somers. Galbraith, to be specific."

Fen snorted. "Galbraith didn't kill Love," he said impatiently. It occurred to him seriously for the first time that Stagge had not the rudiments of an idea about what had been going on. "What's the nature of his alibi?"

Stagge scrabbled through the papers until he found the relevant entry. "He was alone in his rooms from seven thirty onwards, according to his own account. It seems he's not married, and he could easily have gone in or out without his landlady knowing it."

"Where does he live?"

"In Snagshill. Not far from here. Most of them do. Anyway, he telephoned the chaplain about ten thirty, in reference to the seating arrangements at this morning's service, and found that there'd been a hitch of some sort. So he came round here to talk to Dr. Stanford about it and was with him from ten forty-five till after the murders were discovered. You see what that means—since Somers wasn't killed till just before eleven?"

Fen sighed. "Yes, yes," he said. "I see what it means. Well, who are your three full-time suspects?"

Stagge again consulted his papers. "Mathieson, to start with."

"Oh, yes. The man who's producing the play."

"That's him. He was at this Fasti meeting, with nearly a dozen other people, from nine thirty to ten forty-four. He walked back to his rooms alone and says he got there about eleven. But there's no confirmation of that."

"Where does *he* live?"

"Quite near Love. A fair distance, in fact. It *would* have taken him a quarter of an hour. But as a matter of fact he could have arrived home unobserved any time up to midnight. He's living with a family at a private house—accommodation being so limited in this part of the world—and they were all out till midnight."

"I see. Next candidate, please."

"Philpotts," said Stagge. "That's the chemistry master who found the cupboard had been broken open. He was at the Fasti meeting, too, from nine thirty to ten forty-four. And *he* walked home alone, arriving, he says, about ten fifty-five. That fits the distance all right, but again there's no confirmation. His wife was out at a bridge party till well after midnight, and his children were all asleep. He has eight children," said Stagge informatively. *"Eight,"* he repeated, shocked at such uncontrolled fecundity. "And apparently none of them heard him come in. He sleeps in a different room from his wife—fancy that, with eight children—so the plain fact is that no one set eyes on him from ten forty-four last night till breakfast time this morning."

"Yes," said Fen pensively. "I'd like to digress for just a moment, if I may. Did you talk to Philpotts yesterday about that cupboard?"

"I did, sir."

"Did you find out in what circumstances it's locked and unlocked and what masters have keys to it?"

"All the science masters have keys to it, sir—six of them. And it's always kept locked when there isn't a master in the room, for obvious reasons. Philpotts said they were very strict about that, and as far as he knew, the rule had always been observed."

"Good." Fen took a handkerchief from his pocket and draped it solemnly over his head as a protection against the sun; it made him look a particularly disreputable Bedouin. "It's a small point, but worth settling. And now, the third suspect."

"Etherege," said Stagge. "He's got no alibi for *any* part of the relevant period. He was last seen by Wells leaving Hubbard's Building at ten o'clock. He says he went for a walk and didn't get home till eleven forty-five. I distrust people," Stagge added peevishly, "who go for walks at night. It isn't natural."

Fen meditated. "You know, there's one notable omission in your list," he said mildly after a while.

"Omission, sir? What do you mean?"

"Wells, Superintendent. The impeccable Wells. He was alone in his office, wasn't he, between ten and eleven?"

Stagge stared. "Good Lord, sir, you're quite right. I told my people not to worry about him, as he'd already given an account of himself. And then forgot about him." He produced a pencil and made a hurried note at the bottom of the last sheet. "Wells. Yes, he had the opportunity all right."

"You've checked on all the other employees of the school? Oddments—such as the bursar—as well as the masters?"

"Yes, sir. Even the groundsmen. Not the domestic staffs, though. Do you think I should have included them?"

"No," said Fen definitely. "It would have been a

complete waste of time. You think these reports are reliable?"

"I think so, sir, yes. There were a lot of parties going on last night, so my men were able to cross-check almost indefinitely. The people they exempt *are* exempt, I'm certain of that."

Fen took the papers from him and read them through. Apart from what he had already heard they offered nothing of interest—though he noted that the bursar, the J.T.C. adjutant, the school doctor, and the school librarian had all been playing bridge at the bursar's house between ten and eleven and vouched for one another.

"And the next thing," he said sadly as he handed the papers back, "is to find out about alibis for Mrs. Bly's murder."

Stagge nodded dolefully. "That, as you say, is the next thing."

"When exactly *was* she killed?"

"Plumstead thinks it was about five or ten past eleven."

"Ah. During the gym display, in fact. So Etherege didn't do it. I was talking to him at the time."

"Were there many masters watching the display, sir?"

"Not a great many, I fancy. Nothing like all of them."

"Philpotts?"

"I've never met him. Don't know what he looks like."

"Mathieson, then?"

"No, I don't think he was there."

"Wells?"

"I didn't see him, either. But then I wasn't *looking,* you know." Fen glanced at his companion, whose face was pitifully despondent. "Well, Superintendent, have you come to any conclusion about those five?"

Stagge returned the papers to the briefcase, snapped it shut, and deposited it on the grass by the side of the bench. He looked about him—at the upper windows of Hubbard's Building, at the flawless sky, at the tops of the beeches on the river bank, at the cool, fugitive glint of the river itself. And he did not seem encouraged by what he saw.

"It's difficult, sir," he said at last. "Damnably difficult. I was thinking about it while I waited for you to come out of the Hall." He fingered his moustache, as though uncertain of finding it still there. "Take the murder of Love, for instance. He was found dead at eleven, and Mathieson and Philpotts didn't leave that meeting till a quarter to—barely time to walk there and shoot him."

"There are bicycles," Fen remarked rather obviously.

"Agreed, sir. But time isn't the only difficulty. We're bound to assume that those two knew about his habit of taking coffee with his wife at ten forty-five every evening. And you don't, for preference, go and kill a man when his wife's in the same room with him."

"You might reconnoiter and observe that she wasn't."

"On the other hand, sir, you wouldn't just amble round to your victim's house, with a gun in your pocket, on the off chance that something might have gone wrong with his arrangements on that particular evening."

"All right, I agree about that. But on the other hand, both Mathieson and Philpotts could comfortably have killed Somers."

"Yes, sir. And this is how it works out, as I see it." Stagge clasped his large hands together and bumped them on his knee to emphasize each point as he made it. "The murder of Somers: Mathieson or Philpotts or Etherege or Wells could have done it. The murder of

Love: Galbraith or Etherege or Wells could have done
it. The murder of Mrs. Bly: We can't be sure yet, but
Etherege *couldn't* have done it. Add it up, and it
leaves Etherege and Wells in the trickiest position.
And if Wells hasn't got an alibi for the death of Mrs.
Bly, then it looks as if *he* must be our man. . . . There's
only one difficulty about reasoning in that particular
way: We can't be sure that all three murders were
committed by the same person."

"They weren't," said Fen. "At least two murderers
are involved. And it's four murders, Superintendent—
not three."

"Four, sir?"

"The fourth victim being Brenda Boyce."

"Oh, come now, sir," Stagge began, but Fen interrupted him.

"I'm sorry," he said with deliberation, "but it's quite
inconceivable to me that that girl is alive."

There was a long silence. From the cricket pitch
they heard another scattered round of applause, and
someone quite close by was whistling the "Merry
Widow" waltz. Stagge was visualizing Etherege's ur-
banity, Mathieson's heavily built clumsiness, Philpotts's acid vehemence. And he was not happy.
Though normally a placid man, he was by no means
insensitive, and he was well aware that Fen had
gone a good deal deeper into the case than he had.
He could, had he chosen, have officially demanded to
hear Fen's theories, but he did not like working in
that way, and moreover he was far from certain that
it would get results from a man of Fen's tempera-
ment.

There's no doubt, he thought, that I've fallen down
on the job. Too complicated. Too complicated by half.

Fen sensed something of all this, and his conscience
was stirred.

"Look here, Superintendent," he said, "it must be

clear to you by now that I have some fairly definite notions about all this. And you're sensible enough, I think, not to take it amiss if I say that as far as I can see, you haven't."

"I admit it, sir," said Stagge with a certain dignity. "It's all a bit beyond me at present, and I see no point in concealing the fact. I'm entirely in your hands."

He waited. Fen frowned and examined his nails.

"The point is this," he said slowly, "that I'm morally certain of the answer to all the questions confronting us, but I haven't got absolute proof. There's a case of sorts, but it might very well collapse in court, and that's the last thing we want to happen; as you're aware, no one can be tried twice for the same offense. But I'll tell you what I'll do: Give me till midnight to find my proof; and if I haven't got it by then, you're welcome to anything I can tell you."

"That's fair enough, sir. And I wish you luck with it."

"What will you be doing for the rest of the day? Where can I get in touch with you?"

"Well, sir, I'm going back to Castrevenford now to get some search warrants—for Wells's house and Philpotts's and Mathieson's and Etherege's. The manuscript, you understand, and possibly the gun. Not that whoever is guilty won't be prepared for that, but one must do what one can. Anyway, I'll leave instructions at the station that you're to be told where I am if you telephone."

Fen got briskly to his feet, brushing fragments of laurel leaf from his lap. *"Marchons alors.* The suspects will no doubt be swarming at the headmaster's garden party, so I shall go there. I'll let you know what happens."

Stagge smiled. "Good hunting, sir," he said.

Fen strode across the school site to the gates and out into the suburb of Snagshill. It was a prosperous residential area of quiet streets, large, well-built houses, and colorful gardens, redolent of moneyed respectability and inhabited chiefly by elderly folk. But today it was more animated than usual. Parents and boys strolling to or from the headmaster's house greeted Fen respectfully, and in the case of those who had been at the speeches, with positive warmth. In the normal way this would have flattered his self-esteem —for he had a good deal of self-esteem, though he habitually regarded it with a detached and mocking eye—but on this occasion his response was no more than automatic. He was too busy making plans.

He had been right, he thought, to tell Stagge that there was not enough proof as yet for the case to go to the public prosecutor. The common-sense demonstration, in the matter of the manuscripts, could be demolished by an able K.C. in a few minutes. There were alternative explanations for both Somers's wristwatch and Love's unfinished statement. Yet the solution remained obvious; it could hardly be anything else.

The murderer had made two particularly glaring mistakes; it was not impossible that he could be induced to make another, the more so as he would have no idea how far the investigation had gone. Fen set himself to work out in detail an idea that had been revolving vaguely in his mind since Stagge had told him of the alibi reports. It was not, he reflected gloomily, a particularly plausible trap, but it was the best thing he could think of at the moment, and a nervous, overhasty person might be taken in by it. If it failed, it failed, and that was that; they would not be worse off than they were already, and the murderer must at all costs be prevented from doing *nothing*.

The only trouble with the scheme was that it required an agent—someone capable of acting, someone with a subtle command of histrionics. . . .

He came in sight of the headmaster's house. It stood apart from the other buildings of Snagshill, in fairly extensive grounds—a mellow Queen Anne dwelling place with a bold roof hipped back at all the corners, plain chimney stacks, and a noble front doorway. He could see a uniformed constable standing at the gate to ward off gate crashers. And walking toward him, away from the garden party, was Weems, the music master.

Weems. . . .

Fen had taken note of Weems when he was accompanying the school song and had thought at the time that he looked exactly like a Renaissance intriguer. He was a youngish man, suave, dark, and graceful, with a cold eye, a Machiavellian air, and unimpeachable clothes. His left eyelid drooped slightly, giving him, disconcertingly, the appearance of one about to impart a lewd confidence. Looks were deceptive, Fen knew; but if Weems's acting ability matched his smooth self-confidence, he could be very useful.

Fen looked about him. For the moment no one, except for the constable, was in sight. He accosted Weems, and for five minutes they talked.

Undeniably Weems lived up to his looks. He showed no surprise at what was requested of him and asked no questions; Fen had the impression that he would willingly have poisoned the headmaster if only the plan proposed had been tortuous, subtle, and complex enough. All he said when Fen had explained matters was:

"And when do you want me to do this?"

"Before dinner, in any case. As soon as you plausibly can."

"Very well. Do I take it that that person is the murderer?"

"That person," Fen agreed, "is the murderer. But please keep the fact to yourself until you hear from me again."

Weems raised his eyebrows. "My dear sir . . ." he murmured deprecatorily.

Fen went on toward the house, satisfied that Weems was absolutely to be trusted.

The headmaster had omitted to supply Fen with a ticket for the party, and he was arguing acrimoniously with the constable, who did not know him, when Mathieson appeared on his way out. Fen said:

"For heaven's sake, Mathieson, vouch for me."

"It's all right, Constable," said Mathieson. "This *is* Professor Fen."

The constable, defeated but still suspicious—he had had no one so far to repel, and the lack irked him—stood aside. Fen said:

"How's the play going?"

"All right," Mathieson replied. "The new girl isn't a patch on Brenda Boyce—her French is of the Stratford-atte-Bow variety—but she'll get through. Will you be there?"

"I hope so," said Fen. "Good luck to it." He went on into the garden.

The second relay of tea was in progress. On a broad, close-clipped lawn, bounded on one side by rose beds, on another by tall, shady beeches, and on a third by the house, stood groups of Old Boys and parents, perilously balancing cups and plates. Boys wandered about in a condition of unnatural civility, offering biscuits, sandwiches, and cakes. Long trestle tables were laden with crockery, food, silver tea urns, and presided over by matronly women in white coats. The headmaster, still gowned, was chatting affably to a small group of parents, who listened with the strained and reverent attention of applicants to the Cumaean Sybil. Mr. Merrythought was eating pansies with a self-righteous air. Small rain clouds assembling against the sapphire sky were apprehensively examined, but they came too late to throw a blight on the day. Fen, contemplating the cheerful, crowded, untroubled scene, reflected that the staff and the police had kept their melancholy secret remarkably well.

Unsolicited, several boys rushed to fetch him tea and cakes, and for some time he talked amiably to them about ghost stories, in which respect he was sorry to find their education deficient. He was earnestly recommending Mr. De la Mare, Mr. Hartley, and Dr. M. R. James to their attention when he caught sight of Galbraith and remembered that there was a question he had to ask. So he excused himself courteously and took the secretary aside.

"I believe," he said, "that you're an expert on old manuscripts."

Galbraith smiled. He was a quiet, unobtrusive man with one of those complexions which even an hour's sunlight will turn brown.

"Hardly an expert," he said. "But it's a recreation of mine, yes. Forgeries—that kind of thing."

"Just so. The point is that something to do with old manuscripts has cropped up in connection with the business last night, and I was wondering if Somers had spoken to you on the subject any time recently."

"Yes, he did. Quite recently—I think it was Wednesday last. He gave me a detailed description of what he thought might be an Elizabethan manuscript and asked me if I could tell him whether it was genuine or not." Galbraith hesitated. "I never mentioned it to the police because I'd no idea it was important."

"Nor had we," said Fen, "until this afternoon. But anyway, were you able to reassure Somers?"

Galbraith shrugged. "Good heavens, no. Not without seeing the thing and making a good many tests. Forgery's a highly skilled business nowadays."

"Yes, I suppose so."

"You see," said Galbraith, mounting his hobbyhorse with celerity, "you often get, for example, genuine bits combined with imitated bits by photographic engraving. And then another device is to——"

"Yes," said Fen. "Yes." He was not really in the mood for a lecture. "Was Somers disappointed?"

"He seemed to be. I advised him to be exceedingly careful if he was proposing to buy anything of the sort."

"And he didn't reopen the subject?"

"Not that I remember."

Fen thanked him and thereafter gave himself up to exercising sociability. Twenty minutes later, while explaining the plot of his detective story to a bemused father who had not been at the speeches and who evidently took him for one of the staff, he was interrupted by a light tap on the arm, and turning, saw a plump, pretty young woman of about sixteen whose dress and complexion betrayed an invincible determination to look older than her years.

"You're Professor Fen, aren't you?" she said. At which the bemused father, seeing his chance, mumbled something inaudible and edged surreptitiously away. Fen agreed to the identification.

"I've seen your photo in the papers," the young woman proceeded, "and I've followed all your cases."

"Ha!" Fen exclaimed, much pleased. "That's more than Crispin's readers manage to do. Can I help you in any way?"

"I'm Elspeth Murdoch," the young woman explained, "and I'm at Castrevenford High School." She paused, dramatically. "I don't know if *you* can help *me,* but I think *I* can help *you.* . . . I can tell you how to find Brenda Boyce."

† 12 †
A GREEN THOUGHT IN A GREEN SHADE

Fen stared. Then he took Elspeth by the arm and drew her away from the conversing groups that surrounded them. She followed him obediently to the shade of a beech tree sufficiently isolated to prevent their being overheard, where she sat down and arranged herself demurely on the grassy bank. In spite of puppy fat, Elspeth was attractive and aware of the fact; she had dark blue eyes, brown hair with a hint of bronze in it, a slightly snub nose, rather full lips, and a figure that in a year or two would be perfect. Fen settled down cautiously beside her, plucked a long grass, and put the clean, plump lower extremity of it into his mouth.

"Now," he said. "Tell me about it."

"My brother's at the school here," said Elspeth, who apparently felt the need to account for herself. "So of course I came to the speeches. Or rather, I didn't come to the *speeches.* Too hot. The high school has a whole holiday on Speech Day, you know. Partly because of the play, but also there are a good many girls like me who have brothers here."

"Yes, no doubt," Fen responded patiently. "But about Brenda Boyce. . . ."

"I oughtn't to have been quite so definite," said Elspeth, "because I don't actually *know* where she is, and I don't actually *know* that I *know* where to find her. Only I've been thinking, and there's a possibility, you see."

"Indeed?" Fen was a little dazed by so much qualification; in manner it reminded him of articles in learned journals. "Well, perhaps you'd better explain."

Elspeth drew a deep breath. "In the first place I'm damn sure Brenda hasn't eloped with anyone."

Fen had produced his cigarette case. He offered it to her, but she shook her head regretfully.

"I can't while Mummy and Daddy are around. They have a silly prejudice against me smoking. Of course, I smoke a lot when I'm on my own," she added quickly, "only I don't let them know about it because—well, you know how parents are. They like to go on treating you as a kid years after you've grown up."

Fen lamented, in suitable phrases, this disadvantage of the parental instinct, in the meantime lighting a cigarette for himself. "What makes you so certain," he asked, "that Brenda hasn't eloped?"

"Well, I know her pretty intimately, you see, and she just isn't the sort of person who would. She'd never be swept off her feet by an affair, because she's quite hardheaded. I sometimes wonder if she has any *deep* emotions at all."

"Miaouw," said Fen gently.

Elspeth grinned. "All right, I *am* being catty. But you mustn't think she's not a friend of mine; I really do like her. . . . *Men,* of course," said Elspeth with a worldliness that Madame de Pompadour might have envied, "she liked men all right. But she'd never go off with one. That letter to the Parry is a fake."

All of which, Fen reflected, confirmed the Parry's opinion; and springing from such divergent viewpoints, it was almost certainly the truth. It occurred to him to ask how Elspeth had come to know of the letter.

"Oh, these things filter through," she answered airily. "As a matter of fact, I got it from Jean Carvel, who got it from Gillian Pauncey, who got it from——"

"Yes," Fen interrupted swiftly. "All right. Never mind about that now. What else?"

"If the letter's a fake," Elspeth proceeded, frowning with concentration, "that means one of two things: *Either* Brenda's gone off on her own, for some different reason—and I believe she'd have told me or Judith Lindsay if she was going to, because she could have trusted us, you see, and she was never secretive about anything—*or* she's been kidnapped. That's logical, isn't it?"

"Impeccably," said Fen. "But I'd like to digress for just a moment, if you don't mind. You say she would have told you or this other girl if she were going off on her own—running away from home or what not—and that she wasn't secretive. That being so, didn't she mention anything about what upset her at the rehearsal of *Henry V* the evening before last? Something did, you know. Quite seriously."

"It's funny about that." Elspeth clasped her hands round her knees and looked earnest. "It just happened that I didn't get a chance to talk to her at all during school yesterday. She does history, you see, and I do English, and at lunch we sat at different tables, and after lunch she was talking to Miss Parry, and after school she went off quickly, and I had to stay behind for a meeting. But Judith noticed there was something the matter with her and asked her what it was, and she said she *dared* not tell. And Judith said she was crying a little," Elspeth concluded soberly, "and we've none of us ever seen her cry before, not even when she broke her wrist at hockey."

"Unpleasant," said Fen sympathetically. "Anyway, go on with what you were telling me."

"Okay," said Elspeth more cheerfully. "I was saying she'd either gone off on her own or been kidnapped; and *I* think she's been kidnapped—ransom, you see, because her father's pretty well off."

"But in that case, why the fake letter?"

"To delay pursuit, of course, and keep the police

running round registry offices until she'd been got well away to a place where she couldn't be found. Now, let's get down to details. She left school, all right, at four o'clock yesterday afternoon, because I've found several girls who saw her. Usually she biked, because it's almost four miles to her home, but her three-speed's being mended at the moment, so she had to walk yesterday. She was a fast walker, and she should have been home by five. Only she wasn't. So she must have been kidnapped on the way there."

"I'm bound to admit"—Fen spoke apologetically—"that some such notion had already occurred to me."

"Don't get impatient," said Elspeth with severity, "because we must get this straight. One false step in our reasoning and we could go miles astray." Abashed, Fen murmured words of contrition. "Now," Elspeth resumed, "the point is that on the road between the school and Brenda's house there's only one place that's lonely enough for anyone to dare try and kidnap her in daylight."

Fen, who had been reclining comfortably on the small of his back, sat upright. Up to the present he had had scant hopes of the usefulness of this conversation, but now he was interested.

"And that is?" he asked.

"Melton Chart."

"What's Melton Chart?"

"It's a wood just outside Castrevenford, on the west of the river. A big wood, too. People have actually got lost in it and died of starvation—they found a tramp's bones there only last year, and five years ago the bodies of some children they'd been searching for for five days." Elspeth enunciated these lugubrious details with a certain relish. "But of course, the road only goes through a corner of it. Do you see what I'm getting at?"

Fen tapped ash into a buttercup, and instantly regretting the action, blew it carefully out again.

"In a way," he answered with reserve. "You mean that Brenda has been"—he narrowly avoided saying "killed"—"hidden somewhere in this wood."

"Exactly. And that's where my knowledge comes in. As I said, the wood's big, and it'd take days to search it thoroughly. But if we could find some kind of a trail and put a dog on to it——"

"But it would have to be a trail of something specific after this lapse of time," said Fen. "Aniseed, creosote, blood—something like that."

"Blood is just what I think we may find."

Fen was startled. "What makes you say that?"

"I'll tell you." Elspeth looked about her and lowered her voice. "Years ago, when we were only kids, we used to play a sort of war game in the fields near Melton Chart."

She eyed Fen rather self-consciously. "You know the silly things children do. . . . Anyway, there were two sides, and we took prisoners and all that sort of thing, and Brenda used to treat it all frightfully seriously. If she played a game, she *played* it, whatever the consequences to herself or anyone else.

"Well, there was one time when she did the most amazing thing—she could be absolutely reckless when she liked. She was the leader of our side, and while she was out alone, scouting, she was captured by the others. Once you were captured, you had to stay captured until some member of your own side found you and touched you. The enemy took you wherever they liked, and once you were there, you were bound in honor to *stay* there and not make any sign or sound that would help your own side to find you. Only while you were being *taken* there you could yell out or do anything you liked. We worked out who'd won by the number of unransomed prisoners at the end of two hours or whatever it was.

"Well, of course, we *had* to get Brenda back, as she

was our leader, but we didn't have any idea where they'd taken her, and she was too far away when she was captured for us to hear her calling. We hunted about, and after a time we noticed that a little mongrel we'd got with us was frightfully excited about some spots of blood he'd found in the road, and there was a trail of it, and he followed the trail, and *we* followed *him,* and in the end he led us to where Brenda was." Elspeth paused for breath. "And do you know what she'd done?"

Fen admitted that he could only guess.

"Well, she had a tiny penknife in her pocket, and when she saw she was captured, she managed to get it open without taking it out and held it hidden in her hand and bent down as though she was pulling up a stocking and gave herself a terrific cut on the leg with it, under her skirt, so they wouldn't notice. She knew we'd got the dog, you see, and she thought it might follow the blood, and it did."

Elspeth had become much excited during her narrative. "So there it is," she concluded. "Brenda would be certain to remember the trick, because we all talked about it for months afterwards. And she still carries the same penknife. I'm sure if she was kidnapped, she'd have done it again, on the off chance that it would help."

By now Fen was thoroughly attentive. "My dear young lady," he said reproachfully, "why on earth haven't you told someone about all this before?"

"I'm an idiot," said Elspeth with a penitential expression that greatly became her, "but the fact is I've only just remembered. And I recognized you, and I'd seen you talking to the superintendent, and I knew it must be about Brenda, so I thought you were the person who ought to know."

The third and last relay of tea was now in progress, and the composition of the groups on the lawn had substantially changed. Fen stared absently at them and threw his cigarette end into the hedge. He said:

"Well, we shall certainly have to take action about this. I'll talk to Stagge."

"Oh, no, please, not *him.*" Elspeth spoke with venom.

"But why ever not?" he demanded, wondering how the easy-going superintendent could possibly have aroused such animosity.

"He got my father's driving license taken away," Elspeth explained sulkily, "and Mummy *won't* drive, and I'm still too young, so we have to *walk* everywhere."

It was, Fen agreed, an exasperating situation. "But at the same time," he added, "we can't just keep this to ourselves."

"Why not? Why can't *we* trace Brenda and beat the police at their own job?"

"Well, for one thing, someone's got to supply us with a bloodhound."

Elspeth pointed at Mr. Merrythought, who, dazed and comatose after his floral banquet, was sprawling owlish and unfriended at the edge of the lawn.

"What about him?" she said. "He's a bloodhound, I *think.*"

She spoke in the tones of one propounding an unanswerable proposition, but Fen had answers to it.

"He's *far* too old," he objected. "And not, from what I've seen of him, at all a reliable dog."

"Oh, please, Professor Fen," she pleaded, her large blue eyes spectacularly plaintive, "couldn't we just *try?* If you go to the police, they're sure not to let me help, and as I thought of it in the first place, that'd be *damnably* unfair."

Fen considered. He had sound reasons for believing that Brenda Boyce was no longer alive; if she had been, amateur sleuthing, in the light of Elspeth's information, would have been indefensible. But as things were, he saw no particular harm in it, and it would have the additional merit of lending colorability to the trap which, with Weems's connivance, he had set for the murderer.

"Very well," he said, "we'll try. When can you start?"

"Now," said Elspeth unequivocally. "Have you got a car?"

"Yes."

"That's good," she said. "But before we go, I'd better introduce you to my parents, otherwise they'll have doubts about your intentions. You know—*News of the World* and all that." Fen was shocked. "Come along."

In the event, and for reasons that need not concern us but which included Fen's insistence on changing into cooler clothes, it was seven o'clock by the time they set out, and the sky, which in the earlier part of the day had been as blue as a redstart's egg, had clouded over, with promise of a drizzling rain. Mr. Merrythought had developed an unconvincing coyness, and for a long time they were unable to lure him into the car.

"He's just perverse," said Fen after all kinds of blandishment had failed. "I think the thing to do is to shoo him away."

They tried this, and it worked. Mr. Merrythought leaped at once into the driving seat, where he settled down to lick the steering wheel—which was soon covered with slimy, disgusting smears—and to gaze stonily through the windscreen. A further interval elapsed before they were able to shift him. When they eventually succeeded, Elspeth grasped him firmly and courageously by the collar while Fen, after hurriedly wiping the wheel, got Lily Christine under way. Alarmed at the motion, Mr. Merrythought dabbed a paw apprehensively over the side, like a swimmer about to enter cold water; but he soon saw that there was no chance of escape and resigned himself to a sullen hebetude.

Directed by Elspeth, Fen drove from the headmaster's house to the main road, turned off it about three-quarters of a mile from the school gates, and bumped along a number of narrow lanes whose banks were crowned with clumps of mignonette and rockroses.

"It's a shortcut," said Elspeth by way of apology. "We could have gone all the way round by the main road, but it would have taken much longer."

"This is all right," said Fen as he swerved to avoid a vagrant domestic fowl. "Is Mr. Merrythought still with us?"

Elspeth turned to look. Mr. Merrythought, bouncing about on the rumble seat, looked truculent, suspicious, and far from easy in his mind regarding the purpose of their expedition. Occasionally he lunged at a gnat or a mite which whisked past his nose, lost his balance, and fell heavily against Fen's back. But at least he was managing to remain in the car.

"He's okay," Elspeth reported. "And we haven't far to go now."

They passed fields of green wheat, sheep grazing, an ancient, timbered farmhouse. The ground rose, bringing gentle contours, fertile and richly wooded, into view. The pastures were speckled with buttercups and daisies. There was a smell of hay in the evening air, and the sun, westering, seemed tangled in the high branches of a coppice of elms. By a large black barn overlooking Castrevenford town and the quicksilver coils of the river they turned left, into a more even road, and soon the trees grew thicker about them.

"Here we are," said Elspeth.

Fen stopped the car. Mr. Merrythought, jolted into a temporary submissiveness, stared impassively about him. It was very much darker beneath the trees—quieter, too—and no living creature was in sight.

"Not very populous," Fen observed. "You're right in saying this is a likely place for it to have happened. Well, what's our plan of campaign?"

"I suggest you drop me here and drive on till you get to the edge of the wood," said Elspeth. "The thing is, you see, that we've got to *find* the blood before we can start. If we separate now, we can work up the bank, looking for it, until we meet, or until one of us finds it."

"Both sides of the road?"

Elspeth shook her head. "Not at first, anyway. You can see there's not much wood on the left. It's the other side we must look."

"All right. Who's going to have Mr. Merrythought?"

"You can," Elspeth said as she climbed out of the car. "He seems to like you."

"Everyone says that," Fen remarked, nettled. "And I don't really think it a compliment, even if it's true, which I question."

"Yell out if you find anything," said Elspeth, ignoring this complaint. "Halloo my name to the reverberate hills."

Fen raised his eyebrows. "Bless us," he said. "A literary young woman."

Elspeth grinned. "I'm doing it for Higher Cert.," she explained. "See you soon."

So Fen drove on, as commanded, and in about half a mile emerged from the tunnel of trees. He parked the car, got out of it, and beckoned to Mr. Merrythought.

"Now," he said, "you're supposed to be a bloodhound. Find some blood."

The road was tarred and fairly narrow. On his left, as he faced back into the wood, was a high bank overgrown with bromegrass, through which, here and there, the yellow blink of a tormentil was visible.

Dilapidated signboards admonished incipient tres-
passers. The weak, diffused evening light played
patchily on the pale yellow oak leaves, and the scent
of the birches was in the air. Mr. Merrythought sniffed
about, displaying more goodwill than was habitual
with him, and Fen began his search.

In the graying light it was not an easy task, and the
proliferation of summer growths was not helpful.
Luckily there were considerable stretches of the bank
where, thanks to bramble and bracken, it was obvious
that no one had climbed, and he was able to concen-
trate on the more accessible points, some of them
worn by undaunted trespassing to mere mud streaked
with chalk. But even so he was pessimistic regarding
their chances of success; and when, at the end of
nearly an hour's careful work, he heard Elspeth's distant shout, he did not seriously believe that she had
found what they were looking for.

† 13 †
A SENNET: ENTER SECOND MURDERER

Yet it proved that she had. He ran to meet her, with Mr. Merrythought lurching quite rapidly along behind him, and discovered her earnestly studying a little dark splash, filmed with grit and dust, at the edge of the road. In this Mr. Merrythought at once displayed a perceptible interest; no doubt the triumphs of his nonage were recurring in some obscure fashion to his mind, for he uttered a growl of satisfaction and began nosing his way slowly up the bank.

"That's it!" said Elspeth, her eyes sparkling with excitement. "I bet you that's it!"

"It may be," Fen said cautiously.

"Oh, don't be so tiresome; of course it is."

"I don't want to be discouraging," said Fen. "But even if it's blood, it may be only a wounded rabbit, you know."

"Never mind. We must follow. Have you got any paper on you?"

"Paper?" Fen queried. "What on earth for?"

"If we're going far into the wood, we must leave a trail," said Elspeth practically. "Otherwise we shall take hours finding our way back, particularly in the dark. We might *never* get back, and our bones would be picked clean by ravens."

"Ravens?" said Fen, envisaging this charnel scene without pleasure. "Heaven forbid." He felt in the pockets of his raincoat and produced, rather to his own surprise, a small Bible.

"Fifteen hundred pages," he remarked. "That ought to take us some distance, if we use it sparingly."

Mr. Merrythought was finding some difficulty in negotiating the top of the bank; he was making noises that suggested that he suffered from rheumatism. Fen gave him a good push in the hindquarters, and they scrambled up after him. The edge of the wood was inhabited by dense clouds of gnats. Gorse was blooming in plump, compact yellow buds and—with nettles, brambles, and huge, pagodalike fronds of bracken— constituted the greater part of the undergrowth. There were small blackened areas, decimated by fire. Flowers of purple columbine drooped on their stems. The trunks of the trees were encircled with ivy. The bizarre, slightly menacing hush of the forest engulfed them.

Mr. Merrythought, his nose to the ground, set off in what Fen optimistically interpreted as a purposeful fashion.

Their progress during the next half-hour—with darkness growing fast and Fen tearing pages from the Bible and dropping them onto the ground—was sporadic. Partly this was due to the fact that a lot of the time was spent in pushing their way through thickets of resistant virgin vegetation—their clothes, as Elspeth sadly observed, would never be the same again—and partly it was due to the ambiguous demeanor of Mr. Merrythought. At the end of Leviticus, for example, after a fine initial burst of speed, he appeared quite abruptly to lose interest in the whole affair and turned aside to investigate rabbit holes. Well on in the book of Proverbs, again, he came to a sudden standstill and gazed prolongedly at some distant object (what it was, and why it should so enthrall him, neither of them could make out) with the elevated and spiritual air of Cortez surveying the Pacific from a peak in Darien, so that Fen, who misdoubted the quality of Mr. Merrythought's intelligence, began to wonder if in fact he was trailing anything in particular.

Unfortunately—though in view of what happened subsequently one had better, perhaps, say fortunately —they could not write off Mr. Merrythought's efforts as no more than the delusions of senility. Although Fen darkly suspected that he simply imagined he was being taken for a walk, on two occasions his torch, which in the increasing obscurity was much needed, did show them traces of what might be blood, and these were just convincing enough to keep them going, without, however, imbuing them with any serious hopes of the ultimate success of their enterprise. Moreover, a nagging anxiety was at the back of Fen's mind; if by some fantastic chance Mr. Merrythought were actually leading them to Brenda Boyce, they would find her dead, horribly dead perhaps; and to Elspeth the shock of such a discovery would be very great. Fen became silent, debating the best course to pursue in such circumstances. And the amiable chatter with which Elspeth had enlivened the earlier part of their walk faded and died. She was demoralized, to tell the truth, by the fact that her best skirt and stockings were being slowly but inexorably torn to bits, and only pride prevented her from suggesting that they should give up and go home.

"My God, it's creepy," she said with a shiver.

And certainly there is something disturbing about a large wood in the twilight. Apart from the distant cry of a nightjar, the silence was absolute, and now that the light was almost gone, the trees seemed to crowd in on them as they walked, like an ambush in readiness to strike. Elspeth was glad she was not alone, for if she had been, it would have been difficult to hold at bay the impression that someone or something was keeping pace with them. Once or twice she could have sworn that a pale shadow was moving among the trees, that the bushes were being moved by some person on a course parallel to their own. "And this poor boy was followed, and at last pursued and overtaken, and either torn in pieces and somehow made away with, by a horrible hopping creature in white, which you saw first dodging about among the trees, and gradually it appeared more and more plainly." It was a pity, Elspeth reflected, that she should remember such a sentence at such a time.

Something tenuous and filmy covered her face. She gave vent to a little shriek.

"Only a spider's web," said Fen cheerfully as he shone his torch on her.

"Sorry," she said, shamefaced. "I don't know what's the matter with me."

They pressed on, and soon the rain began to fall, lightly at first, then hissing and rustling in the leaves above their heads. Despite her protests, Fen made her put on his raincoat. He turned up his collar and whistled the Funeral March from the Eroica Symphony between his teeth. He noted that they had reached the third chapter of the Acts of the Apostles; at the Revelation of St. John the Divine they would be compelled to stop and retrace their steps.

In the middle of the First Epistle of St. Paul to the Corinthians, however, Mr. Merrythought took action on his own account. His progress during the past few minutes had been perceptibly slower, and now he sat down on his haunches with an air of finality; it was clear that he did not propose to go any farther. What was not clear was whether or no they would be obliged to carry him all the way back. They halted beside him.

"And that," said Fen, "would appear to be that."

"I must apologize," said Elspeth stiffly, trying to keep the tears of vexation and disappointment from her eyes, "for bringing you on a wild-goose chase."

"My dear girl," said Fen gently, "there's no need for apologies. I came of my own free will, knowing there was a possibility of our failing. You see——"

"Shush!" said Elspeth abruptly. They listened. Elspeth was alert, her superstitious fears gone. She realized with a fleeting surprise that even in her present coldly rational state the sense of some third person near them had not vanished, but for the moment such considerations were irrelevant. She strained her ears.

"What is it?" Fen whispered.

"I thought I heard someone calling."

Fen looked at her doubtfully. "Are you sure it wasn't an owl?"

"N—no, it wasn't. At least, I don't *think* so. Didn't you hear anything?"

"No. I didn't."

For fully a minute they stood motionless.

"No good," said Elspeth at last. "I must have been imagining things."

Fen sighed. "Home, then?"

"I suppose so."

"What we're going to do with Mr. Merrythought I can't imagine. He doesn't look capable of moving, to me, and as far as I can see——"

"Listen!"

And that time they both heard it—a thin, weak voice, not very far off, crying for help.

"My God," Fen muttered, "you were right. What direction did it come from?"

But Elspeth seized the torch from his hand without a word; it seemed that she, at least, had no doubts. She went off at a run.

"Come on!" she called.

Fen followed. Mr. Merrythought, tottering to his feet and fearing, probably, that he was about to be basely abandoned to starvation and the night, followed Fen,

baying horribly the while. Brambles caught at their
clothes, and they stumbled on tufts of grass and moss-
covered roots. Fen fell into a puddle placed there by
Providence for the purpose and arose from it spat-
tered and grimy, only to be sent reeling again by Mr.
Merrythought's headlong rush. An owl, alarmed at
their trampling, rose with a shriek and a whirr of
wings from the lower branch of an elm.

In less than a minute they had come out into a clearing bordered with larches, where the twilight still lingered. Small pools of daisies glimmered ghostly
white. They paused uncertainly.

But Mr. Merrythought did not pause. He marched
straight to a clump of bracken and sniffed at it inquiringly. They joined him, and he lay down and gazed up
at them with the fatuous complacency of a hen that
has laid a particularly large egg.

Among the bracken a girl of Elspeth's age was lying.
Her gold hair was tangled and matted, her large eyes
were red and puffy with weeping, there were purple
bruises on her slender throat, and one black-stock-
inged leg was unnaturally distorted.

But Brenda Boyce, by a high mercy, was alive.

Elspeth kneeled down beside her. "Brenda!" she
said breathlessly. "It's me—Elspeth."

Brenda's face was very white, and tears of relief and
exhaustion were running down her cheeks.

"Take me home," she whispered. "Please take me
home."

Elspeth swallowed; her mouth was dry. "Oh,
Brenda, are you badly hurt?"

Fen touched her on the shoulder, and she moved out
of his way. He had a flask of whiskey in his hand.

"Drink this," he said. "It will do you good."

"Please, I only want. . . ."

"Come *along* now," he said, amiably but firmly. "I want you nicely drunk, in as short a time as possible. . . . And keep the torch steady, Elspeth. No, bless your heart, don't shine it into the poor girl's eyes. . . ."

He raised Brenda's head, cradling it in the crook of his arm, and put the flask to her lips. She gulped the spirit down. It seemed to revive her a little, for she attempted to smile through her tears.

"Whiskey always did make me feel sick," she murmured. "I wish you had a gin and lime."

"You've got guts, young woman," Fen told her with real admiration. He turned to Elspeth, whose nervous reaction was issuing in floods of silent weeping.

"Stop that ridiculous boo-hooing," he said sternly, "and do something useful. You must get to a telephone straight away." Elspeth dabbed at her eyes and nodded. "Take Lily Christine if you think you can manage to drive her. Ring up the police station and tell the superintendent what's happened. If he isn't there, insist that they get in touch with him immediately. Say we need a doctor and an ambulance without a moment's delay. Then wait in the road and lead them back here."

"Shall I leave you the torch?"

"Good heavens, no. You'll need it to follow the paper trail. . . . Just a minute. Take off that coat, please." Elspeth obeyed, and Fen spread the coat over Brenda. "That's better," he said. "For the love of God, Elspeth, stop havering and run away."

"But is she——"

"She's perfectly all right." Fen laid the back of his hand against Brenda's forehead. "Not even feverish. There isn't the slightest danger, and she'll be completely recovered inside a week. At the same time we don't want to sit about on damp bracken any longer than we can help. So be quick."

Elspeth got hurriedly to her feet. "All right," she

said. "I'm going. Bye-bye for now, Brenda. Shan't be long."

She ran off into the wood, and Fen turned back to Brenda, slipping off his jacket and folding it to make a pillow for her head. She was a damnably attractive child, he thought, with a finer and more delicate beauty than Elspeth's, though more definitely leggy and coltish; but that would pass in a year or two, and in the meantime Fen inwardly applauded the enterprise and good taste of J. H. Williams. Of course, it was a miracle that she lived, and he could hardly be blamed for not knowing that the murderer had muffed his job. Strangulation was a risky business, certainly, those marks on her throat. . . .

The rain, heavy in that exposed place, was soaking through the thin silk of his shirt. He moved his shoulders uncomfortably.

"You'll catch cold," Brenda whispered.

"Not a chance," he said cheerfully. "You must be cold, though, after being here all last night."

"And h-hungry," she answered weakly. "My throat's not so bad now, and the cut on my leg's healing up, b-but my other leg hurts terribly. I think it's b-broken."

"May I look?"

"Yes. Yes, I s'pose so."

Fen felt the leg, very delicately, in the darkness.

"Not broken," he diagnosed presently. "You've dislocated your knee, and that's not quite so bad, though I know it's hellish painful." He smiled at her—a futile exercise, since they could barely see one another. "Would you like me to put it back?"

There was a long pause before she said:

"W-will it hurt?"

"It may," said Fen with candor, "and it may not. You can never be sure."

And after another pause: "All right," she said. "I

s'pose it's got to be done some time, so it may as well be now. Go ahead."

She closed her eyes tightly, bit her lip, and waited, drawing a little confidence from the feel of his firm, careful hands on the projecting bone. There was a moment of rebellion as he began to straighten the leg, but she stifled it. Every separate muscle and sinew shrieked in protest; she yearned to cry out but would not. Then, quite suddenly, there was an audible click, followed by a blissful sense of normalcy and well-being. She opened her eyes gratefully.

"It hardly hurt at all," she said wonderingly to the dim form kneeling beside her.

"Good," said Fen briskly. "It's very swollen, of course, and you'll have to stay in bed for a few days, but otherwise you'll be all right."

He took off his tie and bound it round the knee. "There. That's the best I can do for the moment. Damn this rain. But we'll soon be out of it."

"I feel *much* better," said Brenda. "Tell me who you are and how you managed to find me."

"My name's Gervase Fen."

"Oh, yes!" Brenda, whose voice had grown stronger, raised herself on one elbow. "Elspeth's always raving about you. She'll be excited, all right."

Fen searched about for a more comfortable position in the bracken. "Nature," he observed gloomily. "I can't say I've ever had very much use for it."

"And was it Elspeth who told you about the blood trail?"

"It was," said Fen, pushing aside a frond that appeared to be seeking entry into his mouth. "Only she didn't remember about it till late this afternoon." He grabbed at something on the back of his neck and cast it into outer darkness. Brenda sensed the movement.

"What's the matter?" she asked.

"Spiders."

"Yes, they've been crawling all over me. They make me yell normally, but I felt so rotten I hardly cared."

"More whiskey?"

"Yes, please."

Fen handed her the flask. "Sottish wench," he murmured. "Still, you deserve it." She drank moderately and returned the flask.

"Lovely," she said. "You know, I didn't think *anyone* would remember about the blood-trail business, but I had to do *something.* And what I was really afraid of was that people'd take that blush-making letter for gospel."

"I don't think anyone believed in it for a moment," Fen told her.

"Why not?" she asked, curious.

"The general opinion was that you had more sense than to go off with a man. And besides, Miss Parry maintained that the style was all wrong."

"Yes, baby stuff, wasn't it? Bad psychology."

"Peg's Own Paper," Fen agreed.

Brenda was silent for a time. "I thought no one was ever coming," she said. "I *couldn't* move, and I shouted and shouted, and it wasn't the slightest use. And I've fainted God knows how many times and been sick twice."

"All over now," Fen consoled her. "In an hour or so you'll be safe at home. . . . smelling like a distillery," he added, and she laughed.

The rays of the torch that Elspeth carried had long since vanished among the trees. Pitch darkness was all about them, and the small noises of a wood at night were dominated by the hiss of the rain, which was falling more heavily now.

"If you leaned on me," said Fen, "do you think you could hop a yard or two? We'd be more sheltered under the trees, and I don't want you to develop pneumonia in addition to all your other troubles."

"Rain won't hurt me," Brenda answered rather scornfully. "But we'll try if you like."

"Right." Fen stood up. "Wait just a moment while I do a little reconnaissance."

He took a few steps away from where she lay, groping in his pocket for matches. What happened then took him completely unawares.

He heard a stealthy rustle in the undergrowth close by.

Danger.

For an instant he stood paralyzed and incapable of thought, gazing helplessly into the darkness. He had no weapon, no light but what a match would give. He could not locate the direction of the sound. But he knew that a killer was close at hand, and that he himself was responsible for it. He cursed aloud.

The beam of a powerful torch shone out suddenly from among the trees, dazzling him. The rain slanted across it like needles. But it illuminated him only momentarily, moving quickly away until it rested on Brenda's supine form. At its source he glimpsed the sheen of black metal, and he saw Brenda look toward it and open her mouth as if to speak.

For a second the tableau held, transfixed as though graven in stone. Then suddenly it was broken. Mr. Merrythought, baying savagely, launched himself at the light. There was a violent detonation and a streak of flame. Brenda screamed. Then the light vanished, and there were footsteps racing away through the trees, with the dog in pursuit.

Fen stumbled back to where Brenda was.

"Are you all right?" he called. "Are you all right?"

"Yes," she said, and relief surged through him. "I— I'm all right. I'm frightened, though. What was it? What happened?"

"Someone took a shot at me," Fen lied. He felt for

her hand and grasped it firmly in his own. She was shivering.

"No," she said in a small voice whose clarity he mistrusted. "It was me. It was me they were shooting at. Will they come back?"

"I shouldn't think so."

"They will, you know. *Oh, God, why can't they leave me alone?*" Brenda broke into hiccuping sobs. "I can't stand any more. I can't *stand* it. . . ."

"Steady." Fen squeezed her hand in a deliberate attempt to hurt. "Try and hang on for a bit."

The sobs subsided. "Oh, Christ," she whimpered, "what a bloody little coward I am. . . . It was only . . . you see, I've been through all this once. It's so bloody *unfair.* . . ."

"Come on," said Fen. "We're going to make a move now."

He helped her to stand. She staggered, one arm round his neck. The raincoat dropped unregarded to the ground.

"All right?" he asked.

She gave a little gasping laugh. "I can manage."

On an impulse he kissed her gently on the forehead. "Bless you, my child," he said lightly. "Now, as quietly as possible, and no talking, please."

Melton Chart was silent again. From a snuffling, exhausted sound at his feet, Fen deduced that Mr. Merrythought had returned. As they staggered—alas, too audibly—toward the shelter of the trees, he reviewed the situation, and a coldness seeped into his veins. Someone had tried to shoot Brenda; that person would not, in the circumstances, stop at a single attempt. He himself could not leave Brenda. She was incapable of the swift, evasive movement that was their only chance of escape. They would be hunted through the wood like maimed and helpless animals. Their assailant would return, track them, spotlight them from a safe distance, and take aim at leisure. They were completely at his mercy.

And the damnable, the sickening, thing about it all was that he, Gervase Fen, had arranged it. He had set a trap and with blind, incredible folly walked into it himself, dragging Brenda with him. Weems had done his work well, he reflected; he had his proof now. But it seemed unlikely that he would live to demonstrate it. Perhaps Stagge would get there in the end, he thought, with the discursive light-headedness which, as he had noticed on two previous occasions, extreme peril does sometimes evoke. If Stagge sat down and meditated for a week . . . if seven maids with seven mops. . . . The point was to work out how long Elspeth had been gone. They might be able to hold out until help came. Half an hour? No. More like ten minutes. . . .

The rain soaked into them. It seemed an aeon before they reached the edge of the trees, with Mr. Merrythought panting noisily at their heels. Let it be done quickly, Fen thought. Better that than a dragging, futile, undignified attempt to escape.

It seemed that his wish was to be granted. They stopped short as the light flared out again, at a distance—Fen calculated—which meant that if he attempted to rush it, he would be dead before he was halfway there. And it was held in a very steady hand —the shadows that it threw were motionless, with the sharp, unreal contours of shadows in a stage set. Of the figure behind it nothing could be seen except the slim, well-cared-for hand that held the revolver.

Fen checked the instinct to flight, swiftly turning his back on the light to shield Brenda with his body. Futile enough, he knew; one bullet for him, one for her, and so an end. She looked up at him, and her shadowed face was strangely calm and untroubled, almost childlike in its innocence.

"Never mind," he said.

But he had reckoned without Mr. Merrythought. He had reckoned without Mr. Merrythought's recurrent homicidal fits. The labor and excitement of the evening had clearly had a baneful effect on Mr. Merrythought's constitution, for now, enraged beyond belief, he was foaming at the mouth, growling, yelping, and capering monstrously, with his eyes bloodshot and the hair standing up along his spine like a porcupine's quills.

And for the second time he rushed at the light.

It shifted almost imperceptibly to keep him in view, and the shot rang out when he was halfway toward it. Turning, Fen saw him stagger at the impact of the bullet. With any other dog, and in particular with any other dog of Mr. Merrythought's venerable years, it would have been enough. But it seemed that Mr. Merrythought's apoplexy abolished his normal physical limitations. He went on, scarcely less swiftly than before. The assailant fired again, wildly, and missed. The next instant, with a bloodcurdling snarl, Mr. Merrythought was upon him.

The torch fell to the ground and rolled, creating a moving chiaroscuro among the tree trunks. Deafened by the uproar, Fen saw an indistinct shape racing out of the gloom. He went to meet it, and they came together with a jarring impact. Fen hit out at random, and pain flooded up his arm as his knuckles came in violent contact with the hard metal of the revolver. It struck his knee as it fell, and in that instant his antagonist eluded him and pounded away.

Fen did not attempt pursuit. He groped for the gun, picked it up, retrieved the torch, and returned to Brenda, who had sunk to the ground. She was numb, speechless.

"That's settled him," Fen said quietly. "He won't have another gun or another torch with him, so he'll go away and leave us in peace. It's all over, my dear."

A single tear trickled down her face. For a minute or two they heard Mr. Merrythought's far-off baying. Then it ceased, and quietness came home again to Melton Chart.

But beneath a distant tree Mr. Merrythought blinked, because his eyes were darkening, and thrust his hot muzzle into a clump of wet grass. The varied, delightful scents of beast and bird were fading in his nostrils as the life-blood ebbed out of him. He had fought like a gladiator, but now he could do no more. He did not whimper; he growled softly to himself. And in this fashion, irate, suspicious, and undaunted to the last, he waited for death.

Half an hour later there were many lights in the wood. Stagge and Elspeth were accompanied by the bearded doctor and by two stretcher-bearers. Fen thought that he had never seen so blessed and enchanting a sight.

† 14 †
EXIT, PURSUED BY A BEAR

The doctor emerged from Brenda's bedroom with an air of professional complacency. He rubbed his hands at Fen and Stagge, who were waiting in the narrow, green-carpeted passage outside.

"You can talk to her now," he said. "What she's been through would have killed most people, but she doesn't seem to be much the worse for it, to judge from the amount she's eating. I'm going home, anyway."

"The knee's all right?" Fen asked. His hair was tousled, he lacked both jacket and tie, and he looked like one of the unemployable.

"Perfectly. Throat'll be sore for a time, of course, and if she wasn't so damn hungry, she wouldn't enjoy swallowing very much. Subconjunctival ecchymoses. But they'll clear up in a week or two. It was an amateurish attempt."

"Fortunately," Fen murmured. The doctor swung his bag at them in farewell and departed. They entered the bedroom.

It was small and decorated in pastel shades. A fire burned in the diminutive grate, and the pale blue curtains were drawn across the windows, shutting out sight though not sound of the downpour in the darkness outside. A pajama case shaped like a panda peered at them myopically from the mantelpiece. The dressing table, which Fen, startled, recognized as genuine Louis Seize, bore more fards and unguents than were desirable for a girl of Brenda's age. *The Poetical Works of Shelley, Horses and Horsemanship,* and a tattered copy of a work by Mr. Peter Cheyney, brightly

jacketed, were held together by a decrepit wooden
duck—distinctly a sentimental remnant of nursery
days—and a thing that looked like a model of Cleopa-
tra's needle. The air was faintly scented with chypre
—on perceiving which Stagge, whom a puritan upbringing had led to associate olfactory delights of a
nonculinary order with ungodliness, frowned slightly.
A white-clad nurse fussed about, tidying. Elspeth was
there; Brenda's parents were there. And Brenda herself was propped up against pillows in a flimsy black
nightdress and a yellow satin bed jacket, consuming
chops and peas, from a plate on a bed table, with the
greatest possible gusto.

Fen was relieved to note that the embarrassing emo-
tional excitements of their homecoming had somewhat subsided. Brenda had wept; Brenda's mother
had wept; Elspeth had wept; the servants had wept;
and Brenda's father had shaken hands repeatedly
with everyone. Fen had been offered dressing gowns,
fires, airing cupboards, and brandy; all except the last
he had refused with a stern and spartan air. But now
the crisis had passed, and a calm cheerfulness pre-
vailed.

"M'm," Brenda said through a mouthful as she saw
Fen. "Do come and sit down, Professor Fen. Are you
hungry?"

"Not a bit." Fen spoke with truth, although he had
had no dinner. And as he looked at Brenda, he mar-
veled at the resilience of youth. He himself was still
shaken. There is something peculiarly unnerving
about resigning yourself to death and then finding
yourself alive and well; and a subsidiary but important effect is to make you feel vaguely ridiculous, as
though you had sat down on a chair that was not there.
Brenda, however, seemed completely unperturbed.
The color had returned to her cheeks, and she was
even disposed to be mildly flirtatious.

Mr. Boyce, a small, glossy, prosperous-looking, middle-aged man, shook Fen's hand for about the ninth time.

"I'm eternally in your debt, sir," he said. "Brenda has told us everything that happened."

"You must thank Mr. Merrythought," said Fen, "and so must I. But for him, neither of us would be here. Well, Brenda, you seem to be completely recovered."

"Swallowing's bloody," said Brenda incautiously; at which her parents made simultaneous noises of protest and dismay, and she blushed fierily. "But otherwise," she went on hastily, "I flourish like the green bay tree." Fen saw what Miss Parry had meant about Brenda's prose style. "Thanks awfully for everything, Professor Fen. Mummy, have you got his tie?"

"Yes, dear. Here it is, Professor Fen. It has been pressed. But I'm afraid your jacket's still very damp. I'll have it cleaned and send it on to you."

"Please don't trouble," said Fen as he crossed to a mirror and adjusted the tie round his neck. "I can take it away with me as it is."

They engaged in polite altercation on this topic, during which Stagge—as was not surprising—became a trifle restive. He cleared his throat and addressed Mr. Boyce.

"If you've no objection, sir, there are one or two questions I should like to ask your daughter."

"Of course." Mr. Boyce was hurriedly apologetic. "Yes, of course. My dear, we must leave these gentlemen for the moment." He hesitated. "As regards the immediate future——"

"I shall be leaving a reliable man on guard here for tonight, sir," said Stagge, "though I believe that now your daughter's had a chance to tell us what she knows, there'll be no further danger."

"I'm very glad to hear it." Mr. Boyce mopped his

brow, which was damp with emotion. "But until this fellow's caught——"

"Until then, sir—and"—Stagge eyed Fen eloquently —"we hope it won't be long—I'll make myself responsible for her safety."

"Good." Mr. Boyce turned to his wife. "Come along, my dear. And you'd better be getting home, Elspeth, or your people will be wondering what's become of you. We'll be back later, Brenda. And I hope you gentlemen will join me in a drink before you leave."

Fen smiled at Elspeth and extended his hand; at which—to everyone's surprise and Brenda's secret annoyance—she flung her arms round his neck, kissed him passionately, burst into tears, and fled from the room. Mr. and Mrs. Boyce, after a mute interchange of grimaces over this phenomenon, followed her.

Fen, Stagge, and the nurse were left alone with Brenda. The nurse merged discreetly into the background, where she rattled medicine bottles to give an impression of activity. The two men settled down in chairs beside the bed. Fen lit a cigarette. And:

"Now," said Stagge.

Brenda, having finished the chops and peas, had set to work on a large peach melba. At Stagge's monosyllabic injunction she grinned suddenly.

"I think," she said, looking mischievously at Fen, "that the maestro ought to give a demonstration of his powers."

"In what way, miss?" Stagge asked.

"Tell us in advance everything I'm going to say."

Fen smiled back at her. "Far be it from me to steal the limelight," he remarked mendaciously, "but of course, if you insist."

He produced a pencil and pocket diary—which proceeding Stagge contemplated with evident disfavor— tore a sheet from the latter, and scribbled busily for a few minutes. Then he handed Brenda his notes. Her eyes widened as she read.

"I was only joking," she said, "but you *do* know. And yet I don't see how anyone but me can know, and *I* haven't told you." Then her face fell. "Oh, but I suppose he's confessed."

"Not a bit. That," said Fen rather grandly, "is pure deduction."

Brenda saluted solemnly. "Sorry, maestro. . . . Oh, but there's one thing you've got wrong."

"Is there?" Fen was not greatly dismayed. "Sorry to let you down."

Stagge scraped his feet along the floor. *"If* you please, miss," he begged.

Brenda finished the peach melba with unheard-of rapidity, was approached by the nurse with some nauseous potion, swallowed it unblinking, demanded a cigarette, was given one by Fen in spite of the nurse's halfhearted protests, and leaned back against the pillows, smoking with the uneasy elaboration of a novice.

"It all began," she said, "the evening before last, when we were rehearsing *Henry V.* I was playing Katharine, you see, and I suppose now they've given Sheila Wotherspoon the part, and she's got a stupendous bust and can't act for nuts. . . . Well, anyway, I arranged to meet Jeremy Williams in the Science Building afterwards. It was all quite innocent, you know," Brenda said, wriggling slightly beneath the sheets and eyeing the nurse in an attempt to assess her potentialities as an informer. "We were both interested in—in—well, in flowers, you see. And anyway, Freud says——"

Stagge coughed discreetly.

"All right, then, I'll spare you Freud," Brenda agreed. "Well, I left the rehearsal before Jeremy did and went straight to the Science Building and upstairs

to the biology lab, where we usually—I mean, where
we'd said we'd meet. And I waited there—in the darkness, of course, because I didn't dare switch on a light
—for such a long time that I began to get nervous.
Jeremy didn't show up, and I couldn't imagine what
was keeping him, and I don't really like labs, and it
was creepy."

Fen could visualize the scene easily enough—the
gleam of jars and bottles and pipettes in the weak
starlight, an articulated skeleton perhaps, its
scrubbed bones luminous, the macabre wall charts of
the lymphatic system, and the musty, pungent smell
of frogs spread-eagled in pickle. A rather sordid setting, he reflected, for the naive ecstasies of calf love.

"Then about a quarter past ten," Brenda was saying,
"I decided I'd better give up and go home, because I
knew Jeremy had to be back at his house at ten. I
thought he'd stood me up, and I can tell you I was
pretty wild about it."

"One doesn't like," Fen murmured, "to miss a cosy
chat about flowers."

Brenda looked blank for a moment. Then she gur-
gled pleasurably. "Touché," she said. "One up to you,
maestro. . . . Where was I? Oh, yes. Well, I was just
going to get the hell out of it when I heard footsteps
coming up the stairs. And, my God, was I scared. I
knew it couldn't be Jeremy at that time, you see, and
it struck me that I was either going to be found by that
prig Wells, who'd be sure to report it to the headmaster, who'd be sure to report it to Miss Parry—or else, if
I managed to hide somewhere, be locked in for the
night. The second prospect wasn't so bad, of course,
because I could easily open a downstairs window and
climb out. It was the thought of being found that
shook me, because I couldn't think of *any* plausible
tale to account for being there, and some people"—she
assumed an expression of mock gravity—"simply

won't believe you when you say you're interested in flowers.

"Well, the point is this, you see, that the chemistry lab and the biology lab are side by side and *connected;* in fact, you can only get to the biology lab through the chemistry lab. So I hid myself behind the connecting door and looked through the crack into the chemistry lab. And a man came in, carrying a torch.

"That struck me as queer to start with, because if he'd had any business there, he'd surely have switched on the lights. He was walking pretty quietly, too, and at the time I couldn't make out who he was. I just waited and watched and prayed he wouldn't come into the biology lab. And actually, he didn't. He stood still and listened for a moment and then went up to one of the cupboards in the chemistry lab and shone his torch on it. The cupboards have glass fronts, you know, so that you can see what's inside. Obviously he didn't find what he wanted in the first cupboard, so he went on to another—did quite a round of them, in fact, before he got the right one. Then he hauled out a heavy screwdriver and jammed it between the doors and forced the cupboard open. And when the torch shone on his hands, I could see he was wearing gloves."

Involuntarily Brenda put a hand to her throat to touch the bruises there.

"He took a small glass bottle out of his pocket," she went on after a moment, "and got a jar out of the cupboard and poured something from it into the bottle —not a great deal, I should say. He poured it very carefully, and there was a kind of steam rising from it, and even then I had a suspicion of what it was, and that scared me even more. Well, he corked the bottle tightly and put it in his pocket and put the jar back and closed the cupboard. You can imagine I was pretty much on edge, but I had the sense to watch where he put the jar so that I could make sure what it was he'd taken.

"And then it happened." Brenda made a despairing gesture. "The corny old farce situation one's seen hundreds of times. In brief—I sneezed. I felt it coming, and I couldn't do a thing about it. Stifled it a bit, of course, but it was still a God-awful noise."

"You should have pinched the bridge of your nose," Fen told her.

"Should I? I never knew that. Anyway, I didn't. And you can imagine how I felt. I'd have given my soul for it to have been Miss Parry, instead of a criminal with a bottle of that stuff in his pocket.

"Still, there was nothing I could do about it. He'd heard. And for a moment I thought he was almost as frightened as I was. He didn't move at once—just stood there as if he was uncertain what to do. Then he said, 'Who's that?' in rather a shaky voice. That cheered me up a bit, so I kept still and said nothing. But—but in the end he found me.

"I think he was relieved to see who it was. Anyway, he said, 'What the devil are you doing here?' very sharply but still in a whisper. And I whispered back —God knows why *I* should have whispered—'Anyway, I'm not committing a burglary.' That was pretty damn foolish of me, and the way he looked at me then made me go cold all over. He said: 'You've seen more than's good for you, young woman. Do you know what it was I took?' I nodded. He said: 'If you say a word about this to anyone, you'll get that full in your pretty face, and it won't be pleasant. And if by any chance you should think of trying to put yourself under police protection, just remember that I'm not working alone. If I go to prison, I have friends who'll wait any number of years to get even with you. As it is, you're lucky I don't kill you here and now. Now get out of here, and keep your mouth shut.' "

All this Brenda narrated in a manner that was a strange mixture of remembered fear and histrionic effect. She was enjoying herself—being, as Mathieson had said, a very good actress and well able to get her effects across—but she was still half frightened, and by a curious irony this fact blurred rather than emphasized the verisimilitude of what she was saying.

"He grabbed me by the arm and led me out of the building," she went on, "but on the way I managed to get a look at that cupboard and make sure what he'd stolen." Brenda glanced at Fen. "And this is where you went wrong. It was sulfuric acid."

"Vitriol," Fen explained, "is only another name for sulfuric acid."

"Oh," said Brenda. "Humblest apologies, maestro. . . . Anyway, when we got outside he sloped off into the darkness—and there I was."

Stagge was unable to restrain himself any longer. "But who *was* it?" he demanded. "Surely you *must* have seen who it was?"

"Oh, yes," said Brenda. "It was Somers. Michael Somers."

Stagge put a hand dazedly to his eyes and rubbed at them as if to assure himself that he was not dreaming. Evidently this was not what he had expected.

"Somers?" he echoed. "You're certain, miss?"

"Of course." Brenda's tone was slightly contemptuous. "I'd never spoken to him, but I knew him perfectly well by sight. We used to pass one another on our bikes when *he* was going into town and *I* was on my way home from school."

The superintendent made a gesture of resignation. "Very well, miss. Go on, please."

"Well, of course I was horribly upset," Brenda

resumed. "I'd seen *The Phantom of the Opera* and all
that sort of thing, and nobody wants half a pint of
sulfuric acid chucked at their face. I went off home,
hoping to God Mummy and Daddy wouldn't notice
how upset I was. But they did, and they tried to question me—poor pets, they knew I was holding out on
them, but what the hell could I *do?*—and next morning—yesterday morning, that is—they rang up Miss
Parry, and *she* questioned me and seemed to imagine
I'd been raped or something, and I was afraid she'd
tell Mummy and Daddy that was what had happened
and they'd believe her, and one way and another, what
with being scared as well, yesterday was about the
most *bloody miserable* day I've ever spent."

Brenda paused for breath, wiped a suspicion of
tears quickly from her eyes, and stubbed out her cigarette on a plate.

"Of course, I knew I ought to have gone at once to
the police and damned the consequences, and in the
end I *would* have, only he'd said he had friends who'd
settle with me if anything happened to *him,* and
though I knew he was probably lying, it *might* have
been true, and I couldn't have a police guard for the
rest of my life, and so . . . ." Brenda left the sentence
unfinished. "I don't really believe in long-delayed re-
venges—*Valley of Fear* and so forth—but I s'pose they
must happen *sometimes.*"

"It's very understandable, Miss Boyce," said Stagge
sympathetically. "You *would* have done better to
come to us, but if I'd been in your shoes, I'm not at all
sure that *I'd* have had the nerve to do it."

She seemed consoled by this admission. "Well," she
said, "I was worrying about it while I walked home
from school yesterday afternoon—and about other
things, too. People knew there was something I was
hiding, and if *he* got to hear about that, he'd imagine
I was going to break down sooner or later and let the

cat out of the bag, as I probably would have, and he'd take action about it. I wished I had my bike, because the road's lonely once you get out of Castrevenford, but my three-speed had given up the ghost. I'd phoned Mummy during break and asked her to fetch me in the car, but she couldn't because she had people in to tea. So I had to walk.

"I knew Melton Chart was going to be the worst bit. There wasn't a soul about, and I hadn't got halfway before he suddenly came out of the trees—Somers, I mean—and slid down the bank. And he had a revolver. I thought: 'Well, this is it.' But I wasn't going to give up without a struggle. I'd got my penknife in my blazer pocket, and there was just a faint chance someone would remember about the game."

"Game?" Stagge queried. They explained. "Oh, ah," he said. "Yes, I get you. Go ahead, miss."

"He said: 'Don't make a sound or a false move. We're going for a little walk together.'" (Somers's phraseology, Fen reflected, had been deplorably melodramatic; but possibly Brenda was paraphrasing.) "But I had to take the risk, of course. I cut my leg open to work the blood-trail business—I was desperate, and I can tell you it was a pretty savage cut—and luckily he thought I was pulling up a stocking and didn't notice; it only took a second, anyway. Well, then I put on a terrified victim act to delay setting off for a minute, because I wanted there to be some blood *in the road* to give a starting point. I didn't dare *look,* of course, but by the time he hustled me up the bank and into the wood I thought I must have succeeded.

"Well, he marched me a long way into the wood, with the gun pointing at my back, and I can tell you" —Brenda had grown rather pale at the recollection— "that I never want to have to go through anything like that again. I thought every second was going to be my last. . . . We got to the clearing where you found me,

and he brought out a paper and a pencil and an envelope and dictated a kind of ridiculous farewell letter
to Miss Parry. I s'pose he wouldn't let me write it in my
own words for fear I'd put in some sort of a concealed
message.

"Then he made me describe exactly where my study
was. If I'd had any sense, I would have described
someone else's study, and the letter being found there
would have made you all suspicious, but at the time I
was so frightened that I never thought of it. A moment
later—I was standing with my back to him—I heard a
thud as he dropped the gun on the ground, and before
I knew what was happening, he'd grabbed me by the
throat. I struggled, and we both fell, and there was an
awful pain in my leg, and I don't remember anything
else till I woke up in the darkness. I couldn't move, so
I lay there till you and Elspeth found me."

The long recital, combined with the injuries to her
throat, had made Brenda very hoarse. She coughed,
painfully and prolongedly. The nurse hurried forward with a soothing draft.

And Fen was wondering, not very relevantly, why
Somers had preferred to strangle Brenda rather than
shoot her; perhaps he had derived a sensual pleasure
from the thought of his fingers about her white neck.
. . . But it was difficult to think objectively about such
a mean and cowardly crime.

"He bungled it," Fen remarked. "Thought you were
dead when you were only unconscious. You've been
very, very lucky, Brenda."

"You're telling me," said that young woman
throatily but emphatically.

Stagge was regarding Fen with considerable curiosity. "And you knew all this in advance, sir?"

For answer, Brenda handed him Fen's notes, and he
read them aloud.

" 'You saw Somers break open the cupboard in the

Science Building, and steal vitriol. He threatened to kill you if you spoke of it. He met you in Melton Chart on your way home from school, dictated a fake letter, made you tell him the whereabouts of your study, and attempted to throttle you.' M'm." Stagge nodded condescendingly; his humility did not run to admitting complete bafflement in front of a third party. "Accurate in every detail."

"And what now?" Brenda asked. "I s'pose you'll arrest him?"

"Oh, dear me, no," said Fen. "Somers is well beyond the reach of mundane laws. You see, Brenda, there was a lot happening while you were lying in Melton Chart. Not to put too fine a point on it, three people have been murdered—and one of them is Somers."

She stared incredulously.

"But this evening!" she exclaimed. "Who—why——?"

Fen stood up. "That remains to be seen. But you'll be well guarded, so you needn't worry. We must go now, and you must get some rest."

He leaned across the bed and kissed her gently on the tip of her attractive nose.

"Oh!" said Brenda mischievously. "Taking advantage, are you? But I should have thought you could have done better than that."

"I'm a married man," he told her severely, "so it's no use your flaunting your charms at me. Besides, think how nice it will be to go back to Jeremy and the smell of dissected crayfish."

"Devil!" she said, smiling. "Do come back tomorrow and explain things." She was tired; her eyelids were drooping.

"I will," Fen promised. "Pleasant dreams."

They left her in charge of the nurse, with a constable on guard in the passage outside.

"I hope she'll be all right," Stagge said anxiously as

they went downstairs. "I've a good deal of admiration for that young lady."

"She will," Fen answered with confidence. "I don't think anything can possibly happen to her now."

It was already close on midnight, and presently, after drinking whiskey with Mr. Boyce, they took their departure. The two cars—Lily Christine and Stagge's little Morris—were parked outside the gate, and they halted there for a moment before setting off. The rain had almost ceased, a cool wind had sprung up, and the clouds were parting like the curtains of a proscenium arch to display the stars.

"I see half of it, sir," said Stagge slowly, "and I could kick myself for not having seen it before. But, damn it"—he struck the palm of his left hand with his right fist—"I can't understand the *other* half. I'm still foxed about two of the murders."

"It's all over, Superintendent." Fen spoke rather wearily. He was carrying his jacket over his arm, and the wind blew chill through his damp shirt. "We've got hanging evidence now."

"Well, sir, our next move is up to you."

"We must have the whole thing out. And I think"— Fen was pensive—"that the headmaster had better be there."

They entered the cars and drove back through Melton Chart to the headmaster's house. But the headmaster, they were informed, was still over at the school. Fen took the opportunity to towel himself briskly, change his clothes, and swallow three aspirin —a drug he held in uncritical reverence—as a precautionary measure. Then they drove to the study in Davenant's. The site was bare and deserted in the beams of their headlamps.

The headmaster was alone. He was sprawled in an

armchair, drinking whiskey and staring at the cold grate. His long nose looked greasy in the lamplight, his sparse black hair was dishevelled, and his eyes were blank with fatigue. But he roused himself at their entry to pour them drinks. He had been sitting there, he explained, for the last half-hour, having got rid of a diehard remnant of parents who insisted on harassing him after the play was over.

"And how did the play go?" Fen asked.

"Oh, well enough," the headmaster said vaguely. "Yes, well enough, I think. But where have you been, my dear fellow? I haven't set eyes on you since the garden party."

Very briefly, Fen narrated the events of the evening and the evidence of Brenda Boyce.

"Good God," the headmaster mumbled. "Somers . . . good God. I didn't like the man, but I should never have dreamed . . . ." He relapsed into silence, twisting his fingers together. Stagge glanced at Fen.

"I *ought* to know, sir," he said. "I *ought* to be able to work it out on my own. You couldn't give me a few hints?"

Fen raised his glass and drank before replying.

"The nature of Somers's alibi," he said, "the wrist-watch, Love's statement about a fraud, the common-sense view about the manuscripts, the alibi reports, and the attempt to kill Brenda this evening."

Stagge considered these arcane indications in silence.

"No good, sir," he said at last. "You'll just have to tell me." There was a hint of bitterness in his voice.

Fen put his glass on the mantelpiece. "In the first place, you realize that it was Somers who killed Love."

The headmaster twisted round in his chair. "But I understood that he couldn't——"

"Just one moment, sir, please." Stagge raised a hand in warning. "Yes, I'd got as far as that. But——"

"But you want to know who killed Somers—and Mrs. Bly. Very simple." Fen smiled faintly. "Who *could* it have been except——"

He checked himself, listening, then strode to the door, flung it open, and peered outside. No one was there, but:

"Wait," he said, and disappeared. Only a few seconds had ticked away when they heard his voice from beyond the windows.

"Quickly!" he shouted. *"Quickly, for God's sake! He's getting away!"*

† 15 †
ROUT

The conclusion of the case was a strange blend of farce and tragedy.

On emerging from Davenant's, Fen had heard footsteps hurrying away across the turf in the direction of the school gates. Pausing only to yell at Stagge and the headmaster, he set off in pursuit. It was unlikely, he thought, that the murderer would have any satisfactory means of leaving the country, but to lose him now might just possibly be to lose him forever.

Fen had hardly begun to follow, however, before he heard the slam of a car door and the whirr of a self-starter somewhere in the drive. He broke into a run. A hundred yards ahead of him powerful headlights blazed out of the darkness, and a long, low shape moved swiftly away toward the main road.

"Hell and damnation," said Fen. He turned back to meet Stagge and the headmaster, who had rushed from the study at his summons. "There he goes," he said tersely.

Each of the three men flew instantaneously to his own car. Fen was the first away. He turned by the simple process of ignoring lawns and flower beds, and leaving a train of devastation and ruin in his wake, rattled vociferously down the drive. Although doubting in his heart if so petulant and eccentric a vehicle as Lily Christine could keep pace with what looked remarkably like a Hispano-Suiza, he was determined to be in at the finish if it were mechanically possible. Stagge followed, and after him came the headmaster. Their little fleet passed through the gates.

Fen was just in time to see the Hispano's taillight
disappearing from the main road into a turning that
he recognized as leading toward Ravensward. And it
soon became apparent that this evasive action had
been a distinct mistake on the part of their quarry, for
the side road was so narrow and tortuous as to vitiate
the difference in capacity between his car and their
own. Moreover, although the headmaster continued to
follow Fen with the unquenchable faith of a martyr,
Stagge had kept on along the main road. He knew of
a detour and hoped to cut the Hispano off. But unluckily he had underestimated the detour's length, with
the result that he rejoined the procession in precisely
the position from which he had left it—namely, between Fen and the headmaster.

They sped on grimly through the night, sending
watchdogs into paroxysms of frantic barking, startling placid cattle, bedeviling the dreams of sleeping
rustics. Suburbia gave place to arcadia. Trees, hedges,
barns, cottages, and telegraph poles fled past them
like leaves before an autumn gale; benighted wayfar-
ers took to the ditches; hens were crushed unhoused
beneath their wheels. And soon they came to Ravensward itself—over the humpbacked bridge, past the
Beacon, past the diminutive green, and so along the
lane where Mrs. Bly's cottage was situated. Stagge
knew that their quarry, seeing the disadvantage
under which he labored, was making again for the
main road.

But it was here that Lily Christine began to display
symptoms of disaffection—disaffection that quickly
merged into open mutiny. Strange popping sounds
reverberated beneath her bonnet, developing with
horrid swiftness into a noise like gang warfare with
submachine guns. A belated courting couple,
clutched in a passionate embrace beneath the hedge,
leaped apart as though a flaming sword had been

thrust between them. The accelerator ceased to function; the engine died; the car lost way. With a spec-
tral groan, Fen pulled in at the side of the lane and
watched Stagge and the headmaster sweep past him
unregarding.

"Help!" he yelled after them in rather a futile fashion. "Help!"

The courting couple, approaching, resolved itself
into the familiar figures of Daphne Savage and Mr.
Plumstead.

"Good Lord," said Daphne, "it's Professor Fen. But
what on earth——?"

She stared inquiringly. Fen climbed out of the car.

"It's useless," he announced somberly. He was easily daunted by setbacks.

"Broken down?" Mr. Plumstead asked, not very in-
telligently. "I'll fix it for you." He suffered from the
common delusion that he understood cars. "Gaskets
gone, I expect."

Fen eyed him without optimism.

"It always seems an extraordinary thing to me," he
said, "that scientists should traipse about, boasting of
all the benefits they've conferred on mankind, when
they've never succeeded in inventing a single thing
which can be relied on in an emergency to work."

Mr. Plumstead did not reply to this observation. He
already had the bonnet open and was engaged, to all
appearances, in dismantling the entire engine. Bits of
metal clattered onto the ground at his feet. He
breathed stertorously.

"Isn't he clever?" said Daphne admiringly; and
when Fen showed no disposition to confirm this judgment: "But what exactly is *happening,* Professor
Fen?"

Fen briefly explained, while Mr. Plumstead went on
with his labor of decimation.

"Heavens," said Daphne, impressed. "But who——?"

She interrupted herself. For a minute past, the
sounds of the chase had been beyond earshot, but now
they heard a car approaching from the direction in
which it had gone, and when it came into view, Fen
recognized it by the numbers of supernumerary lights
as being the Hispano-Suiza. It was obvious what had
occurred. In an attempt to shake off his pursuers, their
quarry had turned in at a gate or drive, switched off
his lights and his engine, waited for them to go past,
and then come back on his tracks. The maneuver had
gained him a little distance, but that was all, for Fen
could already see the lights of the other two cars returning in his wake.

"Quick!" he screamed.

Startled, Mr. Plumstead knocked his head against
the radiator pipe and emerged clutching it
bemusedly.

"Push the car across the road!" Fen commanded.

A wild flurry of disorganized activity ensued.
Mr. Plumstead thrust Daphne masterfully out of
the danger zone; Fen leaped for the brake handle;
and together, by gigantic efforts, they got Lily Christine on the move. But the Hispano was already very
close; it was on top of them; and a second later, its
wheels skidding on the wet-grass verge, it had
scraped past.

"Hell!" said Fen.

Lily Christine, moving under her own impetus,
swung across and buried her nose affectionately in the
opposite bank, blocking the lane entirely. And they
had barely time to appreciate the necessary results of
this situation before Stagge's car and the headmaster's pulled up an inch short of them with a tortured
stridulation of brakes and tires.

Stagge's face, a dim white blob, appeared at the
driving-window. *"Get that blasted car out of the
way!"* he yelled.

They hastened to obey. Without another word, the two pursuers set off again.

"Stop!" Fen cried pitifully. "Wait for me!"

They did nothing of the kind. Stagge, having his duty to do, could not afford to delay even an instant, and the headmaster, imbued with an unseemly, dionysiac lust for the chase, had eyes and ears for nothing else. The roar of their engines died away. Fen slumped down on the grassy bank. Mr. Plumstead returned to his destructive toil. And Daphne stood in gloomy silence, watching them.

Presently they again heard a car approaching, this time from the direction of Ravensward village. Fen scrambled to his feet, stared toward it, and was instantly possessed by something like hysteria.

"He's done it again!" he ejaculated. *"Quick!"*

Undeniably he had, for the car they saw was certainly the Hispano. But this time Stagge had been prepared for the trick, and the distance between hare and hounds was perceptibly less. Fen and Mr. Plumstead strained frantically at Lily Christine's scarlet chassis.

And then, incredibly, it all happened as before. True, the Hispano had even less room to spare, and given another second, they would have stopped her once and for all time and probably have been horribly killed into the bargain. But she squeezed through, miraculously, and once again, being unable to check Lily Christine's progress rapidly enough, they succeeded in bringing Stagge and the headmaster to a standstill. Only this time Stagge's car actually hit Lily Christine, broadside on, propelling her, crab-wise, two or three inches along the lane.

They could not see Stagge's complexion, but they visualized it—correctly—as being purple with fury.

"Are you *mad?*" he demanded in a cracked and frantic voice. "Are you all MAD?"

They bent anew to their humiliating task. On this

occasion, however, Fen abandoned Lily Christine without even troubling to put on the brake and leaped in beside the headmaster just as his car was moving off. Daphne scrambled somehow into the back, and Mr. Plumstead, though his reactions were slower, managed to jump onto the running board, where he held on as though legions of devils were attempting to dislodge him. Fen had a glimpse of Lily Christine's vitals spread forlornly over the surface of the road, and the next moment they were away.

"Exciting, isn't it?" said the headmaster blandly.

His engine was a powerful one, and he had no difficulty in keeping up with Stagge, though the speedometer needle was hovering round sixty. Ahead of Stagge, the Hispano was slowly gaining. Soon they came to a long stretch of road, straighter and broader than hitherto. At the far end, still diminutive to them, was a bridge even smaller and more perilous than that in Ravensward village. A steep slope fell away to the right of it, protected from the road only by a fragile fence of wooden posts and wire. All three cars rushed toward it.

"Nearly at the main road," the headmaster muttered. He was crouched over the wheel like a racing driver. "We'll lose him there, I'm afraid. Look, he's pulling ahead already."

But the end was at hand. It is well known to all motorists that for some inscrutable reason the most gigantic lorries in the manufacturers' catalogs are invariably to be met with at the most impassable points of the most exiguous lanes, at the unlikeliest hours of the day and night. So it was now. The Hispano was no more than a few yards away from the bridge when a stupendous shape loomed up on the opposite side. The Hispano had slowed down for the bridge, but it was still traveling far too fast to be able to stop in time. They saw it swerve—saw its metal flank punched in like paper by the lorry's radiator. Then it wheeled, crashed through the fence, and disappeared down the slope. The next moment there was a violent explosion, and the night sky was lit up by fire.

The lorry driver dragged on his brakes and jumped down from his cabin, cursing. The two pursuing cars pulled up, and Stagge and Mr. Plumstead, traversing the gap in the fence, raced down the slope toward the burning wreckage. They disappeared into the conflagration and after what seemed an eternity emerged again, dragging a blackened and distorted figure.

"Jesus," the lorry driver muttered. "Poor devil. But it was his own bloody fault."

There was a second explosion. Heat swept up at the lookers-on. The conflagration became a raging furnace.

And Fen, hitherto motionless in the road, was galvanized into activity. He began to run down the slope toward that core of white heat. But he was not halfway there before his arm was gripped from behind, and he turned to look into the blackened face of Stagge. The superintendent was badly burned, and the glow of the flames made him seem the denizen of some choleric inferno.

"I shouldn't, sir," he warned. "Even if you wanted to sacrifice yourself, you'd never get it out of *that*. And anyway, it may not even be there."

Fen halted, recognizing that the attempt was futile. He nodded toward the shriveled, unidentifiable human form near which Daphne and Mr. Plumstead and the lorry driver were standing.

"Dead?" he asked.

"No, sir. Alive. But only just. I must get him to hospital straight away."

"Get yourself to a hospital," said Fen. "He's got to die in any case."

"Nothing seriously the matter with me," said Stagge grimly. "I can manage."

He limped away. Fen turned his eyes back to the blazing wreckage. The headmaster came up to him.

"Who is it?" he demanded. "For God's sake, Gervase, *who is it?*"

Fen stared at him almost uncomprehendingly. With even greater urgency, the headmaster repeated his question.

"My dear fellow," said Fen, "I didn't realize you were still in the dark. . . . It's your secretary, of course. Galbraith."

† 16 †

ECLIPSE

"So I spent the morning tidying up loose ends," Fen said. "Saw Weems, saw Stagge, chatted to Etherege—incidentally, he supplied me with one of the missing links—visited Brenda and told her all about it, and wound up by drinking beer at the Beacon with Daphne and Mr. Plumstead."

"Is Brenda recovering?" the headmaster asked.

"Oh, yes. Rapidly."

"And Stagge?"

"He wasn't as badly burned as I thought at the time. He's bandaged up, of course, but not in bed. As for Plumstead, getting Galbraith out of that car doesn't seem to have harmed him in the least. He must be a salamander. He's taken a liking to the Beacon and is going to spend the rest of his holiday there."

It was the afternoon of the day following the speeches, and Fen and the headmaster were seated in the study in Davenant's. Beyond the windows the site was almost deserted, for most of the boys were spending the day with their parents. Last night's rain had broken the spell of fine weather, and the sky was overcast. A cool, steady wind was blowing—so cool as to have induced the headmaster to light his fire. And Fen's long, lanky body was sprawled almost horizontally in the leather-covered armchair, his green tie with the mermaids flowing over his left lapel, his undisciplined brown hair projecting in spikes from the crown of his head, and his ruddy, clean-shaven face warmed to a comfortable glow by the combined effects—gastronomically somewhat nightmarish, but pedantry in drinking bored him—of Mr. Beresford's bitter and the headmaster's Haut Brion.

"Galbraith . . ." the headmaster murmured, "I still can scarcely believe it."

"Why?" Fen demanded. The psychology of the affair interested him, and he was anxious to hear the headmaster's views.

"Because I've worked with the man for so long, in close collaboration, without ever dreaming he had such atrocious potentialities. I can't think, you know, that this is a case of 'there, but for the grace of God.' He must have been abnormal—and I never suspected it for a moment. I used to imagine I was a tolerable judge of character, but I shall never trust myself again."

"Did you, in fact, know very much about him?"

"Nothing," said the headmaster. "I've been thinking it over, and I realize that I knew precisely nothing, except for a few vague and innocuous details about his past. If I'd appointed him myself, I might have known more, but I simply took him on trust from my predecessor, who recommended him highly. And he *was* an efficient secretary—quiet, competent, tactful, unobtrusive. Too efficient, I suppose. If I'd thought about it, I would have realized that *something* must be going on behind the professional facade. But apparently he was quite normal until this business of the manuscripts came up. I can only suppose that he had persistent dreams of moneyed grandeur, and that the huge sums involved simply knocked him off his mental balance."

"And Somers? Are you surprised at his being involved?"

"Not so much. I disliked him, as I've told you, but he hadn't been here long, and I didn't know him well. . . . But look here, Gervase, you promised at lunch to give me a complete account of the business. This morning's papers had nothing but a bare statement of the facts, and there are a great many things I don't understand."

"What exactly do you want to know?" Fen asked, yawning. He was a heavy sleeper, and two truncated nights had made him very drowsy.

The headmaster got out his pipe. "First of all, how you reached your conclusions—step by logical (I trust) step. Then a chronological narrative of events, bringing in the whole background."

"That's a large order," Fen murmured. "It'll keep us here till teatime."

"No matter. My hands are tied till I get a substitute for Galbraith. Do you know"—the headmaster strayed momentarily to the consideration of his own troubles —"the only stopgap I could find was some dim-witted girl from the local commercial college. Things are going to be chaotic for the next few days. And I know what tomorrow's post bag will be like: endless letters from parents who've read the papers, ranging in tone from nervous apology to downright abuse."

Fen stretched out his hand to take a cigarette from the silver box on the desk.

"The key to the whole business," he said, "can be summed up in two words: invisible ink."

"I'd gathered that," said the headmaster, offering matches. "But begin at the beginning, please."

Fen looked rather surly at this injunction, but his sigh indicated resignation.

"Very well. The first news I had of the case—you told me almost as soon as I arrived—was of Brenda Boyce's assignation in the Science Building, her subsequent alarm and refusal to explain it, and the breaking open of the cupboard in the chemistry laboratory. Later on we heard of Brenda's disappearance on the way home from school. Well, there was plenty of material for conjecture in all that, but, as I said at the time, the

number of possible explanations, sinister and otherwise, was legion. I made a provisional interim as-
sumption that the two things were connected—that
Brenda had seen the burglar and been frightened into
silence. But it was no more than the vaguest of un-
confirmed hypotheses, and I was perfectly ready to
abandon it at any time if necessary. Besides, at that
stage the theory presented a number of difficulties—
obvious difficulties enough, and so I needn't expatiate
on them now. In particular, Brenda's disappearance,
combined with Miss Parry's view that the farewell
letter was a fake, made it clear that *if* she had wit-
nessed the burglary, then it had had implications beyond and above the implications of common theft,
since those who commit petty larceny very seldom go
to the trouble of kidnapping witnesses and fabricating
elaborate hoaxes to account for their disappearance.
I concluded, therefore, that—granted Brenda *had* wit-
nessed the burglary—it was a crime of more than ordinary importance. Beyond that, everything was hazy
and obscure."

"This exposition is overcautious," the headmaster
commented. "After all, it'd be stretching coincidence
too far to suppose that Brenda's kidnapping *wasn't*
connected with the burglary."

"Coincidences do happen," said Fen. "And I'm trying to keep to what was plain and unarguable. I want,
in fact, to emphasize that every conclusion I reached
in this instance was perfectly obvious and incontrovertible; and we didn't actually come on anything incontrovertible until we investigated the murders of
Love and Somers.

"You remember that while we were waiting for
Stagge to arrive, you filled in the victims' background
for me. Two things you told me proved important later
on—though remember, I paid no special attention to
them *then:* They were (one) the regularity of Love's

habits and (two) Love's puritanism. I stored them in my mind, along with all the rest, for future reference; and when the police turned up, we all went across to the common room.

"Now, the first and most startling oddity about Somers's murder was that electric fire, and I was thinking about it while they took their photographs and went through all the other routine. In the first place, of course, it might have been some sort of a red herring; the problem about that theory, however, was that the fire didn't *suggest* anything; it was *pointless.* Can you think of any reason, however fantastic, why, having shot a man, you should switch on an electric fire in order to mislead the investigators?"

The headmaster, after a moment's rather perfunctory thought, admitted that he could not.

"Very well, then. I didn't entirely dismiss the red-herring theory, but it seemed more likely that the fire had been *used.* Only—used for what?

"Bodily heat? Of course not; it was a stifling night. Cooking? Well, there were no evidences of cooking—as there would have been if the cooking had been innocuous—and how cooking could be sinister, and connected with a shooting, I was at a loss to see. Warming the corpse? But as I pointed out at the time, the fire was too far distant. No, the thing had to be considered in broader terms. Scientifically speaking, the function of heat is to produce chemical change. And that reflection, I need hardly say, rang a bell: chemical change—the cupboard in the chemistry laboratory—Brenda's rendezvous in the Science Building. But chemical change in what and for what purpose? Someone might have been burning papers, but an electric fire isn't at all a convenient agent for that purpose . . . and so forth. I won't weary you with a complete list of the possibilities and the objections to them. I was led at last to a consideration of the reports;

and you'll agree that as regards the reports, chemical change by means of heat could only mean invisible ink.

"Was there any confirmation of this possibility? There was. I refer, of course, to the sheet of clean blotting paper, similar in kind to that which Wells had put in the pads earlier that evening, which was found in Somers's breast pocket. The top of the pad at which he was working, you recall, was covered with mirror images of the comments he had written on the report forms; and Wells reported that each and every pad had its exact quota of blotting paper. Now—I argued—if Somers had, for some reason, written the reports in invisible ink and warmed them up at the fire (while wishing, as he obviously did, to give the impression that he had written them normally between ten and eleven), he would have to do something about the blotting pad, which could not plausibly be left virgin and unsullied; and *what* he would do would be to take a sheet of the stuff at some previous time—the identical brand being supplied by the school stationer to boys and staff as well as to Wells for use in the common room—cover it with the appropriate marks of his writing, bring it along inside his mark book, and pop it into the pad. Only—knowing Wells's meticulous habits—he'd be careful to remove a clean sheet from the pad to take away with him, in case someone should count the sheets and discover an extra one. Do you follow me?"

"Perfectly," said the headmaster. "And I can see more confirmation coming."

"Of a lesser sort. You mean, of course, the insistence on times. But don't let's go ahead too fast. I was convinced that invisible ink *had* been used—but why? It required no very great effort to decide that Somers wished it to be thought that he had been busy in the common room between ten and eleven when in fact he had plenty of time to be away from it on some private errand. And what errand? Well, presumably something illegal. He had carefully supplied himself with an alibi; if he were to come under suspicion, he could make exactly the suggestion *I* made, rather maliciously, to Stagge—namely, that his efforts be imitated and the minimum time needed for their accomplishment ascertained. That minimum would be arranged so as to be close on an hour. And Somers could then say: 'You see? I just shouldn't have had time to do'—whatever it might be.

"And other evidence strengthened this hypothesis—the fact that Etherege knew exactly how many reports Somers had still, apparently, to write, the fact that Somers asserted he'd have them finished by eleven, the fact that he asked Wells to call him at eleven, the fact that he could rely on Wells being about at ten to witness his arrival and the start of his supposed labors. But what—I asked myself—was all this *for*? *Why* did Somers want an alibi?

"Well, I'd already heard about the second murder, and in the absence, so far, of contradictory evidence, I thought it eminently probable that Somers had wanted his alibi in order to commit that. But there was an unknown quantity in this carefully contrived equation: Someone had murdered Somers himself. And I felt that I mustn't accept unreservedly the explanation I've just postulated of the invisible-ink business without examining the possibility that this x—this unknown—had had a finger in it. There were, it seemed to me, two alternatives: (one) that the invisible-ink business had been deliberately contrived by x in order to be discovered and so point to Somers as the murderer of Love; or (two) that the invisible-ink business had been contrived by x so as to give himself an alibi for the murder of Somers."

"Both of which theories," the headmaster interrupted, "would necessarily involve Somers's complete innocence."

"Exactly. *And they would also involve his coopera-tion.* There was never any doubt that the writing on the reports was his."

"I suppose they *might* have been forged," said the headmaster apologetically.

"Oh, my dear Horace"—Fen groaned—"forging a signature effectively is one thing; forging ninety-seven separate reports is quite another. And besides, have you ever tried forging in invisible—that's to say, colorless—ink? Virtually impossible, I assure you—it's difficult enough when you can see what you're doing."

"All right," said the headmaster hurriedly. "I agree that Somers must have written the reports."

"I'm glad you agree," said Fen, without, however, displaying any special jubilance at the event. "And—I repeat—the two alternatives I outlined a moment ago must therefore have involved Somers's innocent cooperation. Now—I ask you—is that possible? What *conceivable* tale could our *x* have invented in order to induce him to embark, unsuspicious, on such an elaborate and incredible scheme? If anyone ap-proached *you* with such a suggestion—whatever the pretext—you'd think him insane. No, I was forced back on my original idea that Somers had contrived the whole business to provide himself with a colora-ble alibi.

"So what? The next oddity was the broken wrist-watch, and the dilemma which *that* implied I in-dicated at the time. Somers had, of course, said it was broken in order to get Wells to call him at eleven, but it would have been quite unnecessarily thorough for him to have broken it himself, since watches are inex-plicable things which stop and start again for no rea-son perceptible to the lay mind. Besides, he would not

have put it back on his wrist *the wrong way round.*
I've worn my watch as Somers wore his for as long as
I can remember, and for as long as I can remember
I've never once caught myself absentmindedly strap-
ping it on in the unaccustomed though more usual
way. Clearly x had tampered with the watch. But—in
heaven's name—why?

"The position of the hands made no kind of sense
and offered no kind of clue, and the only conclusion I
could reach was that x had been intent on confirming
Somers's alibi, in order to give *himself* an alibi for
Somers's murder. You see, it cut both ways. If it could
be proved subsequently, from the reports, that Somers
had done fifty-five minutes' work, then clearly no one
could have killed him, on the face of it, before five to
eleven, and x could be supplied with an unbreakable
alibi for that time—sufficient reason, I thought, to
make him anxious that the invisible-ink camouflage
should not be discovered and to suggest to him that he
should finish the scene-setting which Somers had
begun."

"I see a snag," the headmaster interposed. "The
point you've just made implies that x was aware of
Somers's alibi plan—and murderers, from what little
I know of them, don't confide such things to other
people if they can possibly avoid it."

Fen threw his cigarette end into the fire. "Agreed,"
he said. "I'm sure Somers didn't confide in anyone. But
I'm also sure that x, entering the common room and
killing Somers, deduced from the general state of
affairs exactly what I did. He may even have come on
Somers heating the report forms at the fire—a complete giveaway."

"I grant you that, but there's still a snag. The business of the supposedly broken watch wasn't in any
way essential to Somers's plan: It was a trimming. So
how could x have possibly known that Somers told

Wells his watch was broken—unless, that is, x was either Wells himself or Etherege?"

"Or unless he happened to be listening outside the common-room door," Fen amended. "That's what must have happened, in fact, though since Galbraith died without speaking, we shall never be certain. I thought of your objections at the time, and it seemed to me that the keyhole hypothesis must be correct—or else that Etherege was x."

"Why not Wells?"

"Because Wells *hadn't any alibi*, by his own account. It's quite pointless to help make it seem that a man hasn't been killed before five to eleven *and then not give yourself an alibi for five to eleven and onwards*. No, from that moment I wiped Wells completely off the list of suspects, which was useful, as I could then safely accept his assertions as true. The watch was pretty conclusive, you know. Our x had obviously broken it in order that Somers's assertion to Wells might seem to have been true. For if Somers's watch was found ticking away merrily and showing the right time, the police would wonder why he'd lied, would investigate his doings closely, might well discover the invisible-ink hoax. And bang would go x's delightful alibi.

"The other facts we turned up in the common room can be summarized briefly; thus—(one) he was shot through the left eye by a .38 revolver, probably silenced, at a distance of about six feet; (two) unseen access to the building—and, correspondingly, egress from it—was possible by way of the downstairs windows; and (three) Somers had sprained his wrist a week previously.

"Of these, (one) was neutral, noncommittal, and unenlightening, (two) confirmed my idea that Somers could have been galloping about the neighborhood while he was supposed to be in the common room, and (three) might, I thought, have been of incidental use to him in concocting his alibi plan. Actually—I may as well say this at once—it later proved to be meaningless or at least inessential.

"This, then, was the position I'd reached by the time we left the common room: that Somers had either killed Love or had been engaged, or intending to engage, in some illegal activity between the hours of ten and eleven; that Somers's murderer would be found to have an alibi from about ten to eleven onwards but probably not for some part of the preceding time; and that therefore Wells was not Somers's murderer, whoever else might be.

"There are one or two other things which I ought to mention. The formulae for invisible ink are innumerable, but very few of them, as it happens, come out black when appropriately treated—and of course it was black ink Somers was supposed to be using; in fact, the *only* one I could remember at the time was dilute sulfuric acid. Now, I couldn't but remember that something had been stolen from a cupboard containing, in Philpotts's words, 'for the most part, acids.' And really, it was no longer possible, in the circumstances, to regard the disappearance of Brenda Boyce as coincidental. I assumed—rashly, perhaps, but not unreasonably—that Somers had pinched sulfuric acid, that Brenda had seen him at it, that he'd tried to scare her into silence, and that subsequently, afraid she'd give him away nonetheless, he'd carried her off somewhere and killed her. You see, so long as he went on with this alibi scheme —and for reasons which I'll be coming to he felt he had to have an alibi—she was an appalling danger to him. Let her once say that he'd stolen the vitriol, and the police would wonder why, and the invisible-ink camouflage would go up in smoke, and that would be the end of him. So I still believe I was justified in thinking, until we actually found her, that Brenda Boyce was dead."

Fen yawned prodigiously.

"I don't pretend," he said, "that I made my deductions in quite such a turgid and laborious fashion as all that; but those, anyway, were the logical processes at the back of my mind.

"We went on to Love's house; and that crime, as Stagge remarked, was pretty featureless. The only interesting thing about it was the unfinished statement I found in a drawer: 'This is to put on record the fact that two of my colleagues at Castrevenford School are associated together in what can only be described as a fraud, which. . . .' And the word 'colleagues,' you remember, was half crossed out, as though he'd thought better of it. By the way, there's no doubt that this document was what it seemed to be; that's to say that it couldn't have been a red herring. The writing was undoubtedly Love's," Fen mumbled rather indistinctly, "and the ink showed it hadn't been written later than the morning, and it was quite incredible that someone had forced Love to write it and then gone off, and that Love had done nothing except put it in a drawer to mislead the police after his own murder. . . ." Fen's eyes closed peacefully.

"Wake up!" the headmaster admonished him sharply.

"I heard you," said Fen irritably, and shook himself like a dog emerging from a river. "I was never more alert and quick-witted in my life. What was I talking about?"

"Love's statement."

"Oh, yes, I remember. Well, the paper was certainly genuine. And to me, at least, there were two very striking things about it.

"Thing number one: 'can only be described as.' As I told Stagge, that meant that the fraud Love was referring to probably wasn't a fraud, in the legal sense, at all.

"Thing number two: the beginnings of an attempt to cross out 'colleagues.' I found nearby a corrected essay in which Love trounced some unfortunate boy for using the word 'ambiguous' to apply to something with more than two meanings—real pedantry, that."

"Love *was* pedantic about words," said the headmaster. "He detested inexactness."

"So I thought. And that was what I was trying to demonstrate when I showed the essay to Stagge, though I'm afraid he didn't see the point. Love had recognized that the word 'colleagues' in the statement was wrong and had set out to correct it; but then, probably, he saw that he'd have to recast the whole sentence and decided that the statement didn't serve any useful purpose anyway and so abandoned it. Still, he'd written 'colleagues' in the first instance, so he must have been thinking of at least one person who, while not a master, was sufficiently close in status to the masters to make the temporary aberration possible. I ruled out masters' wives and families, of course; Love would never have called them 'colleagues.' An employee of the school who was not a master was clearly indicated—or, of course, yourself, for Love's natural reverence would obviously prevent him from calling——"

"That will do," said the headmaster. "There were moments when I almost wondered if I *was* suspected."

Fen chuckled. "You had an unshakable alibi," he said. "Anyway, to conclude this section of my enthralling argument, I need say no more than that the statement suggested a possible motive for Love's murder.

"We talked to his wife. The only useful information she gave us, to my mind, was to the effect that she was

in the habit of drinking coffee with Love every evening at a quarter to eleven, and that the fact was generally known. That cleared up a difficulty which had
been worrying me slightly; for if Somers had murdered Love and arranged the ten-till-eleven alibi to
clear himself from suspicion, then it was essential
that the murder should be discovered *before eleven,*
and that a doctor should get to the scene soon enough
to be able to assert that Love had not died *before
ten.* Do you see what I mean? Somers presumably had
no alibi arranged for *before* ten or *after* eleven; therefore his whole scheme would be vitiated if, for example, Love's body were not found till the following
morning—until, that is, so much time had elapsed as
to make it impossible to say *when* he had died. But
Somers must have expected Love's wife to enter the
study at a quarter to eleven—a habit of which, like
everyone else, he knew, and which served his purpose
admirably.

"Mind you," Fen added in haste, "I still wasn't prepared to swear that Somers had killed Love. But *if* he
had, then that particular problem was disposed of.

"Next morning I was still thinking about this word
'colleague,' and I borrowed a school list from you in
order to check the nonstaff employees. I didn't think
that Love would have referred to the matron of the
sanatorium as a colleague, or Sergeant Shelley, who I
later found was an unashamed Cockney, or the head
groundsman or Wells or the proprietor of the school
shop; but he might so have referred, temporarily care-
less, to the J.T.C. adjutant, the bursar, the librarian,
your secretary, or, less probably, the school doctor; so
I kept them all in mind.

"Stagge met us here. He said that both bullets had
been fired from the same gun—a fact which didn't
necessarily militate against the provisional picture of
events which I was building up, for Somers might

well have shot Love, returned with the gun to the common room, and laid it down; while x, entering the common room, could have picked it up, shot Somers, and gone away with it. (I couldn't be sure this *had* happened, please observe; but it was not impossible.) Stagge, with your assistance, did some preliminary work on alibis, and I asked you if you'd heard a car during the previous evening. I'd already calculated, you see, that it would take a quarter of an hour to walk from the common room to Love's house, and presumably about five minutes to cycle. It was conceivable, though not likely, that Somers (insert the usual qualifications on your own account, please) had used a car; but in any case you said you'd not heard one.

"Later on, I had two rather useless interviews—with Etherege and Sergeant Shelley. I was hoping Etherege would be able to produce something definite in the way of motive, but he was a broken reed in that respect. However, he was able to confirm the fact that everyone was aware of the regularity of Wells's and Love's habits—and Somers would have *had* to be aware of it if he had made the plans I provisionally suspected him of. Etherege also said that Love's manner had been brooding and injured recently, which fitted in not only with the statement about a 'fraud' but also—the 'injured' part of it—with the fact that Somers was Love's particular blue-eyed boy. I asked about Somers's sprained wrist, which I vaguely thought might have been a fake, but apparently it wasn't. I also asked if Somers had always used black ink, and Etherege said he had, which meant that Somers would have been obliged (mental reservations as before) to use one of the rare invisible inks which turn black, for fear that suspicion might be aroused by a sudden change of color.

"From Shelley I got nothing beyond the fact that the revolved and silencer had been stolen from the ar-

mory, and that it was physically possible for almost
anyone to have taken them. Stagge and I searched
Somers's rooms, unsuccessfully; I noticed that he'd
been reading *The Fourth Forger* but didn't make anything of it at the time. Nor did I make anything of the
fact that Somers had withdrawn a hundred pounds
from his bank on the morning before he was killed.
We hadn't found the money, so we assumed—and I
still assume—that the murderer stole it.

"Then came the murder of Mrs. Bly. As you know,
that led on to the discovery of the manuscripts sub-
plot. Motive became clear, and a good many other
things along with it. Somers had been going to buy
the manuscript; Love—for it was almost certainly
Love who had inquired for Mrs. Bly at the Beacon,
and this only could be the 'fraud' of which he spoke
—had been trying to stop the transaction by telling
Mrs. Bly of the real value of the papers. That gave
Somers an overwhelming motive for killing Love;
the probability that Somers was Love's murderer became a certainty.

"All the same, there were problems. How had Love
learned anything about the transaction in the first
place? And why had he said that some third person
was 'associated' with Somers? I found it unbelievable,
you see, that Somers should have told *anyone* about
his find, for fear it might somehow be snatched away
from him at the eleventh hour; certainly he had no
need to tell anyone, for the price demanded was available in his bank—and of all the persons he might have
told, Love—of whose 'commercial puritanism' he
must have been aware—was by far the least likely. I
was inclined, moreover, to think that Love had been
misled about this 'association,' though against this
there was the fact that an x had undeniably murdered
Somers and Mrs. Bly, presumably for the sake of the
manuscripts, of whose existence he presumably

knew. A bit hazy, I agree, but one fact emerged from
the wreckage: namely, that since Somers was one of
the 'colleagues' in Love's statement, and a bonafide
one, then the other, conjecturally our x, must be he
who had provoked Love's incomplete amendment of
the word.

"Then came the alibi reports. And, heavens, they
were revealing! I wasn't looking for a master in any
case, but when I found that Mathieson, Etherege, and
Philpotts had no alibi for five to eleven or after—and
hence had evidently not tampered with the wristwatch to strengthen the invisible-ink hoax—I wiped
them off the suspects list without a further thought.
Wells was cleared for the same reasons. And that left
one person—Galbraith. He qualified for the murderer
in every respect. He was a person whom Love might
have denominated a colleague—and my other four
possibles in the school employment were by some divine miracle playing bridge together at the crucial
time, and so out of it. And his alibi—his only, of all
men—was exactly what I'd been led to expect: not
vouched for before a quarter to eleven but impeccably
vouched for (by you) thereafter.

"And on top of that, Stagge told me that Galbraith
was by way of being an expert on old manuscripts—
a fact which struck me as being morally conclusive.
You see, the only person to whom Somers was likely
to have confided his discovery was—precisely—an expert on old manuscripts. Somers was going to pay a
hundred pounds for *Love's Labour's Won* out of his
not very large balance at the bank; he would naturally
be anxious about its authenticity, and if he could reassure himself with reasonable safety, he would; and
Galbraith no doubt seemed to him, as to everyone else,
a quiet, harmless fellow who was very unlikely to interfere with the transaction or to try to horn in on his
own account. As a matter of fact, I asked Galbraith at

the garden party if Somers *had* applied to him, and he was clever enough to say Yes. It was, after all, a very likely thing for Somers to have done, and although if Galbraith said Somers hadn't we shouldn't necessarily have disbelieved him, he evidently thought it safer to say that Somers had.

"At teatime yesterday, then, the position at which I'd arrived was this: that Somers had certainly killed Love; and that Galbraith had almost certainly killed Somers, and probably—since a third murderer was stretching coincidence rather far—Mrs. Bly as well.

"But of course, there was no substantial case against Galbraith. The ink on the reports could be analyzed— in fact, it has been, with the expected result—and thereby Galbraith's alibi would be blown to smithereens; but the mere absence of alibi isn't proof of guilt; there were other people without alibis. Moreover, the wristwatch clue could be demolished by a clever counsel in no time at all. 'Ladies and gentlemen' "—Fen's voice became imitatively orotund— " 'you know, and I know, that even the best of us is subject—ha, ha—to strange fits of absentmindedness; is a man to be hanged—I put it to you as men and women of sense and discernment—is a man to be hanged for the trivial, nay ridiculous, reason that the unfortunate victim of a brutal murder chanced to adjust his wristwatch in an unaccustomed position?' Plenty of convincing sophistries could be applied, likewise, to the half-crossed-out word 'colleagues' and to the common-sense view that the only person Somers was at all likely to confide in was Galbraith, the expert on manuscripts. Though very significant, it was all too frail for the courtroom.

"Besides, there was just a fragment of doubt left in my own mind. By some millions of miles Galbraith was the likeliest person to be guilty, but I wanted irrefragable proof of it for my own peace of mind as well as for the sake of a jury. So I hopefully set a rather primitive trap.

"I asked Weems to get into conversation with Galbraith and to retail, as a spicy piece of topical gossip, the fact that he had overheard Stagge talking to me about the case. Stagge—as we arranged it—was to have said something on these lines: 'If we can break his alibi, sir, we've got a case to go to the public prosecutor, thanks to that chap who saw him burgle the cottage. But if we can't break his alibi—and it looks completely impossible to me—then he gets off scot-free.' I was to have agreed, and we were then to have perceived Weems's presence and moved hurriedly out of earshot."

"Burglary?" The headmaster was puzzled.

"Guesswork," Fen admitted. "Stagge found signs that Mrs. Bly's cottage had been burgled, and it occurred to me that before embarking on murder, Galbraith would probably have tried to get hold of the manuscript by less drastic methods."

"Yes, I see," said the headmaster. "But what was this fictional conversation intended to make Galbraith *do?*"

"During the course of the evening," Fen explained, "I was proposing to stage a bogus resurrection of Brenda. It was to be discreetly put about that she had been the victim of a murderous attack, and that she was unconscious but expected to live. And Galbraith was to be given the opportunity of trying to kill this supposed Brenda—a lay figure in a hospital bed or something of that sort. Even if we didn't catch him in the act, that the deed had been *attempted* would be proof that Galbraith had murdered Somers."

"Just a moment." The headmaster's voice was plaintive. "How did Galbraith know anything about Brenda?"

"Oh, my dear Horace"—Fen groaned—"if he was

aware of the invisible-ink business, he must have realized the probable significance of Brenda's disappearance, just as I did."

"Oh, yes, of course." The headmaster was abashed. "Sorry."

"But then, of course, the unexpected happened: Brenda actually was alive, and my *ballon d'essai* worked—though prematurely, catching me hopelessly unawares. Someone tried to kill the girl. And that, I need hardly tell you, was incontrovertible proof of Galbraith's guilt."

"How?" Even at the risk of appearing moronic, the headmaster was determined to have everything clear.

"Well, Brenda's sole connection with the case consisted in knowing that Somers had stolen sulfuric acid from the chemistry laboratory. If she lived, she would tell us about that, we should ask ourselves what he'd wanted it for, and by reference to scientific manuals we should very quickly come to the conclusion that he'd wanted it for invisible ink. But, you see, *the only person in the wide world whose safety and immunity depended in any way at all on the invisible-ink hoax's remaining undiscovered was Galbraith; therefore, he was the only person in the wide world, after Somers's death, with a motive for killing Brenda.* I needn't add that his safety did not, in fact, depend on the hoax's remaining undiscovered; but Weems's fictional report made him *think* it did—made him think that once his precious alibi was destroyed, he was lost."

† 17 †
PEACE INDIVISIBLE

Fen paused to filch another of the headmaster's cigarettes, and the headmaster leaned back in his chair with a sigh.

"Marvellous!" he exclaimed admiringly.

"Not at all." Fen's diffidence was for once unfeigned. "Though it involved a lot of detail, the case was unusually plain and straightforward. And when I think of my imbecility in going to Melton Chart unarmed, I blush like an amorous kitchen-maid."

"Now," the headmaster commanded inexorably, "let's have a straightforward narrative, please. There are still things I don't understand about the manuscripts."

"Some of it's bound to be conjecture," Fen warned him. "All four protagonists are dead without telling us anything, and there are episodes which we can only guess at. But a likely reconstruction would run something like this:

"It began last Monday, when, in the Beacon, Taverner told Somers casually of the existence of the manuscript, probably mentioning the name *Love's Labour's Won*. Somers, as an English teacher, would certainly be knowledgeable enough to take an interest, and on Tuesday evening he visited Mrs. Bly to look at the thing, decided it was well worth having, and asked the old woman how much she wanted for it. She, no doubt, mentioned a hundred pounds, in joke at first but later in earnest, since she saw Somers was really anxious to buy it. And he—after some futile haggling—would have said something like 'Well, I'll give you a check.' Being an old and suspicious woman, she would have refused that and demanded cash. He would have said: 'All right, I'll get the money from my bank and bring it to you tomorrow.' And she would have replied: 'No good, because I'm going away to visit my son and shan't be back till Saturday; you can bring me the money *then*.'"

"I can't endure this hypothetical style," the headmaster complained. "Leave out the 'would' and 'must have' and 'probably' and 'doubtless' and tell the story straightforwardly. I'll stop you if you say anything nonsensical."

"I never say anything nonsensical," Fen replied coldly. "But I agree that your suggestion's a good one," he relented. "So here goes:

"Somers didn't at all like the idea of so long an interval's elapsing before this priceless thing came into his possession; he was afraid that Mrs. Bly, suspecting its true value, would sell it in the meantime to someone else, for a much larger sum. So he asked her to sign a Promise to Sell, and she, to whom a hundred pounds was great riches, agreed. (We found this document, by the way, in Galbraith's pocket; he evidently took it from Somers's body.) In his own hand Somers wrote the words: 'I, the undersigned, swear that on payment in cash of one hundred pounds I will hand over unconditionally to Michael Somers of Castrevenford School the manuscript found in my cottage and entitled *Love's Labour's Won;* provided that such payment be made within a week of the date of this agreement.' Mrs. Bly signed, and Somers went off with the paper in his pocket. Since it was a conditional agreement, I imagine—though I'm no forensic expert—that it wasn't legally binding, but Somers didn't realize that, nor did Mrs. Bly, and nor, when he came to hear of it, did Galbraith.

"No wonder Somers was pleased with himself when

he went to the Beacon for a drink last Tuesday evening; for if the manuscript was what he thought, he would be able to live in luxury for the rest of his life. He considered the possibility that the manuscript was bogus and was inclined on the whole to dismiss it. One hundred pounds was too small an amount to be asked for a careful modern forgery; Taverner and Mrs. Bly were a very unlikely pair of agents; and it seemed incredible that a forgery should have been buried at some time in the distant past as an esoteric practical joke. Moreover, Somers had examined the manuscript himself, and though he was not an expert, he knew just enough about such things to make sure that risking his money was worthwhile.

"He read books on the topic of Shakespeare forgeries, and it occurred to him the following morning that he might get the advice of the local expert—Galbraith. Accordingly, he took Galbraith aside, and, secure in the possession of his Promise to Sell, poured out the whole story. Galbraith was interested (secretly *very* interested) and noncommittal. But neither of them was prepared for the fact that Love overheard them, resented Somers's buying the manuscript for so trivial a sum, mistakenly assumed that Galbraith was concerned in the business, confronted them both, informed them that it was his intention to put a spoke in the wheel if possible, and marched off."

Fen made an apologetic gesture. "That's the best hypothesis I can think of; though, of course, it may not have happened exactly like that.

"Somers and Galbraith separated, and in each of them money lust began to do its work. Somers was horrified at the possibility that Love, thanks to his ridiculous scruples, might snatch a fortune away from him; true, he had the signed agreement, but he knew Love's iron determination and didn't put it past him to camp on Mrs. Bly's doorstep until she returned

and then persuade her to break the agreement and
risk an action for breach of contract. Love was, indeed, a formidable opponent who was quite capable of
ultimately preventing Somers from getting his hands
on the manuscript. The conclusion, to Somers, was
inescapable; Love had to die before Mrs. Bly returned
on Speech Day.

"But Galbraith knew that Somers had a motive for
killing Love; consequently, Somers thought, he must
supply himself with a good alibi—and we know what
it was that he contrived. I needn't enumerate all the
various factors which helped him. The chief danger
of the plan was that some other master might enter
the common room and find him absent, but, as Wells
told us, that was unlikely, and if it happened, he could
probably say that he had been in the lavatory; some
risk had to be taken. The chief *problem* was to get
sulfuric acid, since he dared not buy it openly at a
shop; but the cupboard in the chemistry laboratory,
with its flimsy lock, solved that difficulty.

"He robbed it on Thursday evening and was seen by
Brenda. Rather pusillanimously (from his point of
view) he tried to frighten her into silence. Then—or
perhaps next morning—he went off and wrote out the
appropriate number of reports (representing about an
hour's work) in invisible ink. On the Friday afternoon
he learned from Etherege that Brenda had not been
able to conceal her alarm, so he waylaid her, throttled
her (or tried to), and planted the fake letter—a rather
unnecessary trimming—in her study. Everything was
ready for the evening."

"But what about the revolver?" The headmaster
asked.

"Oh, yes, I'd forgotten that. I think that Somers,
passing the armory on Friday afternoon and finding it
unlocked and unguarded, must have stolen the gun on
an impulse. It didn't really matter what weapon he

used, but since the opportunity offered, he took it. That same gun has been used all along, by the way—to kidnap Brenda, to shoot Love, to shoot Somers, and to shoot at Brenda and me in Melton Chart. I'm sorry to say that in the excitement of last night's happenings I made a mess of the fingerprints on it, but at that stage they weren't really required.

"Well, Somers entered the common room just before ten on Friday evening—and must have been somewhat upset to find Etherege there. Etherege, however, went away almost at once, and he unwittingly helped Somers's plan by counting the number of report forms which remained blank."

"That's an important point," the headmaster interrupted. "Obviously the alibi wouldn't stand unless there were some independent witness to swear that at ten o'clock Somers had just so many reports to write. How would he have managed that without Etherege?"

"He would have used Wells, I think, on whose presence he could rely; would have said something to this effect: 'Look here, Wells, I've got a bet on: I've told a friend I can write ninety-seven reports by eleven. So would you mind counting them, so that you can confirm that there actually *were* ninety-seven?' No doubt he had some such fabrication in mind for the purpose."

The headmaster nodded. "Go on."

"Etherege and Wells having departed, Somers closed the curtains of the common room so that no one outside would have a chance of observing that he was not there, went downstairs, and quitted Hubbard's Building by way of a window. I *think* he must have had a bicycle handy—partly because he wouldn't wish to be absent longer than was necessary, and partly for a reason which I'll mention in a minute. Anyway, he proceeded to Love's house, entered the French windows, shot Love where he sat, and returned to the common room; all of which would take him about a quarter of an hour."

"But look here," the headmaster objected; "if Somers had used a bicycle, we should have found it subsequently."

"Unless Galbraith removed it," said Fen, "which he'd have every opportunity to do. However, I don't insist on the bicycle. All I maintain is that Somers must have got *back* by half past ten at the latest. That would have been a squeeze, walking, but not impossible.

"Love's movements during the preceding days we can assess fairly exactly. On Thursday he visited Mrs. Bly's cottage, found her absent, tried to discover where she was, and failed. But he did learn that she was due back on Speech Day, and I expect he had every intention of meeting her on her return and acquainting her with the real worth of the manuscript."

"She might not have believed him, you know," said the headmaster. "She might still have insisted on selling the thing to Somers."

"Agreed, but Somers dared not rely on that happening. Anyway, Love took no further steps before his death, except to begin writing that statement. What he was proposing to do with it defeats me—and it must have defeated him, too, since he never finished it. The only theory I can offer that makes any sense at all is that he felt he wanted a confidant and decided that a piece of paper would be better than none. Much the same impulse goes to the keeping of diaries."

"You don't think, then, that he did confide in any person?"

"Unlikely. I think he would have done if Galbraith alone had been involved, but Somers was a different kettle of fish. Somers was Love's protégé, and for Love to confess that Somers was engaged in a disgraceful (to Love) transaction would be an admission of misjudgment very wounding to his self-esteem. And I expect that in spite of disillusionment Love retained some of his pristine liking for Somers; he'd do his damnedest to prevent Somers from buying the manuscript, but he probably had no desire to hold Somers up to public obloquy.

"In the meanwhile, Galbraith had been active. The circumstantial reasons which influenced Somers in assessing the genuineness or otherwise of the manuscript influenced him too. In any case, he determined that by hook or by crook he must have it. But how? Somers's Promise to Sell seemed to him an insuperable obstacle. He might, of course, wait until Somers had the manuscript and then try to steal it; but if Somers were sensible, he'd take it straight to a strongbox at the bank, and Galbraith would never have a chance of getting near it. Burglary was an interim solution, and he tried that; but probably Mrs. Bly, impressed with the hundred-pound offer, took the manuscript away with her for safe keeping. Anyway, Galbraith couldn't find it. He was driven to the conclusion that Somers must be killed before he could make good his claim to the manuscript on Mrs. Bly's return; and he must have made up his mind that as a corollary Love also would have to die, since Love, alive, would be in a position (a) to put the manuscript out of Galbraith's reach and, (b) thanks to overhearing Somers's conversation with Galbraith, to offer the police a very sound reason why Galbraith should have murdered Somers. With both of them dead, the police would have no reason to consider Galbraith as a potential murderer, since if and when the business of the manuscript came to light, it could not possibly be shown that Galbraith was aware of its existence; he would seem to have no more motive than anyone else.

"Galbraith made no special plans beyond, I suppose, arming himself in some way; he was shrewd enough

to realize that elaborate preparations for murder increase the risk by multiplying clues and traces. On
Friday night he simply followed Somers about with a
view to seizing the most favorable opportunity and
was certainly outside the common-room door when
Somers spoke of his watch to Wells. When Wells and
Etherege left, Galbraith had just time to hide in the
lavatory or in one of the classrooms. Probably he intended to go in and kill Somers there and then, but
Somers himself put a stop to that by surreptitiously
leaving the building. Galbraith may have followed
him to Love's house or may just have guessed what he
was doing, for he knew, of course, that Somers had a
sound reason for wishing Love dead. In any case, it
was quite in Galbraith's interest that Somers should
do that particular job, and he simply waited for his
return (or followed him back to the common room)
and then shot him.

"Having done so, the general condition of affairs
became clear to him, and he saw how Somers's alibi
could be used to create an alibi for *him.* He finished
heating the report forms (if Somers had not already
done so); he tampered with the watch, for reasons I've
mentioned; he opened the curtains so that the scene
should be in every detail what it was when Wells and
Etherege left the room; and he took the hundred
pounds and the Promise to Sell from Somers's body, by
way of confusing the trail. But he made three fatal
mistakes: After wiping the wristwatch and putting
Somers's prints on it, he strapped it back the wrong
way round; he either didn't find, or didn't realize the
significance of, the clean sheet of blotting paper in
Somers's pocket; and—almost incredibly—he left the
electric fire burning.

"The time must by now, I think, have been between
half past ten and twenty-five to eleven. I say 'must'
because at twenty-five to eleven Galbraith rang up the

chaplain, probably from the call box outside the school gates, and it isn't very likely that he killed Somers and arranged the scene between the phone call and ten forty-four, when he arrived at your study (hence, by the way, my insistence on the fact that Somers was back from killing Love by ten thirty). And now comes a problem which you can clear up. That business about the muddle in the chapel seating arrangements—was it a fabrication?"

"No," the headmaster said without hesitation, "it wasn't. The muddle really existed, and Galbraith can't have contrived it on the spur of the moment. I'm bound to admit that he didn't *necessarily* have to bother *me* with it—but it wasn't at all implausible that he should do so."

"I see. Then it was just a convenient pretext, ready-made. On leaving the common room he had to provide himself with a good alibi for about a quarter to eleven and onwards; and there you were at your Fasti meeting, heaven-provided for the purpose. All other considerations apart, you had a complete alibi for the two crimes, and so your word would subsequently be trusted. Galbraith telephoned the chaplain about the seating arrangements to lend likelihood to his belated visit, allowed an interval to elapse sufficient to account for the journey from his lodgings to Davenant's, and arrived just as the Fasti meeting was breaking up."

"He could not rely," said the headmaster rather defensively, "on keeping me talking indefinitely."

"He didn't need to, because Wells would find Somers's body at eleven (and he assumed, of course, that Love's body would be found by his wife at a quarter to). All he wanted was to keep you talking till eleven —and *that* he could rely on, I suppose.

"Next morning he killed Mrs. Bly. There was plenty

of opportunity, since—as I assumed—he had no commitments during Speech Day."

"Not after the chapel service," the headmaster agreed. "I took it he'd be about if he were needed, but I hadn't tied him down to any particular job at any particular time."

"I see. Well, exactly what happened in Mrs. Bly's cottage we don't know. Galbraith wouldn't particularly want to kill the old woman *provided* he could get away with the manuscript unobserved. But since she'd laid eyes on him, she had to die."

"Why?" the headmaster demanded.

"*If* she lived, she could tell the police about Somers's interest in the manuscript; and the fact that after Somers's death Galbraith had stolen it or bought it or what not would make the police realize that he had an uncomfortably pressing motive for Somers's murder."

"Yes, of course. Go on."

"As I say, this part of it is very vague. Possibly Mrs. Bly caught him attempting the theft, or possibly— well, there's a variety of potential situations which you can work out for yourself. What it boiled down to was that Mrs. Bly saw him and that therefore he had to kill her. And he had to stun Plumstead for fear that Plumstead might see him escaping and so be able to identify him subsequently. These tasks accomplished, away he went with *Love's Labour's Won* under his arm.

"And the next thing that happened was that at the garden party he overheard Elspeth Murdoch tell me that she knew where to find Brenda Boyce. That by itself didn't worry him, since like me he assumed that Brenda had been killed by Somers. But hard on the heels of it (at about six thirty, Weems told me this morning) came the report of Stagge's supposed comment on the case. It might be a trap, but on the other hand it might not. If—he reflected—Brenda were by any remote chance alive, she could uncover the invisible-ink hoax and blow his alibi sky-high; and on alibi, to judge from Stagge's comment, his safety depended. He had to make sure, and so he followed Elspeth and myself to Melton Chart. Elspeth told me, when I was visiting Brenda earlier today, that while we were plowing through the wood she had the impression that some third person was near us; but I can't say I suspected anything of the kind myself.

"You know what followed. Not realizing that we were aware of the invisible-ink alibi and that therefore his action was a confession of guilt, he attempted to silence Brenda. And failed. His state of nerves thereafter doesn't bear imagining. When Stagge and I returned here from Brenda's house, he listened outside the door, in a desperate effort to ascertain how much we knew. We chased him, and "—Fen gestured expressively—*"sic transit."*

There was a long silence. Fen was yawning away like a hen with the gapes. And presently the headmaster said:

"I suppose that neither Somers nor Galbraith would have had any difficulty in disposing of the manuscript without the—ah—vendor's identity becoming known?"

"There are various ways in which it could have been done," Fen replied. "And probably both of them were intending to leave the country and live abroad under another name, since a sudden access of riches to anyone connected with the affair would obviously arouse suspicion. No doubt their alibis were only intended to last them till the end of the term—after which either of them could have imperceptibly vanished."

He meditated. "But there's one aspect of the case, you know, of which an alternative explanation is conceivable. Somers may not have killed Love; we may be maligning him. Though as he tried to throttle Brenda, I don't think an additional stain on his memory need disturb our consciences very much."

"How do you mean?"

"Well, Somers clearly *intended* to kill Love. But he may have been killed himself before he could get on with it. In short, Galbraith may have been Love's murderer, since we know that, like Somers, he had a motive. You can take your choice of the two possibilities. We shall never know for certain—but in most criminal cases you get a sediment of the ambiguous or inexplicable left over at the end."

"Did the search of Mrs. Bly's cottage have any results?" the headmaster asked.

"None at all. I really think she must have taken Taverner's advice and burned those letters. Letters," Fen moaned, "Shakespeare letters used as fire-lighters. . . ." He became speechless with dismay.

"Never mind," the headmaster consoled him. "There's that one undamaged page of *Love's Labour's Won* left. Though how that managed to survive, with the rest of it a heap of ashes in the wreckage, I can't imagine."

"I *knew* he'd have the manuscript with him," said Fen, uncomforted. "And all I could do was to stand there and watch it go up in smoke. . . . Still, there is, as you say, that one page—badly scorched but still whole and legible. Stagge let me copy it this morning."

"Oh. May I see?"

Fen produced a sheet of paper and handed it to the headmaster, who donned horn-rimmed spectacles in order to read it.

LOVES LABORS WONNE

The cort of Navarres kinge

1st gent.	And soe you say they are returned hither
2nd gent.	Evn with the swiftnesse of a fledgling brood that dazd with novice flite seeks out againe the boughborne nest, oure gracious lord and Kinge fleering Berowne Dumain and Longaville are soberd home to claim the inviolate pledge taught to them by the lustie maids of Fraunce this twelvemonth since. From out that hermitage sette in the gray Carpathian snowes where Frosts mew uppe the peasant in his lewd abode and Phebus scarce dare ope his radiant face To the fierce hails prickes: our noble Majestie is come againe more kindly to the kibes of lesser men fors own endurance sake. And that Berown which we were wont to say a recklesse whipster void of nice restraint is strangely altered by the lazar house and all those tetters he hath lookd uppon for Rosalindas love
1st gent.	The ladies then are now within the cort
2nd gent.	We attend them hourely: But see where comes the fine fantastick foole Armado and his subtle serving boy
1st gent.	Lets stand apart to hear them?

(Enter Armado with Moth.)

Arm.	Say, boy, say, sweete Socrates: thinke you that tickling lust hath driven my Netta and her wedlock vowes quite out of charitie one with the other
Moth	Why olde knight Id answer you more truly

          had I the sprouting of a beard to com-
          mend me to the ladie: for your beard is a
          sure password to a ladies hart.
Arm.   Her hart little sage: her hart
Moth   Ay and her placket an it please your Inno-
          cence. But imprimis the hart: for a wom-
          ans hart . . ."

"H'm," said the headmaster as he returned the paper to Fen. "I think the Bard must have been a bit off-color when he wrote that. Apparently it's a sequel to *Love's Labour's Lost.*"

"Yes. *Love's Labour's Lost* demands a sequel, when you come to think of it; and there's certainly material for a comedy in the second meeting of the lovers. But I've been wondering whether this isn't a sequel to Shakespeare's play written by someone else. The extreme poverty of style suggests it—though in view of *Titus Andronicus* that isn't really a criterion. And besides, the play might have improved as it went on— might have enshrined a Bottom or at least a Dogberry."

"What about the writing?"

"It does resemble that of the signatures, certainly."

"Do you think it was ever performed?"

"Since Meres mentions it, I suppose so. Of course, it may have been a complete flop, not worth pirating or reviving; sequels often are flops. But there were no signs on the page I saw that it had been used as a prompt copy, if that's what you're getting at."

"How do you suppose it came to be in the cottage?"

"I still postulate a young woman," said Fen, "who demanded from her lover a sample of his work and was fobbed off with this. The letters might have told us—but now, God alone knows. You can read the squabbles on the subject in the academic journals, to which I shall doubtless be contributing. One of the most melancholy things in life is the fact that there's not a single aspect of Shakespeare on which everybody agrees. . . . I've always sympathized deeply with that critic who after years of labor on the problems presented by the sonnets publicly expressed the wish that Shakespeare had *never written them.*"

There was a knock on the door, and Wells entered with a bundle of evening papers. The headmaster scanned the accounts of the case in them.

"No mention of you," he remarked in surprise.

"Certainly not. It doesn't do," said Fen sanctimoniously, "for a man in my position to get mixed up with anything nasty."

The headmaster looked at him severely. "I trust," he said, "that Stagge didn't insist on taking the credit."

"Good heavens, no, he's far too honest and amiable for such a notion to enter his head. It was *I* who insisted he should take the credit, what there is of it. And a devil of a job it was, too. I had to tell him I'd promised my wife never to touch another criminal case and generally lie up hill and down dale before I could persuade him to leave me out of it. . . . But afterwards—*afterwards,* mark you, when it was all settled —he gave me this."

From his pocket Fen took the miniature that had been found in Mrs. Bly's cottage and regarded it affectionately.

"Stagge said: 'It's a funny thing, sir, but there was no one in the room when I discovered this, and I haven't spoken about it to anyone but you. It seems to me you're a more proper person to have it than Mrs. Bly's son in Coventry or wherever it may be; and that page of manuscript, from what you tell me, will make *him* quite as rich as is good for him. So if you're prepared to risk admitting you walked off with it, absentmind-

edly so to speak, in case awkward questions *are* asked,
you're welcome to take it home with you.' "

The headmaster chuckled. "There's nothing more
cheering," he said, "than to hear of a policeman par-
ticipating in some kindly illegality."

Fen put the miniature away again and glanced at
his watch. "Look here; I must be getting back to Oxford and the Honours School of English Literature.
Your local garage-men, by the way, have done a marvellous job with Lily Christine. After Plumstead's
efforts last night I didn't think it would ever be possible to put her together again, but she's running better
than ever. A bit dented, of course," he conceded,
"where Stagge knocked into her. But that can be
remedied when I get home."

"You must have some tea before you go."

"I should like to." Something occurred to Fen, so
that he brightened considerably. "And during tea I
can finish telling you about the plot of my detective
novel."

The headmaster groaned. "Oh, Gervase," he said, "if
you *must* write a detective story—and far too many
dons write them as it is—why not use the events of this
weekend?" The headmaster warmed to his theme. "I
see it as Simenonish, with lots of psychology, to please
the highbrow critics. . . ."

"Galbraith?" said Fen. "Somers? *Love's Labour's
Won?*" He waved the suggestion contemptuously
away into limbo. "My dear fellow, no one could possibly make a detective story out of *them*. . . . Now this
girl in the Catskill Mountains, you see . . . ."

Little remains to be told. The friendship between
Mr. Plumstead and Daphne Savage ripened into marriage; and Mr. Plumstead, who, thanks to having received a garbled account of the affair, erroneously

supposed Fen to have saved him from the hangman, invited Fen to the wedding. It took place during the summer vacation, and as Fen had to be in London in any case on the day concerned, he accepted the invitation gladly. On the morning of the ceremony he caught an early train from Oxford to Paddington.

"Let's hope I don't meet an ancient mariner," he said.